THE RUSSIAN'S ENVY

ALSO BY CAP DANIELS

Book Twenty: *The Abandoned Chase*
Book Twenty-One: *The Gambler's Chase*
Book Twenty-Two: *The Arctic Chase*
Book Twenty-Three: *The Diamond Chase*
Book Twenty-Four: *The Phantom Chase*
Book Twenty-Five: *The Crimson Chase*
Book Twenty-Six: *The Silent Chase*
Book Twenty-Seven: *The Shepherd's Chase*
Book Twenty-Eight: *The Scorpion's Chase*
Book Twenty-Nine: *The Creole Chase*
Book Thirty: *The Calling Chase*
Book Thirty-One: *The Capitol Chase*
Book Thirty-Two: *The Stolen Chase*

Stand-Alone Novels
We Were Brave
Singer – Memoir of a Christian Sniper

Novellas
The Chase is On
I Am Gypsy

THE RUSSIAN'S ENVY

AVENGING ANGEL
SEVEN DEADLY SINS SERIES
BOOK #6

CAP DANIELS

ANCHOR WATCH
PUBLISHING
** USA **

The Russian's Envy
Avenging Angel
Seven Deadly Sins Book #6
Cap Daniels

Published by:

ANCHOR WATCH
PUBLISHING
** USA **

13 Digit ISBN: 978-1-951021-61-0
Library of Congress Control Number: 2024914714
Copyright © 2024 Cap Daniels – All Rights Reserved

Cover Design: German Creative

Printed in the United States of America

THE RUSSIAN'S ENVY

Russkaya Zavist'

CAP DANIELS

Beauty is worse than wine, it intoxicates both the holder and beholder.

— ALDOUS HUXLEY

Tak Mnogo Voprosov
(So Many Questions)

Washington, DC, Late Summer 2012

United States Department of Justice Supervisory Special Agent Ray White ran his fingers across the stubble on his scalp where his treasured headful of slowly greying hair had been only months before. The brain tumor that had been declared inoperable by the specialists at Georgetown Medical Center was resting in a specimen jar somewhere inside a laboratory in Northern Europe after being removed by Dr. Stefan Müller, chief of neurosurgery at Clinique de Genolier, Switzerland. The world's leading brain surgeon had been a life-saving gift from the only person in Ray White's life who'd given him more headaches than the tumor: former Russian assassin turned DOJ Special Agent Anya Burinkova.

White said, "Get your girlfriend on the phone. We've got an assignment."

Special Agent Gwynn Davis stared across White's enormous desk, and instead of dialing the number, she pursed her lips in contemplation. "Uh, boss, you're not supposed to be back at work yet. I'm not sure it's such a great idea for you to . . ."

White lowered his chin and eyed the one real agent left under his command. "Get up."

Gwynn cocked her head. "What?"

White stood from his chair and rounded the island-sized desk. "You heard me. Get up and trade seats with me."

Gwynn slowly pushed herself from the chair and slipped around the other end of the desk. Even more slowly, she lowered herself onto White's chair as he nestled into hers.

The senior agent said, "Okay. Now, you're in charge, and here's your first briefing as acting supervisory special agent."

Gwynn raised a hand. "Wait a minute. This is all wrong."

"Put your hand down, SSA Davis. You said I'm not allowed to be back at work yet, so that leaves you to run the office."

Gwynn sighed, and White said, "You may want to take some notes. Dr. Maxim Bortsov, a plastic surgeon in Los Angeles, is harvesting organs from his patients and selling them on the black market."

Gwynn bit the inside of her jaw to stifle the gasp.

White continued. "Okay, that's it. I'm going home now since you say I can't be here. Good luck." Before he was completely out of Gwynn's former chair, White said, "Oh, yeah. I almost forgot. I'm scheduled to meet with the attorney general at ten. She's going to tell me that our budget has been eliminated and Operation Avenging Angel is over. I guess that meeting is yours now. Have fun."

Gwynn leapt from the plush leather seat. "Wait a minute, Agent White. I wasn't suggesting that I should be in charge. I was just saying . . ."

"I don't care what you were suggesting, Davis. Why would I care? I just had a baseball cut out of my skull. All my hair is gone. My task force got dissolved. Agent Johnny McIntyre was dismissed for cause. The knife-wielding Russian is God only knows where. And the one agent I *thought* I had left decided that she gets to dictate when I come back to work. Does that about cover it?"

"Agent White, I'm sorry. I didn't mean . . ."

White slid back onto the chair. "It's falling apart, Davis. The task force that was supposed to be my swan song is crashing down around me, and I'm supposed to just fade away into oblivion and collect my pension until I die."

Gwynn motioned toward White's chair. "Please sit back over there where you belong, and let's start again." White didn't move, and Gwynn said, "Please, Agent White."

Finally, he exchanged seats. "Does this mean you think it's okay for me to be back at work now?"

"Of course," she said. "Let's try this again. I'll get Anya on the phone."

"You do that," White said. "I'm going to see if I can find a fistful of aspirin."

Anastasia "Anya" Robertovna Burinkova answered on the fourth ring. "*Da.*"

Gwynn frowned. "Anya?"

"*Da.*"

"Anya, it's Gwynn. Is that you?"

"*Da.*"

Gwynn pressed the speaker button and laid the phone on White's desk. "Anya, say something other than *da.*"

"What do you want, Gwynn?"

"You don't sound happy to hear from me. Is everything all right?"

Anya said, "No, Gwynn. Nothing is all right. What do you want?"

"You're scaring me, Anya. What can I do?"

Anya sighed. "You can tell to me reason why you are calling me."

Gwynn stammered. "Uh, I was calling because we have a mission, but now I'm worried about you. What's going on?"

Anya said, "You are inside Ray White's office, yes?"

"Yes."

"I will be there in twenty minutes or maybe sooner. You will understand when you see me."

White said, "Anya, do you need some help? Are you in danger? I can have a team . . ."

Gwynn glanced down at the phone. "She hung up."

White suddenly lost interest in rubbing what had been his hair. "That's not like her. What do you think's going on?"

Gwynn shrugged. "Beats me. But she said we'd understand when she gets here. Whatever it is, I don't like the sound of it."

White crossed his legs. "You know her better than anyone else. Give me a guess."

"If I had to guess, I'd say it has something to do with Chase Fulton. He's the only thing in her life she's hung up on."

"He's still married to that woman in Georgia, right?"

Gwynn said, "As far as I know."

"Well, find out for sure. Something's definitely going on with her, and I'd like to have a little intel before she shows up and turns this place into a circus."

Gwynn scrolled through her contacts until she found the number for the operation center of the American covert operative who'd been—and maybe still was—the only man Anya ever admitted loving.

A woman answered. "Op center."

Gwynn suddenly wished she'd given some thought to what she would say if anyone answered. "Uh, hello."

The young lady sounded frustrated on the other end of the line. "Op center. Who is this?"

"This is Special Agent Gwynn Davis with Justice. I'm—"

"Hey, Gwynn. It's Skipper. Is everything all right?"

"I'm not sure. I called Anya because we have a mission for her, but she didn't sound like herself. I mean, her voice was the same, but something was off. As far as you know, is everything okay with her? Is Chase, uh . . . is everything okay with him and his wife?"

Skipper stifled a chuckle. "Yes, everything is fine with Chase and Penny, but trust me, I completely understand why that would be the first thing to hit your mind when you think something's wrong with Anya."

Gwynn eyed White. "If it's not Chase, do you know what might be wrong with her?"

Skipper said, "I know what it could be, but that's not really up to me to divulge. I really think you should talk with Anya about it. It's, well, a little personal, and you know how private she can be."

"Is she in any danger?"

"No, it's nothing like that. It's just something she'll have to learn to live with."

Gwynn said, "And it's got nothing to do with Chase, right?"

"Not exactly, but again, I think you should talk with her about it. You haven't seen her lately, have you?"

"No. Why do you ask?"

"Just talk to her," Skipper said. "It'll all make sense if she decides to tell you about it."

Gwynn said, "She's on her way into the office. I was just trying to get a little heads-up on what might be the problem."

"Yeah, I understand, but you'll see soon enough. Listen, I have to run. We're in the middle of an operation. Is there anything else you need?"

"No, that was it. Good luck with the mission."

Skipper clicked off, and White said, "That got us exactly nowhere. I guess we're left to play the waiting game. I'm getting some coffee. Want some?"

Gwynn jumped to her feet. "I'll get it for you. Just chill out and come up with something to tell the attorney general that'll keep us in business."

She returned a few minutes later with two steaming cups and slid one onto Ray's desk. "There you go. Black, no sugar, right?"

He lifted the cup. "That's right. Thanks."

They sipped in silence for a few minutes until Gwynn said, "Have you heard from Johnny Mac?"

White said, "Last I heard, he was trying to get on with the Air Marshals. I wrote a letter for him, but I don't know if it did any good."

"You wrote a recommendation letter for him?"

White nodded. "I feel like it was my fault for putting him in a situation he wasn't ready to handle. If I had made you the acting chief while I was . . . away . . . I'm pretty sure things would've gone differently."

Gwynn huffed. "Yeah, they would've been different, all right. I would've been the one unemployed. Johnny made some mistakes, but they weren't entirely his fault."

White interrupted. "That's what makes this job a bear. Even when things aren't my fault, they're still my responsibility. That's why you and your little Russian doll are such pains in my ass. Everything you do, I have to answer for it."

"But so far, we've always gotten our bad guy in the end."

"It's not bagging the perp that gives me grief. It's all the other stuff you do on your way to the bag."

She raised an eyebrow. "If you're right about us getting defunded, you won't have to worry about that anymore."

White ran a fingertip along the edge of his desk. "I'm going to miss it, you know."

Gwynn smiled at her boss. "I know. And we'll miss you."

"What do you mean, we?"

"Anya and me."

White shook his head. "There won't be an Anya when I'm gone."

"What are you talking about?"

He said, "She's only here for this task force. Once Avenging Angel is shut down, she's unemployed, and she can go back to doing whatever she was doing before we nabbed her."

"What about me?"

White shrugged. "I'll put in a good word for you. You've done some excellent work, but no matter where they send you, it won't be like working with Anya. She's a wild card, and I've been a shield between the brass and the two of you. Nobody else will be willing to become that shield, so you'll get reassigned, but not with Anya."

Before Gwynn could respond, a knock came at the door, and White frowned. "That can't be Anya. She doesn't knock."

Gwynn stood. "I'll get it."

White waved a hand. "Sit back down. Come in!"

When the woman stepped through the door, from her boots to her shoulders, she was the same striking beauty she'd been since the day they apprehended her, but when SSA White looked up, he said, "My God, Anya. What happened to your face?"

TOVARISHCH GENERAL (COMRADE GENERAL)

Anya pressed the door closed behind her and bowed her head. "Is long story, but I am no good for mission now."

White stood and motioned toward the chair beside Gwynn. "Have a seat. Are you all right?"

Anya slinked into the seat and raised an eye barely high enough to meet Gwynn's gaze.

The agent immediately forgot she was a fed and became solely a friend. She took Anya's hand in hers. "What happened?"

Anya squeezed Gwynn's hand. "I lost focus on operation and was taken prisoner. I fought, but there were too many of them, and they were very good."

"Tell me what happened."

Anya sighed but still didn't look up. "I was working on operation in country of Bulgaria with Chase. I was to seduce German cryptologist to collect information about bad people doing bad things. I failed at this, and my body and face paid price."

Gwynn touched a finger beneath Anya's chin and raised her face. "It's not that bad, really. You're still—"

The Russian pulled away. "Do not patronize me. I know truth. I have known from time I was little girl I was prettier than other girls, and this gave to me advantages in some ways." Her tone darkened. "In other ways, it was terrible fate. KGB was very good at exploiting everything, especially pretty young girls. I learned things and did things no one should have to know or do." She turned her attention on Ray. "This is part of reason you wanted me to become Avenging Angel. Now, I am no good for this because I am no longer beauty . . . only beast."

Ray said, "You're still a beautiful woman, Anya."

"This is not true, but is nice of you to say to me this lie. You are not so pretty anymore without hair."

Ray slid a palm across his scalp. "You don't like the buzzed look?"

"I like alive look. You would maybe be dead if not for Dr. Müller. Hair will come back with time."

White almost smiled. "I'd be dead if not for you."

"This is silly," Anya said. "I made only one telephone call to doctor. Nothing more."

Ray lowered his chin. "We both know that's not remotely true."

Anya shrugged. "So, maybe doctor owed to me favor, and saving your life was maybe this favor."

Ray said, "Something tells me there's a lot more to that story."

"Not all stories are long and complicated. Some, like me, are simple."

That sent both Ray and Gwynn into a fit of laughter, and Anya furrowed her brow. "Why is this funny?"

Gwynn caught her breath. "You're the absolute opposite of simple, Anya. Nothing about you is simple. I think you're the most complex person I've ever met."

The Russian cocked her head and considered Gwynn's assessment while Ray stared into the distance as if contemplating the remainder of his life. Perhaps he was.

The temporary silence that filled the office was severed by a piercing tone from the desk phone. Ray snatched the receiver from its cradle. "What?"

His personal assistant said, "Agent White, your meeting with the attorney general has been moved up. She wants to see you now."

Ray stared at Anya, down at his watch, and back at the Russian. "Tell her we'll be there in three minutes."

He eased the receiver back onto the cradle and leaned toward Anya. "Look at me and answer one question."

She slowly raised her eyes to meet his, and he said, "Do you want to continue Operation Avenging Angel?"

She pressed a palm to her face. "Yes, of course, but I cannot. Look at me. I am no longer angel . . . avenging or otherwise."

White rose, lifted a folder from his desk, and snatched a tie and jacket from the hall tree. "Come with me. Both of you."

The Office of the Attorney General of the United States is not a broom closet tucked into a forgotten corner of some obscure office building in DC. It's an elaborately furnished, massive affair that consumes a significant portion of the Robert F. Kennedy Building at 950 Pennsylvania Avenue NW. When one walks into the building, he is immediately stricken with a sense of enormity and history, but when he steps into the office of the AG, he is stricken by nothing short of power.

"Go right in, Agent White. She's expecting you."

He led his two subordinates through the massive double doors and onto the carpet, where he had, on many occasions, stood with his hat in his hand and his ego in check. "Good morning, General."

Without looking up, the AG motioned toward a collection of matching office chairs that could've been two hundred years old. "How many times do I have to tell you to stop calling me General? Sit down."

The three obeyed as the AG pretended to finish something far more important. When she capped her pen, she glanced down at her watch and sighed. "Let me begin by informing you that this is not a negotiation. It is formal notification out of respect by me, for you, Agent White. You've had a stellar career at Justice, and no one would argue that point. However . . ."

White cleared his throat. "If you'll allow me . . ."

The AG continued. "I will not allow you. As I said, this is not a negotiation . . . My God, Agent Fulton. What happened to your face?"

Anya instinctually looked down as the AG rose from her chair and swept around the desk. She stood only inches in front of the Russian. "Answer me. What happened to you?"

Far outside Anya's typical degree of confidence, she spoke barely loud enough to be heard. "I made terrible mistake and allowed myself to be captured, interrogated, and tortured."

"By whom?" the AG demanded.

"This does not matter. These people are now deceased and will never do this to anyone again."

"Did you kill them?"

Anya shrugged. "Perhaps I killed some of them, but not all."

The AG turned to White. "And now I would like to know why you chose not to report the abduction, interrogation, and torture of a special agent under your command, Agent White."

"There are two reasons for that, General. The first is that I only learned of it moments ago. Second, Agent Fulton wasn't on an official operation under my direction or anyone else's at the DOJ."

The highest-ranking law enforcement officer in the United States squeezed her eyelids closed and held up a finger. "Ray, for the love of God, don't do this to me today. I've got enough on my plate without you pouring gravy in my lap."

"Ma'am, if you'll take a look at this file, I think you'll understand why I'm here."

She snatched the file from his hand and returned to her chair. "You're here, Agent White, because I summoned you."

"Yes, of course, General, but . . ."

She glared at him over her glasses. "One more time, Ray. Just one more time with the *General* business, and I'll make you think you're a private in my unit. Now, what's this file all about?"

"Give it a read, Gen . . . ma'am. It'll all make sense."

She slid her glasses up the bridge of her nose and opened the file. After two minutes of reading and turning pages, the file landed on her desk and the glasses came off. "This *is* an interesting turn of events, I must say. Exactly what are you proposing?"

Ray glanced at Anya and back at the only person in the chain of command between him and the White House. "As you can see from the file, Anya—I mean, Agent Fulton—is perfect for bringing down Dr. Maxim Bortsov."

The AG lifted the file, read through it a second time, and then looked up at Anya. "Agent Fulton, how do you feel about what Agent White is suggesting?"

She turned to Ray and said, "I trust him completely."

"That wasn't my question," the AG said. "My question was, how do *you* feel about it?"

"Answer is same, Comrade General. If Ray says is good plan, is good plan also for me."

It was suddenly White's turn to fight back the laughter exploding inside of him.

The AG held up the file with one hand and lifted her pen with the other. "Fine. I'll authorize this one final mission under Operation Avenging Angel, but as soon as it's done, the task force is disbanded, and everyone will be reassigned. Now, get out."

The three rose, White gripped the file, and they followed the general's order.

Inside the elevator, Ray said, "What on Earth made you call her Comrade General?"

Anya smiled through the scars. "She tried to make you feel small, and you are my friend. I will always come to aid of my friends like you and Gwynn."

Ray shook his head. "I'm not sure it qualified as aid, but it was hilarious."

Anya said, "It was not meant to be hilarious. It was meant to be offense to general who does not wish to be called general. In Russia, calling general anything else besides general would mean death. Is not this way in America, I am learning."

"No, it's not, and you're turning out to be a darned good American in my book."

Anya laid a hand against his arm. "Thank you for such compliment. I love being American. Now, like I told general, I trust you, but I would still like to know what is plan."

"You're not going to like it," Ray said, "but it's perfect."

Back inside White's office, he threw off the jacket and tie and settled into his chair. "Have you considered plastic surgery?"

Anya looked away again. "I am ashamed to tell to you truth."

Gwynn took her hand. "You have no reason to be ashamed."

"I should not long to have back face I had before. It happened because I was stupid, and now I should live with reminder so I will never make same mistake."

Gwynn squeezed her hand even harder. "That's ridiculous, Anya. There's nothing wrong with wanting to look like you did six months ago. I mean, ninety-nine percent of the women on Earth would kill to look like you."

"You are making only flattering, but I will admit to you I would do surgery if it could give to me face I once had."

Ray shook the file folder. "Nobody can give you back the face you were born with, but the cosmetic surgeons in LA are some of the best in the world, and we just happen to have an authorized assignment from the general to stick our faces right in the middle of their business."

He handed the file to Anya, and she peered inside. Three minutes later, she said, "This person is killing patients on purpose to harvest organs for sale on black market?"

"Exactly," Ray said.

She frowned. "And you want me to become his patient for surgery?"

"I don't want you to take it all the way through surgery, but I want you inside his practice so we can build a solid case and take him down."

"This is terrible plan," Anya said, then smiled. "And I love it."

3

GOROD ANGELOV
(CITY OF ANGELS)

"Are you in pain?" Ray White asked while trying to avoid staring at Anya's scars.

"Not physical pain, but inside heart, I am sad, and this is also type of pain. You understand, yes?"

He pointed to the scar on the back of his neck and the quarter-inch growth of hair covering his head. "Yeah, I get it. The surgery saved my life, and I'm forever grateful, but I *am* looking forward to my hair coming back."

"Is almost same," she said. "You can wear hat or wig, and I can cover scars with makeup, but we both still know what we are trying to hide."

White said, "Depending on what we learn in LA, you might consider finding a plastic surgeon who doesn't want to cut out your liver. From what I hear, some of the best surgeons in the world are right there in LA, and if we do it right, Uncle Sam will foot the bill."

Anya frowned. "I have two questions. First is, who is Uncle Sam, and second is, what is foot bill?"

"Davis, I thought you were teaching her to be an American. You're failing."

"It's a work in progress," Gwynn said.

Ray rolled his eyes. "I'll make up for your shortcomings, although that may turn into a full-time gig for me."

Gwynn covered her heart with both hands. "That's not nice."

"Nobody's ever accused me of being nice. Now, let's have our daily history lesson. Uncle Sam is an off-the-cuff nickname for the United States. Nobody knows for sure how it came to be, but one theory makes a lot of sense." He paused and tapped a finger against his chin. "Let me see if I can remember the details. If I'm not mistaken, during the War of Eighteen

Twelve, there was a New York merchant named Sam somebody. Maybe it was Wilson, but it doesn't matter."

Anya cut him off. "I have now question number three. What is off-the-cuff?"

"We'll come back to that one, but let me finish my story about Uncle Sam. Apparently, this merchant shipped beef in barrels for the military and militia, and these barrels were stamped with the letters U and S. Of course, that meant the United States, but apparently, a bunch of the sailors thought it stood for Uncle Sam."

Anya covered her mouth with one hand and giggled like a schoolgirl.

"What's so funny?" Ray asked.

"Is cute."

"What's cute?"

Anya regained her composure. "Is cute to watch you pretend to be schoolteacher. I learned all of this as a girl when KGB and SVR demanded that I learn everything about American history. Your story is same I learned in school inside Russia."

White calmed the rising fire in his chest. "You'll pay for that one, *malyshka*."

Anya's eyes lit up. "Very good, Ray." She turned to Gwynn. "This means *little girl* in Russian."

Gwynn nodded. "Yes, I know."

Ray reclaimed the floor. "We're getting way off track, so let's refocus. The two of you are going to LA. We'll have travel arrangements soon."

Anya blurted out, "My Porsche will be there, yes?"

Ray caught himself before allowing his fuse to burn hotter. "Sure, why not? Now, shut up and listen. I have a stack of autopsy reports a foot thick. You two are going to read every one of them, word for word, and find a pattern. All of the dead bodies were patients of Dr. Maxim Bortsov's practice, but here's a kicker."

Anya leaned forward, but Ray held up his hand. "No! Don't say it. You know exactly what a kicker is. You're not doing this to me today. I'm putting up with you for only two reasons. One, your doctor friend saved my life, and two, that Comrade General comment was hilarious."

The Russian smiled. "I am very funny American girl."

"So, back to the kicker. The numbers that Maxim Bortsov and his partners are sending to the morgue aren't dramatically out of line with the numbers from other cosmetic surgeons. They're only slightly higher, but the analysts don't like the feel of the cases that result in the patients' deaths. They tell me it's nothing they can put their finger on, but something simply isn't right in the data."

Gwynn scowled. "So, we're building cases on feelings now?"

White groaned. "I know. I don't love it either, but it's enough to justify dispatching the two of you to check it out. Maybe there's nothing there, but if the big brains down in the basement see a trend, it's there. I want you and Russian Wonder Woman to stick your noses into it and see how it smells. If you tell me it's clean, you'll come back to DC, and all of this will be over, but my gut is with the analysts. There's something going on, and we need to stop it."

Anya asked, "When do we leave?"

"I'd like you to be on the ground in LA within forty-eight hours. Can you make that work?"

Anya sighed. "This will not work for me. I have modeling shoot for Victoria's Secret in two days."

White and Gwynn stared at the Russian for a long moment before she burst into laughter.

White said, "That's right, and I've got the shampoo commercial to shoot. Now, get out of here, and get your butts on the airplane."

* * *

The forty-eight-hour window turned into a one-hour packing-and-prep event, followed by just under four hours on the government jet. Gwynn and Anya landed at Burbank Airport to find that the Russian's Porsche wouldn't join them for the mission. Instead, a brand-new, black 911 convertible waited by the terminal.

Anya examined the car and shrugged. "I guess it will have to do."

With Anya behind the wheel and the top down, they made their way in style to the LA field office of the U.S. Marshals Service.

Ten minutes later, the two were behind the closed door of Deputy Marshal Will Parish, whose eyes couldn't seem to leave Gwynn. He said, "Thank you for coming by in person. These things are usually done via email."

Gwynn said, "I prefer a more intimate arrangement between the DOJ and the local federal authorities, and of course, we much prefer working with the Marshals Service than those other guys."

Marshal Parish smiled. "Indeed. So, what can I do for you, Gwynn? It is okay for me to call you Gwynn, isn't it, Agent Davis?"

"Gwynn is fine, Will."

His smile endured, and she said, "As I mentioned earlier, we're here investigating a medical practice that may have run afoul of some federal statutes. It's boring, clerical stuff . . . nothing like the cool cases you get to work."

"Ours rarely qualify as cool, but fortunately, we don't get mired down in the minutiae like you lawyers with badges."

She shrugged. "What can I say? We're not all cut out for gunslinging, but you're clearly right at home in the Old West."

He leaned back, and his considerable girth strained the buttons of his dress shirt. "Well, now that you mention it, I would call myself a man of action."

Gwynn tilted her head and gave him the thin smile she learned from

Anya. "That's obvious, Will. So, do we need to do any paperwork for you, or is intimate contact what you want?"

The marshal cleared his throat. "If all you're doing is clerical work, I don't see any reason to take this any further than the two of us. You made your impression, and I must say—"

Gwynn stopped him before he could cross a line the federal government doesn't like. "Thank you, Will. If our paperwork turns into a gunfight, you'll be the first guy I call."

He pulled a business card from a holder on his desk, flipped it over, and scribbled on the back before offering it to Gwynn.

She took the card, allowing her finger to linger against his for an extra beat. "Thank you, Will. Is this your personal cell on the back?"

"It is, and please feel free to use it anytime . . . absolutely anytime."

She examined the card. "I must say, this is the most pleasant interaction I've ever had with any other division. Thank you for being so . . . courteous and charming."

He stood. "Allow me to walk you out."

Anya stepped between the two of them. "This is not necessary. We can find way out without you."

Gwynn intervened and tapped a finger against the marshal's card. "Thank you, Will. I hope to see you again soon."

Anya left the parking lot with the new Porsche revving near redline. She laced her way through traffic with both hands gripping the wheel.

Gwynn white-knuckled the edges of her seat. "Hey, what's the rush?"

The Russian slid to a stop beneath a red light. "He was very unprofessional."

"Oh, come on," Gwynn said. "He was just a little flirty. You're the one who taught me to play off that and use it to my advantage at every opportunity."

"He is federal agent."

"So are we," Gwynn said as she braced herself beneath the now-green light.

Two miles farther, Anya finally reeled in her Mario Andretti instinct. "I am sorry. I am being like child. You are beautiful woman, and men always fall at your feet." She bit her lip. "I do not like men also not at my feet. Is silly and jealous, and I am sorry."

"Don't be sorry," Gwynn said. "Trust me, I understand. I've been living it for three years. Everywhere we go, every man in the room drools over you, and I'm just the nerdy sidekick."

"You are not nerdy. Well, maybe little bit, but not all of you is nerdy."

"Stop it and drive. I want to see our bachelorette pad."

Anya frowned. "I do not know this phrase."

"It's where a single woman or single women live. That's us . . . bachelorettes."

The code Agent White provided sent the gate sliding open into the twelve-foot security wall around the luxury condo complex.

Gwynn leaned forward and looked up. "Ours is A-Eleven."

"This is really nice. Who knew places like this fit into government's budget?"

"We're going to have to go shopping," Gwynn said from her room across the hall.

"I do not feel like shopping today. I want to have maybe glass of wine and vegetable on sofa."

Gwynn stuck her head into Anya's room. "Wine and vegetables?"

"Yes, this is American phrase, vegetable out. It means do nothing and be only lazy."

Gwynn chuckled. "It's veg out, but you were close, and a glass of wine sounds amazing. I'll run to the store."

Gwynn made the walk around the corner and stocked up, just in case Anya's vegging turned into a prolonged event.

The cop in Gwynn's head studied every inch of the exterior of the condo complex and made mental notes of the security weak points and position from which they could defend themselves should their mission turn into a West Coast war.

Gwynn poured two glasses of pinot noir and joined her partner on the sofa. "Are you ever going to tell me what really happened to you?"

"I told this to you already. I made stupid mistake and paid price for mistake."

"Yeah, I know that's the summary, but I want details . . . if it's not too painful to talk about."

"Is not painful. Only embarrassing."

"You never have to be embarrassed with me," Gwynn said. "You know that. We're like sisters. We can tell each other everything."

Anya emptied her glass, and Gwynn poured more.

"Word in Russian is *nepravil'no otsenen*. I think maybe in English is *underestimate*. This is what I did. I did not think the men were dangerous. I only believed they were cryptographers with no skill of fighting."

Gwynn drew her feet beneath her as Anya continued. "They were very good and also very fast. There were maybe five or six of them. This is second mistake. I did not know how many people were involved."

Gwynn choked on a mouthful of wine. "Five or six? And you thought you could fight your way out? Nobody wins with those odds."

She cocked her head. "Yes, I win with those odds when I am thinking clearly and not dreaming in daytime of Chase."

"Oh!"

Anya took another sip. "Yes, is true. I cannot always make my mind do what I want. It sometimes thinks of Chase when it should think other things, like not being captured."

Gwynn sighed. "That man really got under your skin, didn't he?"

"Oh, Gwynn, you should see him. He is so tall and strong like Viking, and every person all around him cannot turn away. He is like magnet for people."

Gwynn said, "I know, he's a pretty man."

"No, not only beautiful, but strong. And not only strong with muscles. Strong also with mind and confidence."

"I get it," Gwynn said. "So, these five or six guys kidnapped you?"

"Is maybe not kidnapping. Is maybe more capture. They tied me to chair and hit me." She gently touched her face with her fingertips.

"Were you scared?"

"It was not being afraid. It was accepting I was going to be hurt and maybe killed, but Chase came to rescue me."

Gwynn's eyes widened. "By himself?"

"No, of course not. This would be terrible idea. He brought others, and together, we killed them."

"All of them?"

"Yes, all of them, but this is not best part of story."

Gwynn poured more wine. "I can't wait to hear the best part."

"People who captured me and we killed together worked for company called Ontrack Global Resources. Is long story and does not matter, but they are bad people."

Gwynn leaned even closer. "Stop keeping me in suspense. What's the best part?"

Anya took a long sip. "Others on team told to me when Chase went on ship, where more people from this company were trying to find us, he turned into animal and could not be stopped. He was making these people pay terrible price for what their friends did to me."

"You can't be serious."

"I am serious," she said. "This is what many people told to me after mission."

Gwynn drained her glass. "He still loves you, doesn't he?"

Anya bowed her head and pressed her lips into a line.

Gwynn took her friend's hand. "I know, Anya. I understand, and I'm sorry."

The Russian jerked her hand from Gwynn's. "No! You do not understand. You cannot!"

With Gwynn left sitting on the couch in disbelief, Anya stormed down the hall and slammed her bedroom door behind her.

Gwynn threw her head back and sighed.

She gave Anya a few minutes to melt down alone before knocking on her door. "Can I come in?"

"No!"

"Anya, I really think we should talk about this."

"I said no!"

Gwynn stepped away from the door and slipped into the bath with a second bottle of pinot.

An hour into her self-service spa evening, Gwynn opened her eyes to see Anya sitting on the edge of the tub and flinched. "Geez. You scared the crap out of me. How long have you been there?"

Instead of answering the question, Anya said, "I am sorry for second time today. I am terrible friend. You were trying to be kind and supportive, and I was horrible. I am sorry to you. I need to make you understand."

Gwynn lifted a hand from beneath the foam and took Anya's. "You don't have to explain anything. I understand, and I love you. That's what friends do for each other—we love and understand."

Anya swallowed hard. "No, this you do not understand. My mother was killed, and I was taken by KGB when I was maybe four. I took nothing with me. I had no pictures of my mother. I did not even have toy doll she made for me. I had nothing to remind me of my mother except one thing. She was beautiful woman—maybe most beautiful woman in all of world. As I grew and became woman, every day inside mirror, I could see my mother's face a little more. Her hair was brown and not blonde like mine, but our faces were same. This is all I had left to make me remember my mother, and now it is gone. I do not care that I am not beautiful. I only care that I cannot see my mother inside of mirror now."

4

SERDTSE KATERINY
(KATERINA'S HEART)

The second bottle, coupled with the three time zones they'd crossed, sent Anya and Gwynn over the edge of maintaining consciousness. They slept like the dead, and the morning brought their first check-in with Ray White.

Gwynn made the call while Anya showered. "Good morning, Agent White."

"Morning?" White grumbled. "It's almost lunchtime."

"Not out here on the other coast," she said. "We're calling to check in."

"It's about time," he said. "Anya's appointment is at ten thirty. I emailed her legend earlier today when it truly was morning. She needs to study it and devote it to memory. We can't afford for Dr. Kidney Snatcher to figure out she's a fed."

"I'm just bringing up the email now. Anya will have the legend memorized in no time."

White said, "Why are you speaking for her?"

"She's in the shower," Gwynn said. "I wanted to talk with you privately."

"This doesn't sound good."

Gwynn checked the hallway and listened for running water. "I'll make it quick. Anya had a little meltdown last night."

"Meltdown? What happened?"

"It started in the marshal's office when we made the official notification that we were working on their turf. The marshal—a guy named Will Parish —tried to flirt with me, and I played along because a U.S. Marshal might come in handy. Anyway, the guy never gave Anya a second look."

"So? He likes brunettes. Where's this going, Davis?"

She listened for the shower again. "I have to hurry, but when we left the marshal's office, Anya was visibly upset and driving like a maniac. She made several comments about how unprofessional it was for Marshal Parish to flirt with me."

"That sounds like a pot-and-kettle conversation."

"Exactly, but it didn't end there. After we got to the condo—great condo, by the way—we had a glass of wine and girl talk. It turned into Anya storming off to her room and locking me out."

"That doesn't sound like her. What's going on?"

Gwynn swallowed a mouthful of coffee. "An hour later, she came out and apologized, and she told me why she was so upset."

"What were her reasons?"

"It made perfect sense after she explained it to me. When the KGB took her from her mother when she was four years old, that was the last time she ever saw her mother. She's never seen a picture or anything."

"So, all that drama was because of something that happened thirty years ago?"

Gwynn said, "No, it's a lot more than that. She told me that every time she looked in the mirror, she saw her mother's face looking back at her. Apparently, she remembers her mother looking just like her, but after the brutal beating overseas, she can't see her mother in the mirror anymore. That's what's killing her."

White leaned back in his chair. "Oh."

"Good morning, friend Gwynn. Would you like coffee?"

Gwynn looked up to see Anya coming down the hallway and heading for the kitchen. "No, thanks. I already have a cup, but there's plenty left. Help yourself."

Anya pulled a mug from the cupboard. "I am having only tea."

She paused and covered her mouth. "I am sorry. I did not realize you were on telephone. Forgive me."

Gwynn held up the phone. "It's okay. I was just checking in with Agent White."

"Oh, is Ray. I will be right there."

She put on a kettle of water and joined Gwynn. "Make telephone on speaker, please."

Gwynn pushed the button, and Anya said, "Good morning, Ray. Thank you for two things. First, wonderful apartment. Is beautiful. And second, thank you for new Porsche. Is perfect."

"Don't thank me. Thank the taxpayers. And the Porsche is a rental. It's not yours, so don't destroy it, please."

"I cannot make this promise, but I will try. Friend Gwynn maybe already told you, but I had bad day yesterday."

White said, "No, Davis didn't mention it. Are you okay?"

The Russian said, "Today is much better day, and I have decided yes."

"Yes to what?" White asked.

"Yes to finding best cosmetic surgeon in all of world to make my face again look like before."

Silence consumed the moment until Ray said, "Let's step away from me being the boss for a minute and have a real conversation. Are you okay with that?"

Anya and Gwynn locked eyes, neither knowing exactly how to respond, and White said, "Okay, I know it's weird, but let's just talk like friends."

Silence grew again until Anya said, "We are listening, friend Ray."

Gwynn covered her mouth in a wasted effort to stifle her laughter, and Ray began. "Look, Anya. When all of this began, what seems like a thousand years ago, I read your file."

"I have file?" Anya asked.

"Cut it out," Ray said. "I'm trying to be sincere here. I saw your picture and read your dossier, and I couldn't make the two agree. The way you look belies everything about the skill set you possess. Nobody expects someone who looks like you to be able to take down a small army at will."

Anya said, "If this is compliment, thank you."

"It's not really a compliment, but you're welcome. I'm trying to get to the point without sounding, well, like it's going to sound."

"Is okay, Ray. We are all friends, remember?"

"Fair enough," he said. "The impression I had of you before we met—"

"We did not meet," Anya said. "I killed two of your agents, badly injured four more, and you arrested me. This is not meeting. This is capture."

"Fine, we captured you. And that wasn't easy, by the way."

Anya said, "Is getting easier, apparently."

"Forget about that," Ray said. "The point I'm trying to make is that you are a beautiful woman and one of the most dangerous people on Earth. Nobody could possibly deny that, but who and what you are go much deeper. Those things are just elements of you. They aren't what makes you who you really are." He paused to have a drink. "What I'm saying is this. You're a fascinating and beautiful person because of your heart. It doesn't matter if you forget how to throw knives and you suddenly turn into a troll. You're still that beautiful person because of what's inside of you."

Anya licked her lips and swallowed the lump in her throat. "This is maybe nicest thing anyone has ever said to me. I do not know what to say."

"You don't have to say anything. Just know that your face has nothing to do with who you really are. Those of us who know you see who you really are because we look beyond the physical beauty and deadly skills."

The Russian wiped a tear from her eye before it could come. "I am . . ."

Gwynn reached for her hand. "Agent White is right. To everyone who loves you, you're exactly the same person you were six months ago, and that will never change."

"You love me, friend Gwynn?"

She squeezed Anya's hand and leaned close. "Absolutely. And even though Agent White won't admit it out loud, he does, too."

"Oh, I'll admit it," Ray said. "I'm terrified of you, but I do love you for the friend you are to me. What you did for me with Dr. Müller was the greatest thing anybody has ever done for me. When all of this began, I never dreamed it would ever evolve into this."

Anya regained her composure. "Okay, is now time for boss and subordinates again."

Gwynn shook her head. "Wow, that escalated quickly. So, anyway, Agent White sent your legend, and your appointment is at ten thirty with Dr. Maxim Bortsov."

"I will be ready," Anya said. "But I have one request."

"Let's hear it," White said.

"You mentioned picture in file before you captured me. I must have this picture."

"Are you wearing pants?" White asked.

Anya frowned. "Yes, of course I am wearing pants, but why could this matter?"

White said, "Reach into your back pocket and pull out your cred pack. There's a picture of you on your ID."

"Yes, this is perfect plan, Ray. I will walk into office of doctor, who is stealing organs for the Bratva, and I will show to him my badge and identification and say to him, 'Make me look like woman in picture.'"

White huffed. "Yeah, that's probably not the best plan. I'll have someone scan the file picture and email it to you."

Anya's tone softened. "Do you have also picture of my mother?"

White said, "No. Why would I have a picture of your mother?"

"Is okay. I was only hoping that maybe . . ." She stopped, cast her eyes to the ceiling, and gasped. "I must call Chase! Goodbye, Ray."

Ray said, "Whoa! Slow down. What are you talking about? Why would you call Chase?"

Anya said, "He has picture of my mother."

The tea kettle whistled from the kitchen, and Anya stood. She pulled her cell phone from a pocket, pressed a few buttons, and stuck it to her ear.

"Hello, this is Chase."

"Chasechka, is Anya Burinkova."

"We've been through this, Anya. You're the only person who calls me Chasechka, so we can leave off the introductions. What's going on?"

"I have for you question and also demand."

"Demand? Is that what we're doing now? Making demands of each other?"

"No, I am sorry. This is wrong word. I meant request. I have for you request."

"That's much better. What do you need?"

"Do you remember father's airplane he gave to you when he died?"

Chase laughed. "Yeah, a P-Fifty-One Mustang is pretty hard to forget. What about it?"

"Painted on side of airplane was picture of my mother and words 'Katerina's Heart.' You remember this, yes?"

"Yes, of course. What about it?"

"I need picture of this. Very good and close picture. You can do this for me, yes?"

Chase said, "Well, the truth is, I got that airplane a little shot up a few years ago, and I slid her onto the runway on fire. She's been completely rebuilt and renamed. That painting isn't on the cowling anymore."

Anya squeezed her eyelids closed and forced back the emotion she couldn't precisely name. "This is terrible, but you are not hurt from crash?"

"No, I wasn't hurt, and it was a long time ago. Why did you need a picture of the nose art?"

"Not only nose," she said. "I want all of picture."

"I didn't mean just her nose. When a painting is done on the fuselage of an airplane, it's generally called nose art."

"This is ridiculous phrase. Please tell to me you have a picture of art on nose before it was burned."

"I probably do, but I can't tell you where it is. I'll get Skipper on it. If anybody can find a picture, she can."

Anya said, "This is very important to me, Chasechka. I do not have words even in Russian to tell to you how much I need this picture."

"Just like with most things about you, Anya, I don't understand it, but I'll do what I can to get you the picture."

"This would mean world to me if you could do this. You will please tell me when you find it soon, yes?"

"Yes, I'll either have Skipper call, or I will as soon as we find a picture."

She ended the call and poured the boiling water over her tea bag.

Gwynn leaned into the kitchen. "Do you want to tell me what that was all about?"

Anya blew across the surface of the tea inside her mug. "My father had painting of my mother on his airplane. This is called art on nose. He gave to Chase this airplane, but Chase destroyed it."

Gwynn scowled. "I think it's actually called nose art, but why would Chase destroy an airplane?"

"No, he did not completely destroy airplane. It was only on fire, but it has been built again. Chase probably has picture of my mother, Katerina, from painting on airplane."

Gwynn shook her head. "This just gets weirder by the minute. You need to get started learning the legend Agent White sent you."

Anya opened the email on her phone and spent the next twenty minutes poring over the fictional history of the character she would become in Dr. Bortsov's office.

"Okay, I have all of it inside mind, and I am ready."

Gwynn said, "Are you telling me you memorized four pages in twenty minutes?"

"No, do not be silly. It did not take that long. I was reading other email after I learned legend."

"You're amazing, and I still want to be you when I grow up."

Anya rinsed her mug. "We will trade. I will be beautiful and deadly lawyer with badge and gun, and you will be hideous Russian orphan. When would you like to begin?"

Gwynn rolled her eyes. "Stop it. There's nothing hideous about you, and grown-ups can't be orphans."

Anya flinched and pulled her phone from her pocket. Her face immediately bloomed into excited animation. "My Chasechka. You found picture, yes?"

"Not exactly, but we may have done something even better."

"How can this be true?"

"You should receive an email any minute. Can you stay on the phone with me and check your email at the same time?"

"Yes, I can do this. I will put on speaker. Give to me only one second." She pulled the phone from her ear and pressed the speaker button. "You can hear me, yes?"

Chase said, "Yes, I can hear you. Did the mail come through?"

"I am opening now. Is from Skipper."

"Yes, she sent it from her computer."

The silence that followed could've lasted a thousand years, and Anya squeezed the phone to her chest and slid down the front of the refrigerator until she was resting on the floor.

Gwynn rushed to her side. "Are you all right, Anya?"

Tears streamed from the Russian's face, and she made no effort to stop them. Instead of speaking, she turned the phone around for Gwynn to see.

Staring back at her from the small screen was a picture of the most beautiful woman Gwynn had ever seen, sitting on the edge of a stone bench and smiling up at the photographer.

"Did the picture come through?" Chase asked.

"Is perfect, my Chasechka. Where did you find it?"

"I didn't find it," he said. "Penny did."

Anya blinked a dozen times in rapid succession. "Penny? Why would your wife find picture of my mother?"

"She found it tucked inside one of your father's journals. I sent a shot of the back of the picture, too, but I can't make it out. It looks like it might be written in Cyrillic."

She turned her attention back to the phone and opened the next picture. "It says Place du Bourg-de-Four, Switzerland, nineteen sixty-four."

5

RUSSKIYE RUKI
(RUSSIAN HANDS)

As Anya sat on the kitchen floor, her gaze frozen on the picture of her mother from nearly half a century before, the chime of the doorbell rang through the condo.

Gwynn cracked the door and peered through the narrow opening, where a young man stood holding a package. "Ms. Davis?"

"Yes."

"I have a package for you, but I need your signature."

Gwynn opened the door, signed the electronic tablet, and accepted the package.

Back in the kitchen, there was no evidence Anya heard the man at the door, but she looked up when Gwynn tore open the parcel.

"What do you have?"

Gwynn dumped the contents onto the table. "It looks like it's the new you."

Anya cocked her head but didn't put away her phone. "What does this mean?"

Gwynn extended a hand. "Get off the floor, and sit in a chair like a human."

Anya accepted the offered hand and parked herself in a chair beside the table. She lifted the first of two cards and studied it for a moment. "Is ridiculous name, but insurance card looks real." She picked up the second card and examined the driver's license also bearing Anya's ridiculous new name. "Is okay, but I do not like picture."

Gwynn lifted the license from her. "Nobody likes their driver's license picture, but of course, you look beautiful as always."

* * *

Two hours later, Anya presented the cards to the lady behind an elegantly curved reception desk. "I am Anastasia Belyaeva, and I have appointment with Dr. Bortsov."

To Anya's surprise, the lady behind the desk waved a hand toward an open door and answered in Russian, "Thank you, Ms. Belyaeva. Please follow Kristina."

Gwynn and Anya followed the young lady into a plush waiting area with elegant furnishings and a wine bar tucked away in one corner. "My name is Kristina. Is there anything I can get for you while you're waiting?"

"*Net, spasibo,*" Anya said as she settled onto the sofa.

Gwynn sat beside her, and Kristina made her exit.

"This is really nice."

Anya took in the space. "I do not think we will need insurance card. This is place for people who do not pay with insurance."

"I think you're right, but we'll deal with that when it comes up. Do you see anything that concerns you yet?"

Anya said, "Not yet, but we are looking only at face. We will find way to look inside heart later."

Instead of another hostess, as Anya expected, a dark-haired man with chiseled features came through the door at the back of the room. "Ms. Belyaeva, I'm Dr. Maxim Bortsov, but please call me Max. How are you?"

His accent was almost British, but his features were undeniably Eastern European. Anya and Gwynn rose in unison, and Max's eyes met Anya's instantly. She smiled instinctively, and he followed suit as if she were still the ravishing Russian beauty she'd been only weeks before.

Anya said, "As you can see, I am not well. Thank you, though, for asking."

"Follow me," he said. "Let's have a talk and see what we can do to make you better than new."

He led them into an impressive office that bore no resemblance to anything clinical or that of a typical surgeon.

"You have wonderful taste, Doctor."

He motioned toward a pair of luxurious chairs. "Please have a seat. And who have you brought along with you, Anastasia? If I may call you Anastasia."

"You may call me Ana, and she is my friend, Gwynn."

Max extended his hand. "It's a great pleasure to meet you, Gwynn. Please let me or my staff know if there's anything you'd like."

The two slipped into the chairs, and Max nestled into a third facing the two women. "What brings you in to see me today?"

Anya subconsciously pressed her fingertips against the skin of her face. "I was once beautiful woman like women in your office, but I had . . . accident."

He listened intently and never took his eyes from hers. "Tell me about your accident, Ana."

She looked away. "I do not wish to talk about accident. I wish only for you to make me who I was before."

"I'm sorry to bring up unpleasant memories, Ana. We don't have to talk about anything that makes you uncomfortable, but I will need to see some X-rays and an MRI before we go much further. Are you prepared to have those done today?"

"Yes, of course," she said. "I am in your hands, Doctor."

"Please, call me Max. I've found the less formal we are, the better our results tend to be."

Anya said, "Thank you, Max."

He stood and motioned for the two women to do the same. "If you'll follow me, we'll take care of the imaging, and then we can talk about what we can do to help."

He led them through a well-concealed door and into an examination room even larger than his expansive office. "Make yourselves comfortable, and Andrea will be in to get your X-rays and MRI. Do you need anything before getting started?"

Both women shook their heads, and another flawless young lady appeared, as if on cue, the instant Dr. Bortsov left the room. "Hello, Ms. Belyaeva. I'm Andrea, the radiology technician."

"Hello, Andrea."

The tech smiled and motioned toward a door to her left. "If you'll change into the gown behind the door, we'll get started."

Anya returned wearing the gown, and Andrea helped her onto the MRI table. The process lasted fewer than twenty minutes, and Dr. Bortsov replaced the tech.

He studied the imagery on his computer screen as Anya and Gwynn held their breath. Finally, he turned from the screen. "Ana, whatever caused your injuries was no accident. You've been brutally attacked, and under California law, I'm required to report such things to the local authorities."

Gwynn's heart sank into her stomach, but Anya didn't show any reaction other than to say, "This will not be necessary. I am certain people who did this will never do it to anyone ever again."

"You can't be certain of that, Ana. People like that have to be stopped."

Anya's heart rate never changed. "I killed one of them, and my friends killed other four, so I can be certain. You can make me look like before accident, yes?"

"You killed them?"

"Yes, I told you this. I killed one, and friends killed rest of them."

"How . . ."

"It was not hard. I crushed his skull with leg of chair and stabbed him through neck with broken arm of same chair. My friends had guns. I have very good friends."

The doctor leaned back in his chair and crossed his legs. "Exactly how did this happen, Ana? And where were you?"

"I cannot tell to you these things. Is secret."

He said, "I'm not certain that relieves me of my responsibility to report the incident."

Anya stood. "Come, Gwynn. We will go now. I think you were wrong. He is not best doctor for me."

Before either woman could take a stride, Dr. Bortsov said, "Please. I'm confident we can find a way around this issue without involving anyone outside my office. This is obviously a special case, so unless you're a member of law enforcement, I believe I can feel comfortable keeping the discussion between ourselves."

Anya said, "Do you believe police officers are capable of paying prices you charge for such service as this?"

"One can never be too careful," he said.

Anya pointed to her face. "I am, as they say, living proof of this."

He said, "Have a seat, and we'll continue."

They reclaimed their seats, and Dr. Bortsov said, "Yours is an interesting case in that not only do you require superficial repair, but you also suffered some damage to what I call facial structure. We must begin by repairing the underlying foundation of your face before we erase the scars."

"This means more than one time for surgery, yes?"

"Unfortunately, yes. It is likely you will require at least three, or perhaps four, procedures to restore your face. I have the photograph from your driver's license, but it isn't very good quality. I would like to see several more photographs taken prior to your . . . accident."

Anya said, "I have better idea."

She handed her phone to the doctor, and he studied the screen.

Finally, he said, "This isn't you."

"No, is my mother. Except for color of hair, we were same."

"I see. May I take a closer look?"

Anya said, "Yes, of course."

He led her to a complex examination chair and pulled a light beside his head. "If you will, please close your eyes, lean back, and relax."

She followed his instructions, and he carefully allowed his fingertips to explore every curve of her face. A few soft sounds escaped his lips during the exam, but he didn't speak until he turned off the light and pushed it away.

"Okay, thank you, Ana. You're a cosmetic surgeon's dream. Although your procedures will be long, I see no reason why we can't make you even more beautiful than you were before being—"

She interrupted. "Accident."

He nodded. "Accident, indeed."

"Thank you, but I do not wish to be more beautiful than I was. I wish only to look like my mother again."

"Even still, I'd like to see a few more photographs to ensure that I can meet and hopefully exceed your expectations."

"What is risk of dying during procedures?"

The doctor's eyes widened. "Oh, my. After what you've been through, I must say you are far safer in my operating suite than where you were when your *accident* occurred."

"This does not answer question," Anya said.

Dr. Bortsov answered in Russian. "You will not die in my hands, comrade."

Anya bowed her head and spoke softly in her native tongue. "I am still afraid."

The doctor softened his voice. "Don't be afraid. These hands are worth every penny they earn and more."

Anya looked up as if reassured. "*Kogda*?"

He smiled. "Whenever you're ready. We can schedule the first procedure today, or you can call Andrea and select an available date."

"I would like to schedule now, please."

He nodded and stood. "In that case, I'll send Andrea back in with the calendar, and you may choose a date."

Anya stood, stepped toward him, and opened her arms. The doctor took her in his, and they shared a hug that continued long after it should have.

As he stepped back, Dr. Bortsov said, "Remember, you're in very good Russian hands."

Andrea returned and took the doctor's seat. She slid an electronic tablet to Anya and said, "These are Max's available dates."

Anya pressed her finger against a Monday three weeks away. "This day, please."

"The day is yours," Andrea said. "As with all surgical procedures in our practice, you will be Max's only patient, and he'll be with you every step of the way."

"Is this how all cosmetic surgeons work?"

Andrea smiled. "Oh, no, definitely not. We're a very unique practice. You'll never find another practice quite like this one."

"Perhaps this is good thing, yes?"

"We think it's a very good thing. Now, if you have any questions, you can call me directly at the number on this card." She slid her card into Anya's hand.

"Thank you."

"Of course. We will contact you in a few days to come back in and do some labs and a few more tests before your procedure, but in the meantime, you can continue life as you have been."

Anya raised an eyebrow. "My life as it has been made me look like this. I wish to not continue."

Andrea withdrew. "I'm so sorry. I didn't mean—"

"Is okay. I feel very good in your care. I have very good feeling about all of this."

Andrea relaxed. "I'm so glad to hear that. If you don't have any more questions, you can expect to hear from us in a few days."

Anya stood and hugged the young woman.

The instant Gwynn closed the door in the car, she said, "What was all the hugging about? You barely ever hug me. What were you doing in there?"

Anya opened her hand, revealing a single key and one electronic access card. "Hugging is best way to pick pocket. I have also very good Russian hands."

6

OZHIDANIYE IGRY
(WAITING GAME)

Back at the condo, Gwynn nestled onto the sofa beside Anya. "Look at me and tell me you're okay."

Anya laughed. "Of course I'm okay. I had bad feelings yesterday, and feelings came out in terrible way. This will not happen again. I promise this to you."

"We all have meltdowns sometimes, and you've been through too much. To be honest, I'm surprised it took so long to reach the boiling point."

"Maybe this is true, but it does not give to me permission to be cruel to you. You are better than sister to me."

Gwynn smiled. "The phrase is, you're *like* a sister to me."

"I do not care what phrase is. I said what I meant. I had once sister, and she was terrible. You are better than having sister."

Gwynn's raised eyebrows said she was intrigued. "You've got a sister? How did I not know that? Is she still in Russia? What's her name?"

Anya recoiled. "This is too many questions at same time. I do not know if she is still alive. Is very long story."

Gwynn spread her hands. "Yeah, of course it is. Everything with you is a long story, but spill it, girl. I have to know."

Anya sighed. "Her name is Ekaterina Norikova, and she was captain in Sluzhba vneshney razvedki Rossiyskoy Federatsii. This is Russian Foreign Intelligence Service, SVR."

"Yeah, I know what the SVR is. I want to hear about your sister."

"I was inside prison called Black Dolphin in city of Sol-Iletsk, Orenburgskaya Oblast', Russia. Is prison usually only for men."

"Why were you in prison?"

Anya did the last thing Gwynn could've expected: she smiled.

"I was there because I would not give to Kremlin my Chasechka."

"What? Does Chase know that? Wait. How did you get out?"

Anya's smile faded. "No, Chase does not know why I was inside prison, but he knew I was there. He rescued me from this place and put my sister inside prison instead of me."

"Wait a minute," Gwynn said. "He swapped you and your sister? How long did it take for the authorities to figure it out?"

Anya shrugged. "Maybe they have not figured it out yet. I do not know. This was many years ago, and it was also last time I ever held Chase inside my arms and thought of nothing in all of world except being with him. He gave to me precious gifts. Money from my father, passport, car, gun, and freedom from prison. This is when I ran to Siberia to have time to . . . maybe heal from starving and beatings inside prison."

"So, what about your sister?"

"I do not know. She does not have same mother. In English, this makes us only one half of sisters, but she looked almost like twin to me."

Gwynn relaxed against a pillow. "That's what the world needs . . . two of you."

"This is enough talk of sister and Chasechka. What do you think of Dr. Max?"

Gwynn cast her eyes to the ceiling. "He's cute."

Anya blushed. "Yes, he is, but I was talking about—"

"Oh, I know what you were talking about, but he's still cute, and that English accent . . . How did that happen?"

Anya said, "Is Oxford accent. He is Muscovite. I can hear this when he speaks Russian, but English accent is not natural. I think is accent he learned over many years."

"Well, it works for him," Gwynn said.

"Don't be silly girl. Tell to me what you saw other than beautiful man with fake accent."

Gwynn huffed. "Fine. I think if he's as good as he thinks he is, he may be the best plastic surgeon in the world."

Anya slid her laptop from the coffee table and opened the screen. "I want to show you something I found."

Gwynn studied the screen. "What are these?"

Anya said, "They are before and after pictures of patients of Dr. Max."

Gwynn leaned closer and zoomed in on several photos. "That's amazing."

"Is maybe photoshipped, yes?"

Gwynn said, "I think you mean photoshopped, and you may be right. They look almost too perfect."

Anya cocked her head. "English is not best language for me, but I think perfect cannot be too much or not enough. I think perfect means only perfect and not degrees of perfect."

"Oh, so now you're the grammar queen, huh?"

"If crown fits."

Gwynn said, "Are you seriously thinking about having Dr. Max do your surgery?"

Anya shrugged. "Maybe. It would make our story easier to believe if I go through with surgery."

"Yeah, it would, but what if he decides your kidneys are worth more than your face?"

"If this is concern, we have to make sure he knows fixing my face is more valuable than my organs. There is only one way to do this."

"How?" Gwynn asked.

"Bribery."

"I like it," Gwynn said. "But we have to get Agent White to authorize the expenditure."

"Make call to him."

Gwynn handed her phone to Anya. "Oh, no. He'll yell at me. He can't say no to you. You've got that whole she-wizard power thing over him."

Anya took the phone. "I will teach this power to you when you are ready, Hopper of Grass."

"That's Grasshopper, but teach me, oh great one."

The Russian pressed the button, and four rings later, Ray White's voice-mail answered.

Anya said, "Make call to us, Ray. We need money. A lot of money."

"He didn't answer?" Gwynn asked. "That's not like him. Let's call the office."

A few seconds later, Ray's administrative assistant answered. "Supervisory Special Agent White's office."

"Hey, it's Davis. Is Agent White available?"

"I'm sorry, but he's out of the office for the rest of the week, Agent Davis. Did you try his cell phone?"

"Is everything all right?"

The assistant said, "I think so. He just said he'd be out of the office for at least the remainder of the week. I can transfer you to the staff duty officer if you need something right away."

"That's not necessary, but thank you."

Gwynn ended the call. "He's out of the office all week. Again, that's not like him."

"Is okay," Anya said. "I have money to pay Dr. Max."

"I'm not worried about the money right now. I want to know what's going on with Agent White. I'll try his cell again."

The instant she pressed the send button, a knock came at the door, and Anya leapt to her feet. "I will answer door."

Gwynn nodded and pressed the phone to her ear. Four rings came, and again, the voice mailbox answered. She spun on the sofa and said, "He's still not—"

Supervisory Special Agent White stood in the foyer, waggling his phone. "Looking for me?"

Gwynn ended the call and stood, but White waved his hands. "Don't get up."

"What are you doing here?" Gwynn asked.

He frowned. "That's not exactly how I hoped I'd be greeted, but if you must know, I love LA, and I was bored in the office. I thought you two might like some company."

Anya laced a hand inside White's elbow. "We are happy you are here. We need money."

"What for?"

"For surgery," she said. "I have made decision to have surgeries."

White threw up a hand. "Wait a minute. Surgeries? Plural?"

"Yes. Dr. Max says it will maybe take several times to return my face to normal. He said there is damage to bones and cartilage that must be repaired first. This will be surgery number one. After this, comes surgery number two."

"Yeah, that's how numbers work," White said. "How much is it going to cost?"

"This I do not know, but is excellent plan because I will have excuse to be inside office many times, and also, he is very good surgeon."

"How do you know?" White asked.

"Only from talking with him and from looking at pictures of patients."

He said, "I think you might want to dig a little deeper before you let this guy slice into your face."

"Of course I will do this, but so far, so good."

White said, "Help is on the way. I've got a technical team en route from the Sacramento field office. They'll be here later today, and they'll help us dig through the records and handle any technical requirements we may have during the investigation."

"Can they copy access card?" Anya asked.

White shrugged. "I'm sure they can. Why?"

Anya smiled. "I borrowed key to office from person who is maybe nurse, and also access card from Dr. Max. If we can make copies, I can return originals to office, and they will never know."

"The key is easy," White said, "but I'm not certain about the card. The geeks will have to give it a try. So, let's talk about this money you need."

Anya brightened. "Yes, we have idea. If Dr. Max believes he will make more money keeping me alive than selling my organs, I believe he will not let me die. To do this, we must give to him more money than my organs are worth on Russian black market."

"I like it," White said, "but I can't authorize a Wells Fargo truck to pull up outside of his office. I have to run it up the chain."

Anya motioned toward White's pocket. "You have telephone. Make call to chain."

"It's not that simple. I have to submit a request with supporting documentation. It could take a few days."

Anya waved a hand toward his phone. "Then do it. We cannot drag feet. We must be efficient."

White laughed. "Efficient? That's funny. The federal government is exactly the opposite of efficient, but I'll get on it. You guys got anything to eat? I'm starving."

"We have wine and Frosted Flakes. They are delicious alone but terrible together."

He checked his watch. "Your buddy, Dr. Müller, says I can't have alcohol or sugary foods, so let's find a salad. I'm buying."

They found a sidewalk café and settled in. White stuck to his salad and ice water, but Gwynn and Anya splurged a little since dinner was on Ray.

As the hour passed, Anya studied the faces of passers-by until Ray asked, "What are you doing?"

"I am eating dinner," Anya said.

"No, not that. I mean, why are you watching everybody so closely?

We're not in any particular danger on a sidewalk in LA. We're all armed, and there are police officers everywhere."

Anya laid her fork on the edge of her plate. "Is very strange for me. I have never known feeling like this."

"What kind of feeling?" Gwynn asked.

"I do not know English word for this, but all women here are beautiful, and I am not beautiful anymore. Is maybe jealousy, but I do not think this is right word. Is feeling like I want to maybe be one of those beautiful women instead of being me with this face."

White gave Gwynn a wink and said, "It's called envy, and it's one of the seven deadly sins." He turned in his chair. "Look at them. You're right, most of them are beautiful. They're probably actors working their butts off to get their big break. Some of them may have some talent, but most of them are just pretty faces. Every one of them would kill to have your skill set. They envy you."

"This is ridiculous thing to say, Ray. None of them have for me envy."

White's phone vibrated, and he checked the screen. "Special Agent White."

"Agent White, this is Bryan King with the tech team. We made it to LA, and we'll be set up in a few minutes."

White asked, "Did you bring anyone with you who can copy a common access card?"

"Sure, we can do that in a couple of minutes if it's just a magnetic card, but if it's got a chip, it'll take a while."

"We're on our way."

Ray paid the check, and they were standing in front of the techs only minutes later.

Anya handed over the access card. "You can make copy, yes?"

A tech who looked like the sun had never touched his skin took the card from her hand. "Sure. Nothing to it. How many do you want?"

"Only two, please." She produced the key. "How about this? You can make also key, yes?"

"Even easier," the tech said.

Ten minutes later, the work was done, and Anya said, "Is now waiting game."

"Waiting game for what?" White asked.

Anya stared into the western sky. "For waiting until sun is gone and darkness comes. We have medical office to break into."

7

VOLSHEBNYY MIKAEL
(MAGIC MIKE)

The night consumed Tinseltown, and the stars came out.

As Anya drove down Hollywood Boulevard, Gwynn shot a finger through the air and pointed towards the sidewalk. "Oh, my God! That's Matthew McConaughey."

Anya followed her partner's finger. "You know this person? Is small world, yes?"

Gwynn slapped Anya's arm. "No, silly. That's Matthew McConaughey. Please tell me you know who he is."

"I do not know this person. Why are you so excited?"

Gwynn palmed her forehead. "Are you kidding me? It's Dallas from *Magic Mike*. Do you really not know who that is, or are you messing with me?"

Anya scowled. "No, I do not know this person, but he is too skinny, and beard is not good. Is like beard of maybe billy goat."

"You're insane. He's gorgeous." Gwynn slapped the dashboard. "Slow down!"

The Russian tapped the brakes, giving her partner an extra second to adore her big-screen crush. "Is ridiculous. My Chasechka is much better. He is bigger and stronger and can grow real beard like man."

"Am I ever going to meet your Chasechka?" Gwynn asked.

"Yes, of course," Anya said. "I will call to him to come to us when mission is finished."

"Anya, no. He's married. You can't just summon him at will."

"Yes, I can. Penny will understand. I do not plan to sleep with him— only to introduce to you. Although . . ."

"No! Stop that. Just no."

"You cannot tell to me what I can think inside my head. Is my thinking inside my head only."

Gwynn laughed. "It may be *your* thinking in *your* head, but it's showing all over *your* face. I still can't believe we saw Matthew McConaughey. He's a great actor."

"I thought you said he is magician."

"No, he played a character in a movie called *Magic Mike*. It's . . . never mind. I'll show you when this is over. I think I can force myself to suffer through it one more time."

Anya said, "Magic is silly and is for children."

"Trust me, girl. This kind of magic is for full-grown women."

"I will maybe watch with you magic show, but I cannot promise I will not be bored."

Gwynn's grin said she had every confidence Anya would not be bored.

Anya parked the Porsche two blocks away from Dr. Max's clinic to avoid the security cameras. She said, "We will walk behind parking garage to door on side of building. There are still cameras there, but is very dark, and this will give us best chance of being invisible."

Gwynn pulled her cap low across her forehead and followed her partner, moving silently through the darkness. As they approached the corner of the clinic, Anya pulled a pouch from her pocket.

"What's that?" Gwynn asked.

"Is laser to kill camera."

Anya anchored a small bracket to the wall and slid the tubular object into the holder. Then, she pulled a monocular from her other pocket and held it to her eye.

"Now what are you doing?"

Anya said, "Laser is infrared. This means I can only see it with night vision, but camera will not function with beam inside lens."

She adjusted the bracket until the laser was pointed directly into the center of the camera lens. "There. Is done. Let's go." Anya slid the key into the door and turned.

To their relief, the lock withdrew, and they stepped inside. The instant they were through the door, the alarm system issued its soft warning tone indicating they had only seconds to enter the code to avoid the sirens blaring and police cars lining up outside.

Anya turned to Gwynn. "Put in code."

"What code? I don't have the code."

Anya frowned. "What? You do not have code? What are we going to do?"

Gwynn's shoulders fell, and she sighed. "You got me."

Anya grinned. "Yes, of course I did. I am very good at this game."

She pried the cover from the alarm control panel and spent five seconds defeating the simple device. "Okay, is done. We have whole place to ourselves."

"You have to teach me to do that."

Anya cocked her head. "They did not teach this to you at academy?"

"Not hardly. All I learned there was to trust my partner and don't miss if I have to pull the trigger."

"This is also good things to learn."

They made their way through the darkened hallways of the clinic until they came to the reception area in the front. Anya slipped the original door key onto the desk beside the telephone. "This way, maybe they will believe someone found key and left here for person who lost it."

"Good plan," Gwynn whispered.

"You do not have to whisper. Alarm was set, so no one is here."

"It still feels like we should whisper."

"This is silly. Think about Magician Michael. Maybe that will take mind off of breaking and entering."

"It's Magic Mike, but you're right. That will definitely take my mind off this felony we're committing."

"Is not felony yet," Anya said. "Is only breaking and entering so far. It will become felony only after we steal medical records."

"Speaking of stealing records, I'll take care of that while you find a place to put Dr. McHottie Pants's access card."

Anya split from her partner and waved the access card across the reader beside Dr. Max's door. The light turned green, and the lock clicked. She stepped inside and took in the massive space. Everything about the office screamed financial success. From the framed photos of Dr. Max with Hollywood A-listers to Picasso's *Courses de taureaux*, the doctor's ego seemed to echo through the office.

She let herself settle into his plush chair behind the ultra-modern glass-and-steel desk and dropped the stolen access card to the floor beneath the desk to be discovered later. When her reflection shone up at her from the glistening surface, the reality of her new world came crashing down around her. Instantly, the Picasso lost its appeal, and the vast space felt like a coffin.

Looking away from the desk, she yanked the data collection device from her pocket and jammed it into the USB port on the side of Dr. Bortsov's laptop. The program built into the hardware worked its methodical wizardry, collecting a perfect copy of the contents of every hard drive built into the thin computer.

Anya waited, staring alternately at the flashing light on the tip of the USB device and the carpet between her shoes. Her impatience weighed on her mind until time seemed to pass like waves upon crashing waves of time, dragging her mind further from her task and deeper into her sad realization of the woman who no longer peered back at her from within the mirror.

The office door swung inward, and Gwynn stepped through. "Anya, what are you doing? Let's go."

Anya looked up to see the glowing solid green light at the tip of the data collection device and yanked the flash drive from the computer. "I am sorry. I was—"

"It doesn't matter," Gwynn said. "We've got to go."

"Did you collect records you wanted?" Anya asked.

"I think so, but I won't be sure until we can upload the data and dig through what we have."

Anya said, "I have copy of Dr. Bortsov's hard drive."

Gwynn stopped in her tracks and turned to her partner. "So, we're back to Dr. Bortsov instead of Max?"

Anya kept walking. "Does not matter. I thought you said we must go."

Before Gwynn could investigate Anya's mood swing, she heard a whistle from the front of the clinic, and both women turned to stone. Each of them turned an ear toward the sound and held their breath. The whistle became a rumble, and the rumble was followed by at least one pair of footfalls. A moment later, a rustling sound wafted through the air, and Anya reached for her partner.

When her hand met Gwynn's hip, she gently pressed her toward the rear of the office and farther away from the sounds.

Once around a pair of corners in the hallway, Gwynn whispered, "What was that?"

Anya said, "I think maybe was cleaning people. Did you hear sounds from security system?"

Gwynn grimaced. "Maybe. I thought I heard a faint beep right before the whistle."

"I heard also. I think it was four-four-seven-two."

Gwynn shook her head. "You heard individual tones and identified them? Do you have some kind of sonar in your head or something?"

Anya took a long breath. "What I have inside head is all I have. Outside is terrible."

"Now's not the time for that. Let's get out of here before we have a face-to-face with the janitor."

They crept silently through the same door they used to gain entry and became the night. With a swipe of her hand, Anya recovered and pocketed the laser.

Half an hour later, they laid the data collection devices into the waiting palms of the DOJ technicians.

Ray White looked up from what had likely been a catnap. "How'd it go?"

Anya was first to answer. "Fine."

"Just fine?" he asked. "That's what we're going with?"

Gwynn stepped toward their boss. "We made entry without detection thanks to Anya's IR laser and planted the borrowed key and access card where they could be discovered. I retrieved files from the two computers in the file storage area, and Anya nabbed the data from Bortsov's computer in his office."

"That sounds productive," White said. "Did you encounter any issues?"

Anya huffed, and Gwynn gave her a brief look before answering. "We almost got busted by the cleaning crew, but we got out before they could spot us."

"Do you think they heard you?"

"No, we were on our way out when they came in, but if we'd been a minute slower, it would've been a very different story."

"Code is four-four-seven-two," Anya said.

White said, "What?"

She growled. "Four-four-seven-two is security code cleaning person used to turn off alarm that was not on."

"Did you watch the guy type it in?"

"No, I heard tones. This is all. It is important for you to know code if I am not with you next time."

"Not with me?" Gwynn said. "What does that mean?"

Anya slid three fingertips across the skin of her face. "If maybe I am recovering from surgery or something."

"But you're not planning to run off, right?"

"I do not have this plan. I will finish mission because . . . it doesn't matter. I will finish mission."

White eyed Gwynn and mouthed, "Is she okay?"

Gwynn shook her head.

"Bingo!" one of the techs almost yelled. "Nice work in there. We've got medical records and case files going back almost twelve years. You guys are good."

Anya stepped toward the tech and leaned down to see the screen.

"Check it out," he said. "In addition to the medical records, you guys grabbed almost a terabyte of data from Bortsov's computer. This is like a gold mine."

The two technicians practically buzzed with excitement as they pored over the data flashing across their monitors. "It's gonna take us a while to get through all of this, but we'll run comparative checks between the records we already had and the ones you two snatched tonight."

"How long will that take?" White asked.

"It's an automated process, so it's tough to predict. Maybe four or five hours, but we have dedicated processors for that so we can keep working even while that's running."

"What will that comparative check tell us?" Gwynn asked.

The tech said, "Mostly, it'll verify the data we already had, if it corroborates, but I'm interested to see what's different between what we had and what you picked up tonight. That's going to be the real tell."

Gwynn asked, "What do you mean?"

The tech squirmed in his seat. "I don't know. I mean, I know I'm not supposed to make guesses, but something tells me the files we had were woefully incomplete. We'll get a report on differences, as well as similarities, in the two databases. I'm sure we'll have something for you by morning."

Anya checked her watch. "Is already morning."

The tech rolled his eyes. "Okay, Madam Technical, I'm confident we'll have something for you by nine a.m."

White laid a hand on the tech's shoulder and gave a squeeze. "Check the attitude with my agents. Operators like them are rare, but computer geeks are a dime a dozen."

He nodded. "Yes, sir. I'm sorry. It won't happen again."

"Don't apologize to me," White said. "Talk to the Russian with the knives."

8

DERZHITE SVOI DEN'GI
(KEEP YOUR MONEY)

The tech's estimate of 9:00 a.m. came and went as Ray White paced behind the pair of customized chairs precisely designed to fit the posterior of the computer wizards. "How much longer?"

"I'm sorry, Agent White, but the anomalies are all over the place. It's going to take some time to sort this out. Nothing we expected happened overnight."

White pounded a fist against the side table. "How much longer?"

The tech recoiled. "There's no way to know. If I had to guess, I'd say maybe eight hours, but that's not a guarantee."

White caught his breath. "Would it help if I brought in more techs?"

"Not immediately," he said. "It would take longer to bring them up to speed than to finish parsing this data, but some more help would be nice if we're going to continue operating around the clock. We're crashing pretty hard."

"Crashing?" White yelled. "This guy is selling body parts on the black market. Do you get that? Body parts! And you two are crying about missing a few hours of sleep?"

Gwynn laid a gentle hand against White's back and encouraged him to walk with her. "Let's take a break and have some coffee."

White groaned, but he let himself be led away from the exhausted techs poised at their computers.

Anya slipped onto an office chair and rolled between the two techs as they labored away. "Tell to me your names."

Both men stopped what they were doing and turned to face the Russian.

The first tech wore a terrified look. "You're not firing us, are you?"

"Of course not," Anya said. "I would just like to know your names. I am Anya."

He said, "Yeah, we know who you are, but your ID says your name is Ana Fulton."

"Yes, this is official name for working with government, but my real name is Anya."

"Okay, I'm Bryan, and he's Chris."

"Is very nice to meet you. Please do not be afraid of Ray. He is loud sometimes, but Gwynn and I will take care of him for you. Now, tell to me this anomaly."

"That's easy for you to say," Chris said. "You've got no reason to be afraid of anybody. We're just IT guys."

"Do not worry about him," Anya said. "He is big bear named Teddy."

Bryan furrowed his brow. "I'm pretty sure you meant teddy bear."

"Yes, this is what I said. Now, tell to me about anomaly."

He rolled his chair to the left, giving Anya a clear view of his screen. "Check it out. In the right column are the reported fatalities during surgery with Dr. Bortsov. That list is public information, mostly. Anyway, it's the data we already had, but it doesn't match the records you and Agent Davis acquired last night."

"What does not match?"

He said, "Well, it partly matches. All the names we had match the names officially reported by Dr. Bortsov's practice, but the anomaly happened when we ran the list against a twelve-month mortality list in California."

"Why would you run this comparison?" Anya asked.

Chris blushed. "It was a mistake, to be honest. I was trying to back-door my way into a short-term mortality list to see if any of the patients died within a few days of surgery, and I set the parameters incorrectly."

"What did you find?"

Bryan took over. "That's what I'm showing you on this monitor. Dr. Bortsov's practice performed one thousand two hundred sixty surgical procedures last year. That's the count for the whole practice, not just for Bortsov. Six of those procedures resulted in fatalities in the operating room or within twelve hours of surgery. That's zero point four seven percent, making the clinic's surgical mortality rate slightly above the national average, but not particularly alarming."

Anya leaned in. "I do not see problem."

A new set of data filled the screen, and Bryan said, "Take a look at this. This is the one-year mortality rate of cosmetic surgical patients nationwide. There are just over one point five million plastic surgeries every year in the U.S. Some of those are multiple procedures done on the same patient, so the number of patients is slightly less than one point five million. Try to stay with me. It gets a little math-heavy at this point."

Anya said, "I can keep up."

Bryan continued. "Of the one point five, about eight and a half percent die within one year of their surgery. This is where it gets weird. Dr. Bortsov's patients are dying at a rate of almost eleven percent post-surgery. Most of that eleven percent die between nine and twelve months out."

Anya let out a satisfied sigh. "This is where the killing is happening. He isn't killing anybody on operating table. He is killing them after surgery." She hopped to her feet, kissed Bryan on the forehead, and said, "You are genius. Take break and sleep now . . . both of you. Come back when you feel rested. I will take care of Agent White."

"Are you sure?" Bryan asked.

"You never have to ask if I am sure. If I say something, I mean this something always."

"Yes, ma'am."

Anya found Ray and Gwynn at the neighboring coffee shop, nestled into a booth in the back. She said, "Do you feel better?"

Ray tapped his cup. "Coffee always makes me feel better. Did you get anything meaningful out of Tweedledee and Tweedledum?"

"Do not call them those terrible names. They are very good at their jobs. And yes, I have good information."

She slid into the booth beside White, and Gwynn slid a cup toward her. "We got you a tea, and I've already stirred in the honey."

Anya said, "Thank you. Now, about Bryan and Chris. These are their names. Not Tweedle. I put them to bed, by the way."

White said, "You did what?"

"Yes. I told them to go away and have sleep. They are very tired, and we have already information we need."

White lowered his chin. "They don't work for you, and they said they wouldn't have the data we need for another eight hours."

Anya took a sip of her steaming tea. "This is what they told to you because you scared them. I was kind to them, and they gave to me everything we need."

White groaned. "I can't wait to hear this."

Anya swallowed her mouthful of tea. "According to data, patients of Dr. Bortsov's clinic do not die on operating table in numbers out of line with national averages."

"Yes, they do," White said. "According to the information in the preliminary file, they're dying at nearly twice the national average."

"This is because you did not read data correctly. They are not dying on operating table. They are dying between nine and twelve months after surgery. This is alarming number and real mystery."

White drained his coffee cup. "Run through the numbers with me."

Anya spent the next five minutes detailing what she'd learned from the techs.

When she finished, he said, "How does that happen?"

Anya shrugged. "I do not know, but is true."

Gwynn said, "What if they're doing something to the patients during the surgery that will ensure their deaths nine months later?"

"How?" White asked again.

Gwynn said, "I don't know, but we clearly need to talk to the families of the patients who died long after surgery with Bortsov's clinic."

Anya stepped in. "Also, we need more computer technicians. You are pushing Bryan and Chris too hard."

"You don't get to make those calls," White said.

Anya leaned back and sipped her tea. "If you want good work from smartest people we have, you must have more. Bryan and Chris cannot work twenty-four hours without sleeping and still do good work. Is only option."

"Fine. I'll get a couple more techs, but don't send them to bed anymore. They work for me. Got it?"

"Maybe, but if they are too tired to work, you must let them sleep."

White said, "Whatever. So, what's going on with your decision to have the surgery?"

"Court is where your ball is."

White shook his head. "What?"

"This is American saying. It means you are now responsible for what happens next."

Gwynn giggled, and White huffed. "No, it isn't. The phrase is, the ball is in your court."

"Is same thing," Anya said.

"What makes the ball in my court?"

Anya said, "I told to you that we need money for surgery to make Dr. Bortsov keep me alive."

Ray checked his watch. "I made the request. It's up to the AG's office."

Anya motioned toward Ray's cell phone. "Call them."

He held up both hands. "You're not in charge, so stop giving orders."

She lifted the phone and placed it in Ray's palm. "Please call them. I will pay if necessary, but if government will pay, this is better for me."

White lifted the phone to his ear.

Two minutes later, he ended the call and said, "Keep your money, wherever you keep it. The AG approved a million dollars."

"Thank you. Perhaps that will be enough. We will know soon." Anya drew her phone from a pocket, and when the call connected, she said, "Is Anastasia Belyaeva. I must speak with Kristina."

The muffled sound of hold music escaped the speaker, then she said, "Hello, Kristina. Is Anastasia Belyaeva. I wish to have surgery now."

The back-and-forth continued for a few minutes until Anya said, "Thank you. I will be there at three." She hung up and said, "I have appointment at three o'clock today with Dr. Max. I must have one hundred thousand dollars in cash for this appointment. You can do this for me, yes?"

Ray sighed. "I almost forgot how exhausting you can be, but yes, I'll have the cash for you."

Four hours later, Ray stepped into the lair of the techs and dropped a banded stack of one-hundred-dollar bills in front of each of them. "Nice job, guys. Take the afternoon and evening off. Go drink and smoke, or whatever you guys do, and report back at eight tomorrow morning."

Chris looked up and shied away from White. "Is this some kind of integrity check or something?"

"No, it's not some kind of integrity check. It's my way of apologizing for being an ass this morning. Two more of you guys will be here tomorrow to pitch in. Be ready to bring them up to speed. I don't have time to deal with a learning curve."

Chris and Bryan shut down their computers and vanished at the same time Anya and Gwynn showed up at Dr. Bortsov's clinic with a much more impressive stack of bills in Anya's oversized purse.

Kristina met them in the foyer. "Hello, Ms. Belyaeva. Nice to see you again. Please follow me."

Kristina deposited them in Dr. Bortsov's office in front of the enormous, gleaming desk. "Max will be with you in just a moment. Would either of you care for a glass of wine while you're waiting?"

Gwynn held up a hand. "Oh, thank you, but we can't."

Anya pushed Gwynn's hand from the air. "Of course we can. We would love glass of wine. Thank you. White, please."

Kristina bowed ever so slightly. "Of course. Just a moment."

Seconds later, they sat in the most comfortable chairs in any doctor's office anywhere in the world and sipped their wine.

Dr. Max Bortsov came through the door, running a hand through his hair. "Ladies . . . How good it is to see both of you again. I trust Kristina took care of you."

Anya held up her glass. "She did. Thank you."

He settled into his seat. "I'm so sorry to have kept you waiting. I hear you'd like to move up our surgery date."

"I would," Anya said. "As soon as possible."

The doctor pressed a button on his phone, and his nurse materialized as if from thin air with her tablet in hand.

"Andrea, Ms. Belyaeva would like to move up her date. What do we have available?"

She scanned through her tablet, leaned close to Max, and whispered something.

The doctor pursed his lips and leaned back. "It appears we have an opening tomorrow afternoon. I have two patients to see early tomorrow morning, but yours will be the only procedure, if tomorrow works for you."

Anya's eyes lit up. "This is perfect. Yes, we will take it."

Andrea typed furiously on the tablet. "If it's convenient for you, try to arrive before ten a.m., and don't have anything to eat or drink after midnight. We'll need to do some blood work when you arrive, and we'll have you in the surgical suite just after noon."

"That is fine," Anya said.

Max repositioned in his seat. "This is always the uncomfortable part, but unfortunately, it is necessary. Your insurance will pay a portion of the associated expenses of the procedure, but we provide a luxury service with far more attention than any hospital. I'm sure you understand."

Anya considered playing with the doctor, but instead, she stacked banded cash on the edge of the desk until one hundred thousand dollars formed a neat line in front of her.

Max mentally counted the stacks. "It's always nice to find a well-prepared patient. Andrea will prepare a receipt for you."

"This is not necessary. I trust you to put your hands inside my face and make me again beautiful like my mother, so a matter of dollars does not concern me."

Max tilted his head and nodded slowly. "We appreciate your trust, and you will not be disappointed with the results."

"I am sure I will not be disappointed."

Max suddenly turned his attention to Gwynn. "And may I assume you'll drive Ms. Belyaeva?"

"Yes, I'll drive her," Gwynn said. "But she won't go home tomorrow night, right?"

Max smiled. "No, not after this procedure. This will be an in-patient surgery, and you'll spend the night, but not at the hospital. We have four surgical suites here with accompanying luxury accommodations for post-surgical recovery. Of course, you're welcome to stay overnight as well if you'd like, Ms. Davis."

"Thank you, Dr. Bortsov."

He waved a hand. "Oh, no. I thought we discussed this. Please call me Max. Informality is our status quo."

As the words dripped from his tongue, he focused his attention directly on Gwynn. "Forgive me," he said. "But has your left eye always been smaller than your right?"

Gwynn, suddenly self-conscious, reached for her face. "I didn't realize it was."

Max took Andrea's elbow. "Please bring us a magnifying mirror."

She returned in seconds with a lighted mirror with a convex curve to the glass.

Max held the mirror in front of Gwynn. "It's subtle, but as we age, subtleties tend to magnify. It's a simple outpatient procedure if you'd be interested in having me take care of that for you. The recovery period is brief, with very little, if any, post-surgical pain."

Gwynn turned away from the mirror. "I can't afford the surgery." She glanced at Anya. "I'm not, well . . . I can't afford it. But thank you for offering."

Max shrugged. "We have less expensive and less luxurious options other than our clinic here in LA. We have a clinic in the Dominican Republic, for example. Procedures there, due to several factors, are significantly less expensive than here in the U.S. Give it some thought, and if you have questions, feel free to speak with Andrea or Kristina."

9

DAUN-AYLEND
(DOWN ISLAND)

As Gwynn and Anya stepped through the door of their rented condo, Supervisory Special Agent Ray White looked up from the sofa. "There's my angels."

Gwynn asked, "Should we start calling you Charlie now?"

He chuckled. "No, Bosley would be more appropriate. The angels never actually saw Charlie."

Anya frowned. "Who are these people you are talking about?"

Gwynn said, "When this is over, you and I are pulling a month-long American television session."

"Can we have also wine with television session?"

"You know it, girl."

Ray said, "Enough with the sorority girl routine. What did you learn at the clinic?"

Anya wasted no time. "We learned where Bortsov is harvesting organs."

"We already knew that. According to the data the techs dug up, he's poisoning his patients, and they're dying within a year of their surgery, at which time somebody is plucking their organs out before they're buried."

Anya said, "Yes, this is true, but is only small tomatoes compared to what we found out from Dr. Bortsov today."

"It's small potatoes, but I get your point. What did you learn?"

She said, "We learned they have also cosmetic surgery clinic in Dominican Republic."

White sank into the sofa and let out a long sigh. "That is beautiful. Nice work. How did you figure it out?"

Gwynn said, "Dr. Asshole pointed out that my eyes aren't the same size and that I need a procedure to fix that."

White leaned toward his agent. "They look the same size to me."

Anya focused on Ray. "Perhaps you could maybe have facelift to take away bags below your eyes."

White grabbed his face. "What are you talking about? I don't have bags under my eyes."

She said, "Look inside mirror."

White jumped to his feet and ran for the bathroom. When he returned, he said, "You're right. I do have the beginnings of bags."

Anya said, "This is what Dr. Max did to Gwynn. There is nothing wrong with her eyes. She is perfect, but he made her believe eyes are different. Is psychological strategy, and it works."

White rubbed the skin beneath his eyes. "So, how did that lead to a clinic in the Dominican Republic?"

Gwynn shot a thumb toward Anya. "Moneybags over here threw a hundred grand in cash onto the doctor's desk, and the cash register in his head went off like a slot machine. He started selling me on a procedure to fix my cartoon eyes."

White painted the picture in his head. "Quit freaking out about your eyes. There's nothing wrong with them. But that still doesn't explain the DR connection."

"Oh," Gwynn said. "When I told him I couldn't afford his fee, that's when he brought up the clinic down island."

White chewed his bottom lip for a moment. "Okay, we've got to find a way to get into that clinic."

Gwynn said, "That's easy. I'll take the referral, and we'll get on an airplane."

"Slow down," White said. "It's one thing to undergo plastic surgery in LA for an undercover op, but doing it in a third-world country is a whole other animal. I'm not willing to throw either of you down that rabbit hole."

"We don't have to go through with the surgery," Gwynn said. "We can play it right up to the line and run the same game on them that we ran here. If we can break into a clinic here, surely we can waltz right into one in the Dominican Republic. They may not even have computers down there. Who knows?"

White held up a finger. "Hold that thought, and we'll come back to it. But first, tell me what came out of your request to move the surgery up."

Anya said, "Is happening tomorrow. I cannot eat or drink after midnight, and Dr. Max will perform surgery in early afternoon."

"And you're completely comfortable with that?" White asked.

"Is first step in having again face of my mother, so comfort is not consideration. I must do this. Besides, this is only first surgery of maybe two or three more. I am for Dr. Max goose who is laying golden eggs. He will not kill me until he has taken all of my money."

White said, "I wasn't asking about him killing you. I was asking whether you're sure you want to go through with the surgery. There are risks."

Anya's phone chirped, and she checked the screen. "Is text message from Chasechka."

Gwynn slid toward her partner. "What did he say?"

"He is asking if I can take telephone call from him. What should I tell him?"

Gwynn huffed. "There's only one answer to that question. Take the call."

Anya shrugged and replied to Chase's message.

Seconds later, her phone rang, and she said, "Hello, my Chasechka."

"Hello, Anya. How are you?"

"I am fine. Tomorrow I am having first surgery to repair face."

"Yeah, that's kind of why I'm calling. Do you have a couple of minutes to talk?"

"Yes, of course. I am talking to you now."

"Are you alone?"

"No, I am here with Gwynn and Ray. Also, Gwynn wants to meet you. You will do this, yes?"

"Why?"

"Why what?" Anya asked.

"Why does Gwynn want to meet me?"

"Because I told to her everything about you, and she cannot believe it is true. She has to see for herself."

"I'm not sure that's a great idea, but we'll see."

"So, is yes. We will make plan for this."

"No, Anya. I said we'd see."

"Yes, I know, but for me, this means yes. Thank you, Chasechka. This is now decided, so what else do you want to talk about?"

"It's not decided, but we'll see. I was calling to talk with you about the surgery."

"Yes, I will have maybe three surgical procedures. First is tomorrow and will repair damage to structure of face, bone, and cartilage."

"Are you sure you want to go through with it?" he asked.

"Of course, yes. Why would I not? I will always remember first time you looked at me. You liked what you saw."

Chase said, "You don't know the first time I saw you."

"Of course I do."

He chuckled. "I don't think you do. The first time I saw you, you were on top of a water tower in Elmont, New York, behind a rifle."

"Okay, so maybe I was not thinking of that time, but I remember first time you looked at me from close. Your pupils dilated, and you took long breath. Every girl wants boy to do this same thing. You wanted me."

He stammered. "Uh, I mean . . . I was on an assignment. It was—"

"Is okay, Chasechka. It makes my heart smile even now, all these years later. Is wonderful feeling, and I will never have this feeling again from your eyes if I do not have surgery."

Chase peered through the plexiglass window in the hangar's small office to make sure he was still alone. "That's why I'm calling. I need to answer your question."

"I did not ask question," she said.

"Yes, you did. You asked me if I would want you if I didn't have Penny."

"Yes, I remember this question, and I should not have asked. It made you angry because you thought I might kill her so I could have you."

"No, I didn't really think you'd kill her. It's just that . . ."

"Is okay," she said again. "I will never hurt you or anyone you love. You are dear to me, and I should not have asked question. It was moment of weakness for me."

"There's nothing weak about you, Anya."

She said, "You will always be greatest weakness for me."

Chase caught his breath. "I want you to know something."

"I probably already know this something, but tell to me anyway."

He cleared his throat. "It's about your surgery. I want you to know that you don't need the surgery to be beautiful again."

"This is silly thing to say. Of course I do. I look like monster."

"No, you don't. Maybe I'm biased, but the answer is yes. If there were no Penny, I would—"

"But I am hideous."

He sighed. "Not to me. You'll always be that gorgeous girl with the blonde ponytail up on that water tower. You're still beautiful to me, so if you're having the surgeries out of some strange desire to still make me look at you the way I did back then, don't do it. I love Penny, and I'd never leave her under any circumstances, but you don't need the surgery to make me see how beautiful you are. I already see that, Anya, and I always will."

She swallowed hard and fought back the coming tear. "I do not know what to say. No one has ever said to me anything so good. I will always love you, my Chasechka, even if you cannot love also me."

"I just wanted you to know."

"Thank you," she said. "But I must have surgery for me. Is not for you."

"If that's true, and I have no reason to doubt you this time, I'll pay for the surgery. You got hurt on an operation with us, so it's only right that we cover the cost."

"This is very kind of you, but is not necessary."

"No, you don't need to spend your money on this, and I know it has to be expensive. Let us pay for it. I talked with Penny about it, and she understands and agrees. It's our responsibility."

"This is wonderful offer from you, but . . ." She covered the mouthpiece with her hand and whispered, "Can I tell to him we are on mission and government is paying for surgery?"

White scowled. "Yes, but nothing more than that."

She removed her hand from the phone. "I am working on case with Department of Justice investigating Russian mafia in California. Your government agreed to pay for surgery with one of best surgeons in America. If maybe they change mind, I will take money from you."

A moment of silence prevailed until Chase said, "Just take care of yourself, okay? The world is better with you in it."

"I will see you when I bring friend Gwynn to meet you. Goodbye, my Chasechka." Anya stared at the phone and whispered, "He said yes."

White turned an ear toward the Russian. "About what?"

Anya looked up and smiled. "Nothing. Was only for me. We must find wonderful place for dinner so I can have fantastic meal before being hungry for surgery."

* * *

It took a two-hundred-dollar tip to the maître d', but the three scored a quiet table in the main dining room at Spago Beverly Hills, just past eight o'clock.

After the fourth course, the chef appeared table-side and laid a gentle hand against Gwynn's shoulder. "I trust you are enjoying your dinner."

Gwynn glanced up and gasped. "Oh, my God. You're Wolfgang Puck."

The world-renowned chef bowed almost imperceptibly. "I am, indeed. Thank you for noticing. Dessert is on the house tonight. I promise you will not be disappointed."

When the chef stepped away, Gwynn shot a finger toward him. "That was Wolfgang Puck."

Anya laughed. "Yes, we heard. Are you now also famous chef because he touched you?"

"Cut it out," Gwynn said. "I can't help it if I'm a chef groupie. I love good food, but on a government salary, this is a real treat."

Dessert arrived, and Chef Puck had been correct. Nothing about the array of pastries disappointed anyone.

When they'd finished, Anya paid the check and never mentioned the butterflies in her stomach as she braced for a sleepless night before Dr. Maxim Bortsov's blade pierced her flesh for the first time.

10

PERVYY RAZREZ GLUBOKIY
(THE FIRST CUT IS THE DEEPEST)

Anya's eyes fluttered open, and she slowly scanned the room until Gwynn's face came into focus. "I am alive, yes?"

Gwynn smiled down at her friend. "Yes, you're very much alive, and according to the doctor, the surgery went perfectly."

Dr. Maxim Bortsov stepped through the door, took Anya's hand, and spoke in their native Russian. "Welcome back, beautiful lady. Everything went perfectly. You're the model patient."

To Anya's surprise, her words left her lips in English. "I am okay?"

Bortsov switched to his practiced British tongue. "You're better than okay. I had a marvelous foundation to work with, so you made my job quite easy. How do you feel?"

"I am sleepy and a little, uh, maybe confused."

The doctor squeezed her hand. "That's perfectly normal as the anesthesia wears off. We're going to make you as comfortable as possible, and someone will be by your side constantly for the next twenty-four hours. As soon you're ready, you can have something to eat and drink. I suspect you'll be hungry soon."

"Chase is here, yes?"

Bortsov turned to Gwynn and raised an eyebrow.

Gwynn said, "No, he's not here, but you probably dreamed about him in your sleep."

Anya narrowed her eyes. "No, he was here. He told to me I was still beautiful. I remember this."

Bortsov said, "It's okay. Whoever Chase is, he's a lucky guy, and he's right. You are beautiful. The anesthesia will wear off soon, but we'll manage any pain you experience with some very enjoyable medication. Do you have any questions for me?"

Anya glanced between Gwynn and the doctor. "Are you killing your p—"

Gwynn clamped down on Anya's hand and let out a theatrical laugh. "She and I were talking before you took her back for surgery, and we said you had to be killing your practice by spending all day with only one patient."

The doctor smiled. "On the contrary. My practice is thriving precisely because I spend so much time providing individual attention. We are a concierge practice built on quality, not quantity." He paused and held out his hands. "Well, that, plus the fact that I'm very good at what I do."

Anya let her eyes close. "Yes, of course."

While Anya slept off the anesthesia, Gwynn dialed Ray's number.

He answered almost before it rang. "White."

"Agent White, it's Davis. Anya's out of surgery and doing fine. She almost slipped up and asked Bortsov if he's killing his patients. We have to make sure one of us is with her when she comes out of surgery every time. It was close, but I managed to intercede before it turned ugly."

"Good catch, Davis. Did the surgery go well?"

"According to the doctor, it was perfect. He said she was a model patient."

"How does she look?"

"Really? That's what you want to know right now?"

"No, Davis, not like that. I meant, does it look like anything other than the planned surgery happened to her?"

"Oh, that. No, she's fine, other than the facial surgery. She's still bandaged, so I can't answer the question I thought you asked."

"Stay with her and keep her mouth under control. The last thing we need is a former Russian assassin stoned out of her mind and telling every-thing she knows."

"Apparently, she'll be here for at least twenty-four hours, but I'll keep you posted. Have you made any headway on the Dominican Republic clinic?"

He said, "None, and it's not looking good. I'll brief you as soon as you get our Muscovite Frankenstein home."

"That's not nice."

He said, "Nice has never been one of my filters. Take care of our girl, and let me know if she does anything stupid."

An hour later, with the anesthesia worn off, Anya reached for her face. She wrestled with the IV line and finally probed the bandages with her fin-gertips. "I need mirror."

Andrea, the nurse, stepped through the door just as Gwynn stood from her seat beside Anya's bed. "Welcome back, Ms. Belyaeva. How are you feeling?"

"I need mirror."

Andrea untangled the IV. "There's not much to see. You look more like a mummy than a person right now."

Anya squirmed and pressed the control to raise the head of her bed. "Bring to me mirror or take away IV so I can go to bathroom."

Andrea asked, "Do you need to use the restroom?"

Anya said, "May I have mirror, please?"

The nurse said, "Yes, if you insist."

"Good, then I do not need to use restroom."

Andrea placed a handheld mirror in Anya's hand.

She held the glass close to her face, twisting and turning the mirror until she was satisfied. "Thank you."

Gwynn took the mirror from her. "What was that all about?"

Anya said, "I have still eyes of my mother. This is important to me. When can we take off bandages?"

Andrea said, "We'll change the dressing this evening before you go to sleep, and we'll take another look tomorrow morning and possibly change them again."

Anya snatched the mirror back from Gwynn. "In this case, I will keep mirror. When can we do second surgery?"

"That's up to the doctor," Andrea said. "But it's usually at least two weeks between procedures to allow adequate time to heal from the previous operation."

Anya said, "I do not need to heal before next surgery. This one was for structure of bone and cartilage only."

"You'll have to take that up with Dr. Max," Andrea said. "Are you in pain?"

Anya shrugged. "Not much. I am very strong."

The nurse smiled. "We don't want you to experience any pain at all, if we can make that possible."

"I do not like drugs to make my mind soft."

"You don't have to worry about that. Your partner will be here with you, and you'll always have at least two nurses around the clock. You can relax and enjoy the vacation."

The Russian turned to Gwynn. "You will stay with me?"

"Of course I will. You've got nothing to worry about."

"Is okay also with Ray?"

Gwynn smiled. "Yes, in fact, he'll probably stop by to see you this evening."

"I would like that, but you must tell to him I am inside bandages."

"He knows," Gwynn said. "I spoke with him while you were napping."

Anya turned to Andrea. "Okay, I will have medicine for pain. It hurts."

The nurse pulled a syringe from her pouch and injected the narcotic into Anya's IV. "It will only take a few seconds for you to feel some relief. Just relax and enjoy. If you need anything, let us know."

"Thank you. I will be fine," she said. "I would like to see doctor before I fall asleep. This is possible, yes?"

"Of course," Andrea said. "I'll have him come in. Is there anything else you need?"

Anya turned to Gwynn. "You must be hungry. She will bring for you food."

Gwynn said, "Stop worrying about me. I'm fine."

Anya glanced back at the nurse. "Please bring for her food."

Andrea made a few notes on her tablet and turned for the door. "Dr. Max will be in to see you in just a moment."

Almost before the nurse was out of the room, Dr. Bortsov came in, dressed in a suit that the federal government's one hundred thousand dollars probably paid for. "Hello, again. How are you feeling?"

"Is painful, but I have now drugs to help. I wanted to talk to you before my mind is confused. When can I have next surgery?"

He took her hand. "Let's get through this one first and see how you heal. We don't have to be in a hurry."

"This is not acceptable answer. We will schedule next surgery at earliest possible time."

"You are a woman who is accustomed to immediately having everything she wants, aren't you?"

As the narcotics began clawing at her mind, Anya said, "I cannot have Chase."

Dr. Max leaned in. "I'm sorry. What was that?"

Gwynn said, "I think she—"

Anya interrupted. "I said, when is soonest time for next surgery?"

Dr. Max took a step toward the door, and Anya said, "Where are you going? We have not chosen time for next surgery."

Max turned and flashed his flawless smile. "Don't jump out of bed. I'll be right back. I'm just getting my calendar."

Anya rolled her head to face Gwynn and stared up at her with a nar-cotic-induced peacefulness in her eyes. "You will make for me appoint-ment, yes? I am falling asleep."

When Dr. Max returned with Andrea at his side, Anya was well on her way to the spirit world, but she blinked several times in rapid succession and forced the words from her lips. "Perhaps tomorrow, yes?"

"That's a little ambitious," Max said. "But if everything goes perfectly and you have no complications from today's surgery, it is possible that we could perform your second surgery early next week."

"Yes," floated from the Russian's lips as she closed her eyes, succumbing to the demand of the narcotics making their way through her body.

* * *

The night passed with Anya sleeping soundly, while the nurse returned time after time, routinely injecting the precise dosage of narcotics to keep her comfortable.

When the sun finally pierced the window shade, the Russian was alert, sitting up, and quickly returning to her presurgical wit. "Is time for break-fast, yes?"

Gwynn yawned and stretched. "I guess it is. How are you feeling?"

"Hungry."

Gwynn threw her legs over the edge of her bed. "I meant, how does your face feel?"

Anya subconsciously reached for her bandages with her fingertips. "Is small amount of pain, but I do not wish to have more drugs."

"Maybe a smaller dose just to knock the edge off?" Gwynn said.

"We will see, but for now, I am ready for breakfast."

As if on cue, Andrea stepped through the door with a pair of plates. Anya's held soft scrambled eggs, oatmeal, and yogurt, but Gwynn's was a little more substantial. They ate in silence until the plates were empty, and Anya said, "I am ready for next surgery now."

Gwynn pushed away her plate. "I'm thinking that's not going to happen, but maybe the doctor will let you go home today."

Andrea cleared the plates, and Dr. Max stepped through the door. "Good morning. I trust you slept well, Ms. Belyaeva."

"Yes, I did. When is next surgery?"

Max gave her a smile. "Let's have a look beneath those bandages before we make any rash decisions." He stepped beside the bed and meticulously unwrapped and removed the gauze from her face.

Gwynn grimaced when the final bandage left Anya's face, but the doctor showed no reaction.

He leaned close and examined the bruised flesh. "It looks better than expected."

Gwynn looked away, and Anya said, "I will have again mirror."

Dr. Max said, "Sure, but don't be too surprised. The first day after the type of surgery you had is unpleasant. And remember, we still have the cosmetic bits to do."

Andrea placed the mirror in Anya's hand, and she held it in front of her face. She gasped. "This is better than expected? I look like monster. What have you done to me?"

The doctor laid a hand on Anya's arm. "Trust me. When the bruising fades and the incisions heal, you'll be pleasantly surprised. You're less than twenty-four hours out of surgery, and there was a lot of reconstruction to be done."

"How long?" Anya asked.

"How long for what?"

She said, "How long until I look like my mother again?"

Max said, "This process requires a great deal of patience. Rest assured that the quality of work we perform here is among the best in the world, with some of the shortest healing times in the industry. We are very gentle."

Anya pointed to her face. "This is not gentle."

Max smiled again. "I know it's surprising, but please know that you look much better than I expected for the amount of reconstruction we had to perform. Whatever happened to you was far more violent than you admitted."

Anya ducked her head. "It was bad day for me."

"I'm sure it was, but don't worry. We're going to erase any evidence the incident left behind."

Anya didn't look up. "Thank you, Doctor."

"It's just Max. And based on what I see this morning, I'm comfortable proceeding with the second surgery on Tuesday of next week, but that will require a great deal of commitment from you."

Anya finally looked up. "Commitment from me?"

"Yes," the doctor said. "I'm going to send you home, but you have to promise that you won't do anything besides resting and eating soft foods for the next four days. If you'll do that, I'll place you on the calendar for Tuesday."

Gwynn locked eyes with the doctor. "I won't leave her side, and she won't do anything that doesn't qualify as resting."

He stared down at Anya and pointed toward Gwynn. "You're lucky to have her. She's a good friend."

Anya let the memories of her time with Gwynn play through her mind. Gwynn had come so far from that naïve lawyer with a badge and gun. She'd grown into a knife-wielding, street-hardened fighter, and Anya had been the catalyst for every step Gwynn made. Trust between the two was a bond that couldn't be severed. They'd worn each other's blood and held each other's lives in their hands. They'd failed and triumphed, suffered and cele-brated, but through the years, neither doubted the other. In the toughest moments, when lesser souls would crumble, they did not. When bullets flew and blades pierced the air, the two stood in the face of fear, and likely death itself, to still be standing when the smoke cleared and evil bowed at their feet.

"I am luckiest girl in all of world. Friend Gwynn is more than sister to me, and I love her more than I could ever love myself."

The doctor took a step back. "I wasn't ready for that, but I believe you, and now I know you'll be more than ready for Tuesday."

Gwynn couldn't take her eyes from Anya's. "That's the sweetest thing anyone has ever said to me, and I feel exactly the same."

Dr. Bortsov took another step back. "I won't ruin this moment for the two of you, but Andrea will be in to reapply the bandages, and you're welcome to go home when you feel ready."

11

Seychas My
(We Are Now)

"Are you sober?" Ray White growled only seconds after walking into the condominium.

"Which one of us?" Gwynn asked.

"Both."

Anya said, "I should not drive car, but I am awake. This is maybe not sober, but also not unconscious."

White ceased his line of questioning and studied the Russian's bandages. "That looks like it hurts. Are you okay?"

"I will be. I have number-two surgery on Tuesday."

"Tuesday? Like five days from now?"

"Yes, I am very good patient, and I have also very good nurse."

"They sent a nurse home with you?"

Anya shook her head and took Gwynn's hand. "No, my personal nurse brought me home."

White rolled his eyes. "If I were in a gunfight, Davis would be my number-one choice, but as far as nurses go, you might need to look for a pro."

Gwynn grabbed her chest, feigning offense. "That's hurtful. But are you serious about picking me in a gunfight?"

"Oh, I'm sorry," he said. "I forgot that you forgot that I don't care if I hurt your feelings, and yes, I'd rather have you beside me in a street fight over any man I know."

Gwynn dropped her hands. "Okay, that makes up for the hurt. And yes, I'm completely sober, but I'll be glad to make you a drink if you'd like one."

"Keep your seat," he said. "I'll make my own. Can I get you anything?"

Gwynn raised both eyebrows. "Wow, the great and mighty SSA Ray White is making me a drink. What's the occasion?"

"We'll get to that. What do you want to drink?"

"I'll have whatever you're having."

Anya jumped in. "Also same for me, please."

White glared down at her. "Nothing for you. You're high enough already."

"In this case, I will have tea. Thank you."

Ray returned with a pair of wine glasses in one hand and a steaming mug in the other. "Here. You're going to need it. We may all need a handful of Anya's painkillers before this is over, and that's likely to be a lot sooner than we thought."

Gwynn took the wineglass. "What does that mean?"

"It means we don't have any jurisdiction in the Dominican Republic."

Gwynn froze. "No, that can't be right. If Americans are being killed, surely we can claim some sort of jurisdiction. Can't we?"

White took a sip of his wine. "Look at it this way. If Dominicans were being murdered in the United States, would the DR have any jurisdiction to arrest the Americans committing the murders?"

"That's not really the same," Gwynn said.

White crossed his legs and tossed his cell phone onto the sofa beside Gwynn. "Go ahead, Ruth Bader. Give the attorney general a call and explain to her how jurisdiction works. In fact, put it on speaker because I could use a good laugh."

Gwynn sighed. "Okay, but there has to be a way."

"There's a way," White said. "We could declare war on the island, but that's outside of the AG's authority as well. At most, we can post warnings on the surgeon general and the State Department websites. Outside of that, our hands are tied."

Gwynn turned to her friend. "Aren't you going to help me here? You're the problem solver."

Anya said, "I am not lawyer with badge. I have only badge and no bar card, but is simple inside my mind."

"This ought to be good," White said. "Let's hear it."

"When I am finished with surgery, we will go to Dominican Republic and kill doctors who are killing Americans. This solves problem, yes?"

White huffed. "Oh, yeah, that would do it, but that isn't really what the U.S. Department of Justice does."

Anya sipped her tea. "Yes, but it is what clandestine service of Central Intelligence Agency does."

White said, "That may be true, but I don't think they take requests. Unless I'm mistaken, they create their own target packages, and they don't look for much outside help in that area."

Anya shrugged. "This is not problem. We will call Chase, and he will take care of it for us."

"Absolutely not!" White said. "Just no! That's the last thing any of us needs. We don't hire mercenaries to handle DOJ business."

Anya blew across her mug. "Is not business of DOJ. You said we have no jurisdiction. Is now business of people who are not limited by jurisdictional constraints."

"It's still a hard no. We're not calling anybody, especially not your boyfriend."

Anya flinched at the word and reached for the bottle of painkillers on the end table. After swallowing two more, she said, "There is option not inside box."

White shuddered. "What's that supposed to mean?"

"You know this phrase, thinking not on inside of box."

White groaned. "You do that just to torture me, don't you?"

She smiled and hid her bandaged face behind her cup.

"Something tells me I'm going to regret it, but let's hear this not-in-box idea of yours."

Anya straightened her sitting position. "You said to us this will be final operation for you. You remember this, yes?"

"I remember, but I didn't mean it would be the final mission because I'd be getting myself fired for approving harebrained stunts by the two of you."

"Brains do not grow hair, so listen. You are planning to retire from job when mission is finished, yes?"

White said, "That was my plan. The AG is planning to do away with Operation Avenging Angel when this one is over, and I don't have it in me to stand up another team and start all over. The two of you, plus the brain tumor, have done enough damage to my noggin."

Gwynn asked, "Where's this going, Anya?"

"To Dominican Republic, but not for you, maybe."

"What does that mean?" Gwynn asked.

Anya took another sip of tea and seemed to brace herself against the coming effects of the narcotics she'd just swallowed. "If Avenging Angel is no more, and I am Avenging Angel, this means my job is also finished, yes?"

White said, "That's correct. I told you when this began that you'd be free to go if you fulfilled the requirements of our agreement, and you've far exceeded those expectations."

Anya stared at the ceiling for a moment. "Will I have also retirement?"

White laughed. "Who knows? It wouldn't surprise me, though."

"Perhaps I will ask attorney general. She will know answer to this question."

White said, "Yeah, you do that, and let me know how it goes for you. We're getting off track, so let's keep it in the lane."

"I have first question before rest of plan. Do we have enough evidence to continue this operation here in Los Angeles?"

White said, "Maybe, but what answer were you looking for?"

"I thought answer would be no."

"Okay, for the sake of this discussion, let's say we don't have the evidence we need to continue this investigation."

"If this is true, and also we cannot officially do anything about what is happening in Dominican Republic, this means mission is finished, yes?"

White grimaced. "Not exactly finished, but certainly slowed down. If we can bust this guy on even one charge here in the States, we've got a good shot at shutting down his Dominican Republic operation."

"I have other question. Do you believe Dr. Max Bortsov is part of Bratva?"

White shook his head. "There's no reason to believe he's Russian mafia, but their fingerprints are all over this thing. We just have to follow the breadcrumbs back to the Russians."

"What if there are no crumbs of bread?"

"There are always crumbs whenever the Russian mob is involved. They're not known for covering their tracks."

"This is true," Anya said. "They are men of action who believe laws are for other people and not for them."

"That's why we're so good at catching them," White said.

Anya smiled. "This is not true. We are good at catching them because I understand what happens inside minds of these people, and friend Gwynn is fearless and smart . . . and also beautiful."

White said, "I didn't mean to imply the two of you weren't the reason we're batting a thousand until this mission."

Anya's smile continued. "This is baseball phrase. I have told you that Chase is famous baseball star, yes?"

Gwynn laid a hand against Anya's arm. "Yes, you've mentioned that about a thousand times, and you always get that same smile on your face."

Anya giggled, and White said, "Well, there it is . . . that narcotic goofiness. We're done for today."

Anya blinked several times in rapid succession. "No, I am not finished with thinking inside another box."

"Oh, I think you're finished," White said. "I just hope you'll remember what we were talking about in five or six hours when that dose of whatever you just swallowed wears off."

"I remember this now," Anya said. "I believe Dr. Bortsov is not guilty, but maybe his partners in Dominican Republic are horrible men, doing unthinkable things for only money, and because Bratva insists on this."

White said, "This is going nowhere."

Anya leaned forward. "Is going everywhere. You will retire now, and I will go with you to Dominican Republic to kill these terrible men because this is our mission with or without badges."

"What about me?" Gwynn asked.

Anya never took her eyes from Ray's. "You cannot go. You have career and maybe will be attorney general one day."

Gwynn emptied her glass. "Screw that. I've got a law degree and a bar card. I can make a living anywhere in this country. I don't need this job or my badge for that."

Anya grinned against the fading pain. "Then it is settled. I will have next surgery. We will leave LA and go to Dominican Republic, where we will finish final mission together."

Ray White deposited his glass onto the table beside him and threw up both hands. "Whoa! Wait a minute. That's not how any of this works. We aren't vigilantes who run all over the world killing bad guys."

Anya's eyelids fluttered against the coming sleep. "We are now."

12

ZHIRNYYE LADONI
(GREASY PALMS)

"I think maybe I do not wish to have second surgery."

Gwynn looked up to see her partner pressing her palms against her un-bandaged face. "Why not? What's wrong?"

Anya slowly pulled her palms away from her face and scanned the room. "Ray is not here?"

"No, it's just us. What's going on?"

"It hurts, and I was being foolish child."

Gwynn patted the sofa cushion beside her. "Come sit down. I'll make you some tea."

Anya joined her. "Thank you, but I do not want tea."

"What do you mean you were being a foolish child?"

Anya blew out a long breath. "I told to you before that I have only memories of my mother, and it made me happy when I looked inside mirror and saw her again. It is foolish of me to want to keep this."

Gwynn took her hand. "There's nothing foolish about that. It makes perfect sense."

"It does not make sense anymore. Now that I have photograph of my mother from my father's diary, I do not need to see her only inside mirror now."

Gwynn chewed her lip for a moment and then said, "Can I ask you a question that's going to sound sort of mean, but it's not?"

Anya squeezed her hand. "Of course. You can ask me anything. I have nothing—almost nothing—to hide from you."

Gwynn recoiled. "Almost nothing?"

"What is question?"

Gwynn shook off the comment. "I feel bad for asking, but you can be honest with me, okay?"

"Of course."

Gwynn cleared her throat. "Okay. Here goes. How much of your desire to have the surgery is based on looking like your mother, and how much is based on your desire to look like you did six months ago?"

"I maybe do not understand. These two things are same."

Gwynn groaned. "I knew it wasn't going to come out right, so here's what I really mean. You were the most beautiful person I'd ever seen when we first met."

"You mean when you captured me."

Gwynn sighed. "That sounds so harsh."

"Yes, but is truth."

"The truth sucks sometimes, huh?"

Anya motioned toward her face and tried to smile.

Gwynn said, "You know what? My question doesn't matter. If you don't want another surgery, I don't think you should have another surgery. Your face, your choice."

The Russian glanced toward the kitchen. "Maybe tea would be nice, if you do not mind."

"Of course I don't mind. One hot tea coming right up."

Gwynn filled the kettle and slid it onto the eye of the stove before opening the tea chest. "What kind would you like?"

She waited for an answer, but it didn't come, so she stuck her head around the corner. "What kind of tea—" She stopped herself and whispered, "I'm sorry. I didn't know you were on the phone."

Her curiosity kept her at the corner between the kitchen and living room. Eavesdropping had never been a vice for her, but Gwynn couldn't resist the urge to know who Anya was calling. She listened as her partner said, "Is Anya Burinkova."

Seconds later, Anya said, "Yes, I know this, but is always for me to tell to you who is calling. I will try to stop doing this, but I might not be able to stop. I am sorry." Another pause, and then she said, "I am calling for this reason. A few days ago, you said to me I was still beautiful to you. This was truth and not lie for sake of my heart, yes?"

Oh, my God, Gwynn thought. *She's talking to Chase.*

Anya said, "Please tell to me only truth."

The tea kettle whistled, and Gwynn jumped, barely keeping a squeal from escaping her lips. She chose a tea bag at random and poured the boiling water into the mug.

"Here you go. I got the water a little too hot, so be careful."

Anya took the cup. "Thank you. Is too hot because you were listening to telephone call with my Chasechka."

"No, I wasn't. I mean . . . how did you know?"

Anya smiled against the pain. "I am still KGB-trained spy. I know when someone is listening. And is okay. He said I am still beautiful. He is lying, yes?"

Gwynn smiled and shook her head. "No, he's not lying. To him, you'll always be that young, gorgeous spy he fell in love with all those years ago."

Anya placed the steaming cup on the table. "One day, I will tell you about it."

"About what?"

"About falling in love with man I was supposed to kill."

Gwynn gasped. "You were supposed to kill him?"

"If I could not recruit him to spy for Russia, yes, I was supposed to kill him and feed him to sharks inside ocean."

Gwynn flushed pale. "I can't believe that's how Russia works. The Cold War is over."

"Is not only Russia who does this. Also China, North Korea, many countries in Middle East, and of course, USA."

"No way. We don't kill foreign intelligence officers."

Anya stared back with a blank expression. "Chase is not intelligence officer. He is much more dangerous than this. He is man of action, man of war. He is threat to Kremlin because he cannot be stopped without killing him. Foreign intelligence officers are brave and smart, but most are not warriors like Chase."

"What do you mean?"

Anya lifted her mug, blew across it, and took a tentative sip. "Chase is not spy. He is American covert operative but without limits from CIA."

Gwynn said, "I thought he worked for the CIA."

"No, he does not. He is independent contractor. Maybe this is not correct name, but he is not government worker like you."

Gwynn waved her hands between them. "We're getting off track. We'll have time for girl talk later, and I'm holding you to it. I can't wait to hear everything about you meeting Chase. Right now, though, we've got to talk about your next surgery."

Anya took another sip. "I think maybe I will not have it. I have picture of my mother, and Chase thinks I am still beautiful. This is enough. You think so, too, yes?"

Gwynn closed her eyes and took a long breath. "Anya, I don't know how to say this without hurting your feelings, but I really think you have to move on."

"To where?"

Gwynn sighed. "From Chase. It's not healthy to be so hung up on a guy who married someone else."

Anya furrowed her brow. "But he married her only after he thought I was gone forever. He would make different decision if only he knew . . ."

"If only he knew what?"

Anya said, "If only he knew I would always answer when he called."

"It's called obsessing, and you're missing out on a great life by hanging on to him."

"I have wonderful life. I have you and Ray. I have good job. I own good company in Bonaire inside Caribbean Sea. I have money, best friend, and I am happy. I am not missing out on great life. I have great life."

"Yeah, but don't you want someone to love?"

"I love you and also Chase. This is enough."

Gwynn said, "No, that's not what I meant. Don't you want someone to love you?"

"You love me, yes? And this is also true of Chase. He cannot say words out loud because it would be cruel for Penny, but inside, I know he loves me because love does not end. If it is real, it is forever, even if we cannot be together."

Gwynn slowly shook her head. "Oh, Anya. If only the world were as beautiful as you believe it is."

Anya said, "We are now finished with subject. We must now talk about clinic in Dominican Republic. What do we know?"

"That was abrupt, but okay. We don't know anything about it yet, but Agent White is correct. There's really nothing we can do, even if we find out they're killing Americans."

Anya said, "We need opinion of lawyer without gun and badge. I think Ray is not correct."

Gwynn rolled her eyes. "You know I love you, but Ray White is *never* wrong about the law. He could literally be a law professor at Harvard. Nobody knows the U.S. Code like he does, and if he says we don't have jurisdiction, we don't have jurisdiction."

"This makes no sense. America is best country in all of world. If someone kills Americans, we should be able to capture or kill these people anywhere we want."

Gwynn grimaced. "The law is part of what makes this country the best country on Earth, but the Dominican Republic has laws of its own, and they're responsible for enforcing their laws."

Anya relaxed and seemed to let the sofa absorb her. "Perhaps this is answer. We simply tell to police inside Dominican Republic what is happening inside clinic, and they will arrest people who are responsible. This is simple, yes?"

"It's not that simple either. It's a different world down there. I'm not saying the DR government is corrupt, but most of the banana republics are, let's say, a little less strict about which laws they enforce when it comes to companies or individuals who are maybe greasing a few official palms."

"I do not understand. What is greasing palms?"

"Bribery," Gwynn said. "Sometimes elected or appointed officials in the islands accept massive bribes to look the other way. I'm not saying the DR is corrupt to that degree, but it wouldn't surprise me."

"But is wrong to kill Americans, even if they have greasy palms."

"I agree, but just because it's morally wrong doesn't mean we have the authority to stop it."

Anya closed her eyes and considered Gwynn's words. "Then I was correct. Perhaps we do not have authority to stop it, but we have two things."

"This ought to be good. What two things do we have?"

Anya locked eyes with her partner. "Ability and responsibility to stop it."

Gwynn slumped in her seat. "Ah, the world according to Anya. If only it were that simple."

"It is that simple," Anya said. "It takes only courage and willingness to get our hands dirty. If you are correct about corruption in Dominican Republic, this is opportunity for us, and no one will see us coming."

13

Ubivat' Lyudey, Lomat' Veshchi
(Kill People, Break Things)

Special Agent Gwynn Davis sat in the most uncomfortable chair she'd ever felt and spoke barely above a whisper. "She's going to the Dominican Republic, and I don't think I can stop her."

"You have to stop her," White said.

Gwynn rolled her eyes. "How many people do you know who can control her?"

White leaned back in his chair and propped his feet on the coffee table inside his extended-stay hotel. "Then you have to make a decision."

Gwynn squirmed and realized it wasn't the chair that made her so uncomfortable. It was everything else in the world. "What decision?"

White checked his watch. "How did you get away from Anya?"

Gwynn said, "She's sleeping off the extra dose of pain pills I dissolved in her tea."

"You roofied your partner?"

"No, not really. I'm not planning to take advantage of her. I just wanted her to sleep long enough for us to have this conversation."

"I'm just messing with you," White said. "I'm glad you did. Before we get into the DR and your decision, I need to ask you a girl question."

Gwynn screwed up her face. "Girl question?"

"I think Anya's acting like a girl, and it's freaking me out. Haven't you noticed it? She's not tried to kill anybody or break anything in several days. That's not like her."

Gwynn said, "Yeah, I've noticed, and I'm surprised you did, too. This isn't something most men would understand, but we women base a lot of our self-identity on our looks, and when you look like Anya, every woman around you hates you and envies you all at the same time."

"But you don't feel that way, right?"

Gwynn shrugged. "Sometimes. I mean, I'm confident in how I look. I stay in good shape, and I got lucky with some pretty good genes from my folks, but I'm different. I'm living in a man's world, and I know it. That means I have to work harder and be smarter than everyone around me. I graduated at the top of my class in law school, and I kicked ass at the academy. And thanks to Anya, I'm usually the most dangerous person in any room, as long as she's not there. So, even if I looked like a troll, I've got a lot to be proud of."

"Davis, you don't look like a troll by any means."

She glared back at him. "Are you hitting on me, Agent White? I'm pretty sure that's against the rules."

"Oh, yeah, that's it. I'm hitting on the deadliest person in the room. So, what are you saying? Is Anya suddenly envious of you?"

Gwynn chuckled. "No, that's not it at all. You have to look at it from her perspective. All her life, she's been the most beautiful woman everywhere she goes. The Russians taught her that it was a magic key to unlock any door anywhere on Earth, and they pounded that into her head year after year until it became part of her identity."

"What about the deadliest-person-in-the-room thing? She's still got that."

"She does, but now she believes she no longer has the key to open the door to that room. And there's something else you should know."

White groaned. "Great. What now?"

Gwynn considered how to put it into words, then said, "She's been calling Chase."

White leaned forward. "What?"

"Yeah, I've heard her on the phone with him a couple of times. I think he told her she's still beautiful, and that's keeping her from climbing under a rock."

White let out a long breath. "Oh, boy. That's not good."

"I don't know. Maybe it is good. I think she decided to forego the second surgery."

"Are you serious? Do you think Chase had anything to do with that?"

Gwynn said, "I don't know, but she seems to be putting a lot of stock in the fact that he still sees her as that hot young spy who tried to kill him."

"Oh, she didn't try to kill him," White said. "If she did, he would be dead. But that doesn't matter. Let's get back to the Dominican Republic. What makes you think she's going down there?"

"She thinks it's her responsibility. I think she believes it's up to her to stop the Russian mafia from killing Americans, even if it's happening outside the States. It's like a crusade for her."

White stared at the ceiling for a moment, and Gwynn said, "You're thinking about turning her loose and letting her tear that place apart, aren't you?"

White narrowed his gaze. "That would be irresponsible and absolutely unthinkable. Besides, it would be dereliction of duty if I knowingly allowed a U.S. federal law enforcement officer under my command to embark on a vigilante rampage through a foreign country. And that's exactly why I'm going to fire her."

"Fire her? Why?"

White put on the look of a disappointed father. "Top of your class at law school and kicked ass at the academy? I think you can piece it together."

Gwynn's jaw dropped. "No. There has to be another way."

"If there is, I can't figure it out. But I'm all ears if you've got a better suggestion."

Gwynn's mind churned behind her eyes. "What about me?"

"That's the decision I was talking about when we started this conversation a hundred years ago. That's up to you."

Gwynn stiffened. "But I can't just go down there and kill everybody in the clinic."

"No, you can't. You're not a KGB-trained sparrow assassin. You're an American cop . . . and a damned good one."

"But I can't let her go down there by herself. What if the same thing that happened in Bulgaria happens in the Dominican Republic? What if she's losing her edge and gets caught again? I can't let that happen. You can't let that happen."

"We started this whole conversation on the premise that nobody can control Anya. Ultimately, she's going to do whatever she wants, and if that means she gets herself killed, that's on her. You and I can't carry that kind of guilt around."

"I can't do it," Gwynn said. "If I don't find a way to stop her, I have to go with her. That's all there is to it."

"You're a good cop, Davis. You've got a bright future ahead of you. By any measure, Operation Avenging Angel has been a blazing success, and at least half the credit for that is due to you."

"That's not true," she said. "For the first three missions, I was nothing more than dead weight. Anya taught me a billion things they never mentioned at the academy. This whole thing has been a masterclass in street survival."

"You don't get it," White said. "You're the leash."

"What's that supposed to mean?"

White said, "Anya was—and in many ways, still is—a wild animal. I've never been able to control her, and telling her no is a waste of time. I learned that in the first two days of this thing. But you're the leash that almost makes that wild animal manageable. You're the missing piece between me and her that gives me the tiniest of upper hands."

"I don't know if I like the idea of being called a leash."

White checked his watch again. "Oh, I'm sorry. You must've missed the briefing."

"What briefing?"

"The one where I told you I don't care if you like being called a leash. That's what you are. When this whole thing started, I thought it would be Johnny Mac, but she snapped that leash in no time."

Gwynn almost laughed. "More like she chewed through it."

"You get my point."

"Yeah, I get it, but I want to make sure I understand what you're saying. You want me to talk her out of going to the Dominican Republic, right?"

White groaned and made a sound she couldn't quite identify.

Gwynn said, "So, you *don't* want me to talk her out of going?"

He grimaced and shrugged.

"Okay, now I'm completely confused."

White checked the time again, and Gwynn said, "Do you have a date or something? Why do you keep checking your watch?"

"I've got a conference call with the attorney general and the AAG in ten minutes."

"That sounds important."

"It is," he said. "And I want you to be in on it. How much longer do you think Anya will sleep?"

It was Gwynn's turn to check her watch. "At least another hour."

"Good. That gives us eight minutes for you to make a decision."

Gwynn threw up her hands. "What decision?"

"Don't play dumb, Davis. I graduated in the middle of my class."

"Are you asking me if I want to resign so I can go play vigilante with Anya?"

"I'd never ask you such a thing."

"Then what *are* you asking?"

He said, "My retirement paperwork has already been processed. All I have to do is pick a date. When I retire, I'll no longer be the approving authority for your request for a leave of absence to care for your friend who's recovering from surgery."

Gwynn's jaw dropped for the second time in only minutes. "Oh."

"Yeah. Oh is right. Now, grab us a couple bottles of water out of the fridge. I've got to hit the head before I call the AG."

Five minutes later, White and Gwynn were sitting beside a tiny desk in the corner of the room.

"Are you ready?" he asked.

"Ready for what? I'm not talking. I'm just a fly on the wall."

White said, "You might think of something to say—especially if the AG asks you any questions."

The federal government telephone system at the Robert F. Kennedy Building finally connected White's cell with the telephone on the attorney general's conference room table.

"Good afternoon, Agent White."

Ray cleared his throat. "Good morning, ma'am. I'm here with Special Agent Gwynn Davis."

"Where's your sparrow?" the AG asked.

"I assume you mean Special Agent Ana Fulton. She's recovering from surgery."

"I see. So, as you know, Agent White, this is the follow-up conference to the memorandum for record and case disposition report you submitted last night."

"Yes, ma'am. As I stated in the CDR, I recommend that the case be referred to the Medical Board of California, the surgeon general, and the FBI without official finding from Justice."

"So, you're giving up. Is that right, Agent White?"

"No, ma'am, not in the least. After thorough investigation, in my official capacity as the task force commander, I have found insufficient evidence to justify further expenditure of DOJ resources. Further, I recommend that the special task force known as Operation Avenging Angel be terminated due to mission completion."

"So you've kicked the Russian mob out of the country, have you, Ray?"

"It's impossible to definitively make that determination, General, but my team and I have investigated, eliminated, or tried and convicted five major organized crime operations linked directly to the Russian mafia."

The AG said, "Are you suggesting that five out of six investigations represent satisfactory completion of the mission?"

"In this case, ma'am, I am saying exactly that. There simply isn't sufficient evidence to support the claim that Dr. Bortsov's clinic is engaged in criminal activity that is directly attributable to association with the Russian mafia."

"I see," she said. "You've built quite a career, Ray. You haven't always been easy to work with, but you always got your man in the end . . . until this one. I guess all that remains is for you to pick a date."

White closed his eyes for a moment and bit his lip before saying, "I'd like to have ninety days, ma'am. That'll be sufficient time to close the task force."

"And your sparrow? What will you do with her?"

"She's not a sparrow, General. She's a United States Department of Justice special agent."

"Yes, well, nonetheless, what do you plan to do with her?"

White said, "I plan to keep my word and set her free."

14

SLEDUY ZA DEN'GAMI
(FOLLOW THE MONEY)

Dinner was a catered affair by Pizzeria Bianco in Gwynn and Anya's condo.

Ray White hoisted a slice in one hand and a beer in the other. "To the end of an era."

Gwynn raised her glass of pinot noir, but Anya protested. "Is not ending. Work is not finished."

Gwynn poured another glass of pinot and stuck it into Anya's hand. "You've been off the meds long enough to have a glass of wine, and no one said the work is finished—just the era."

Anya took her first sip. "I know this word *era*, but maybe I do not understand exactly."

White wiped the corner of his mouth. "The federal government is finished with Operation Avenging Angel. We've got ninety days to close up shop."

Anya frowned. "But there is more work. We are not finished."

Gwynn reached for a second slice. "Yeah, we know. That's why at this table, there's no rank. He's not Supervisory Special Agent White, and we're not Agents Fulton and Davis. We're just three friends having wine and pie. Well, two thirds are having wine. Hey, that reminds me. I'm not sure you should be drinking after your brain tumor."

White waved a hand. "A brain tumor couldn't kill me, so I doubt one beer is going to finish me off."

Anya's smile slowly grew as the reality of the situation washed over her. "We are going to Dominican Republic, yes?"

White said, "*We* might not be the correct pronoun, but I can't stop the two of you if you're planning a Caribbean vacation."

Anya turned to Gwynn. "You are also retiring?"

"No, I don't have enough time with the government to retire, but I can take a leave of absence from the department to help care for my friend who's recovering from facial reconstruction surgery."

"This is me, yes?"

"Who else would it be, silly girl?"

Anya raised her glass again. "To best day in all of operation."

White held up a hand. "Don't get too excited. You two aren't exactly going on a sanctioned mission. You won't have any official support, and most of all, there won't be any government funding."

Anya's smile continued. "This does not matter. I have money, and I have friends for logistical and intelligence support."

White peered at the Russian over his glasses. "Not Chase."

Anya nodded with great enthusiasm. "Yes, Skipper is operational analyst, and she is friend." She paused and turned to Gwynn. "Not friend like you, but friend, and she is smartest person I know. She will help."

White said, "You can't just assume this Skipper person will help, and you can't arbitrarily recruit other civilians for a vigilante operation."

Anya said, "I thought you were no longer in charge since official operation era has finished."

White enjoyed a long swallow of his lager. "I don't know what I was thinking. I couldn't control you when you officially worked for me, and I certainly can't do it now that you're on your own."

Gwynn laced a hand through the crook of Anya's elbow. "She's not on her own. As soon as you approve my request for a leave of absence, she's got me."

White leaned back and picked at a pepperoni. "I'm starting to think this isn't such a good idea."

Anya grinned. "Is terrible idea. This is why I like it so much. I will begin making arrangements when pizza is finished."

"Wait a minute," Gwynn said. "Are we sure we need outside help for this one? We could use Dr. Bortsov's referral for my eye work as a cover to get into the clinic in the DR."

White slapped the table. "Did you say referral?"

Gwynn recoiled. "Uh, yeah. Right after Bortsov told me that my eyes were screwed up, he said he'd refer me to the clinic."

Anya leaned close to her friend. "Nothing is wrong with your eyes. Just like rest of you, they are beautiful."

"Oh, no, they're not!" White roared.

Both women froze, and Gwynn said, "I beg your pardon?"

White leaned back, crossed his legs, and put on his most smug look. "If Bortsov refers a patient to the clinic in the DR, knowing what they do down there . . ."

Gwynn's flawless eyes turned to saucers. "That's the textbook definition of conspiracy!"

"Indeed, it is, Miss Magna Cum Laude. Indeed, it is."

White killed the remainder of his beer and yanked his phone from his pocket. Thirty seconds later, he said, "I need to speak with the general."

"You know she hates it when you call her that," came the curt response through the phone.

"She's going to love me for this one," White said. "Just put her on the phone. It doesn't matter if she's in a conference with the president. She'll want to take this one."

"Stand by, Agent White. Let me see if she'll take your call."

"You're not listening," White said. "Put her on the phone."

After waiting longer than he wanted, the voice he'd been waiting for rang through the speaker. "What is it, Ray?"

"You've not officially closed the operation, have you?"

"It's as good as closed," the attorney general said. "And the clock on your ninety-day window to close the books is ticking. What's this about?"

"It's about conspiracy to commit murder, General."

After a brief scolding for calling her general, the AG listened as White laid out the rediscovered case. When he finished, the nation's highest-ranking law enforcement official tapped her nails against the telephone receiver. "Give me an hour to think about it and discuss it with the prosecutor. Keep your phone handy."

"There's one other thing," White said, but the line was dead. He studied the phone in his hand before looking up. "She hung up on me."

Gwynn asked, "Did she blow you off?"

Anya giggled, and Ray glared at her. "That phrase doesn't mean what you're thinking, so stop thinking." He shook his head and said, "No, she didn't . . . shoot down my idea, but she said she needs to give it some thought."

"Why would she have to think about it?" Gwynn asked. "It's the epitome of conspiracy, and it gives us the authority to conduct an investigation overseas."

White said, "That's not automatic. We still need permission from the Dominican Republic to work a case in their banana republic."

Gwynn considered his answer. "Maybe that's what she's thinking about. I can't imagine her not liking the idea of nailing Bortsov on conspiracy."

White said, "Keep in mind that conspiracy isn't a federal crime. It's ultimately going to come down to the state of California."

Gwynn pulled her cred pack and gave it a shake. "The second Bortsov involved a federal government official—me—it became a federal crime. It's all about the jurisdiction, baby."

White said, "Don't ever call me baby again, and Bortsov doesn't know you're a fed."

Gwynn grinned. "Foreknowledge of the victim's status isn't a requirement for establishment of jurisdiction in a federal conspiracy crime."

"But we don't know that Bortsov was conspiring to slice you open and sell your guts."

"That's a little harsh."

"Harsh or not, we'd have to establish that Bortsov had a reasonable expectation that you would be harmed or killed by someone at the clinic he referred you to. How do we establish that?"

Anya piped up. "Follow the money, baby."

White lowered his gaze. "You don't get to call me baby, either, but you're right about the money trail. If we can prove that Bortsov is getting kickbacks by means of so-called referral fees, that establishes foreknowledge."

"Not necessarily," Gwynn said. "If the fees are big enough, it could establish that he had foreknowledge of the potential murder, but if the referral fees are reasonable compared to the price of the procedures they perform in the DR, it'll be tough to argue that Bortsov is getting paid for body parts."

Anya raised her hand as Gwynn and Ray continued their volley. "I have something to tell to both of you."

Gwynn and Ray stopped their exchange and turned to the Russian.

"Thank you," she said. "You are so worried about jurisdiction that you forget that we are talking about human lives. Who cares if jurisdiction is state's or country's? I care that Russian mafia—Bratva—is killing innocent people who only want to have bigger breasts or perfect eyes."

Gwynn sat stunned, but White, ever the civil servant, said, "Of course we care that we're talking about human lives, but in order for us to go down there and put a stop to all of this, we have to check the appropriate boxes in DC."

"This is not true," Anya said. "There are no boxes to check. Is only to get on airplane to Punta Cana. Chase has also airplane, and he is wonderful pilot. He will take us. I am sure of this. When should I ask him to pick us up?"

"Slow down, Pocahontas. This is a government op. We don't beg for rides from civilians. We've got our own airplanes."

Anya scowled. "Pocahontas was Native American woman who had adventure with Lewis and Clark."

White said, "Close, but no cigar, comrade. That was Sacagawea. It sounds like the Kremlin school of American history let you down."

"This does not matter," Anya said. "Why would you call me this?"

"I don't know. It just popped out of my mouth. Either way, cool your jets. We're not doing anything until I hear back from the general."

Gwynn laid a hand on Anya's arm. "I'm not sure what's going on inside your head that has you wrapped around Chase's little finger, but you've got to let that go."

"I do not understand. One minute, we are vigilantes, and next, we are lawyers again with guns. We have to decide."

White jumped back into the fray. "Those files you two lifted from Bortsov's office . . . Were there financials included?"

The two women shrugged simultaneously, and Gwynn said, "I don't know. Ask the techs."

White dialed his phone and pressed the speaker button. "It's SSA White. When you reviewed the files we snatched from Bortsov's practice, were there financials in those files?"

"No, sir. They contract the financials out to an accounting firm, but we have corporate and personal tax filings for the practice, as well as all four surgeons."

"How did you get access to those?"

"We're next-door neighbors to the Department of Treasury, and more specifically, the IRS."

White said, "Interesting. I need you to look for income to Bortsov or the practice from the clinic in the Dominican Republic. It'll likely look like referral fees, but they may be pretty large."

"We're on it, sir. I'll let you know what we find."

White hung up and studied Anya's still bruised and swollen face.

"Here's the plan. If we get approval to proceed from the AG, we'll roll as soon as you've healed enough to be comfortable in the field."

"Is fine. I am ready now."

"I don't think so, but I like the ambition. If we don't get approval, we're back to square one, and you can make that call to Chase Fulton's charter service."

15

KHOROSHIYE GENERALY
(GOOD GENERALS)

Ninety minutes later, SSA Ray White's cell phone rang with no caller ID, and he considered thumbing the button to send the call to voicemail, but something rattling in his gut made him answer instead. "White."

"Are you alone, Ray?"

White pulled the phone away from his face and stared at the screen as if he could see through the digital connection to identify the caller. Then, it hit him. "General?"

"Don't call me that. You know how much I hate it. Get your butt back to DC, and be in my office at nine tomorrow morning."

White checked his watch. "I don't know if I can catch a flight that'll get me there by nine. What's this about, ma'am?"

The attorney general said, "There's a red-eye leaving LAX in less than two hours. Be on it. Nine o'clock, Ray. Don't be late."

White sighed. "We'll be there."

"Not we, Ray. Just you. Don't bring your angels."

"Can you tell me what this is about?"

"Just get here, and don't be late."

Before he could ask another question, the line was dead and Ray was left scratching his head and wishing he hadn't poured himself that second beer.

Gwynn answered on the second ring. "Davis."

"Hey, it's White. Listen, I just got recalled back to DC for a nine a.m. meeting with the AG, so I'm on my way to the airport."

Gwynn said, "Okay, I'll grab Anya, and we'll meet you at the airport."

"No, the general made it clear that you two weren't to be included."

"What's that about?"

Ray said, "I don't know, but I have a theory. It has to be directly related to our request to extend the investigation on the conspiracy argument. I need you to prepare a brief on the supporting case law, if there is any. And if there isn't, write a brief on the statute. We may have to make a legal argument before a federal judge."

"No problem. When do you want it?"

"Have it in my email box when I land in DC."

Gwynn stammered. "Oh, uh . . . you mean right now."

"Yes, right now. I don't want to get blindsided in that meeting tomorrow morning. If you can't do it, find some hotshot Ivy League clerk somewhere and get it done."

"Yes, sir. It'll be in your mailbox when you land. If you've got a minute, I need to tell you about a conversation I had with Anya after we left your place."

"Not now, Davis. Unless it's something earth-shattering, it'll have to wait."

"Okay, but we have to talk about it. It directly involves everything we've done on the past five cases."

"Why do you do this to me, Davis? Let me get through the meeting with the AG, and we'll talk tomorrow. Now, get to work on that brief."

"Yes, sir. Good night, Agent White."

Gwynn ended the call and groaned.

"What is problem?" Anya asked.

Gwynn shook her head. "It's not a problem. I've just got to write a brief on the case law covering our investigation."

"I do not know what this means."

Gwynn grabbed her laptop and nestled onto the couch. "The AG recalled Agent White back to DC for a nine o'clock meeting tomorrow morning, so I have to do the research and provide him with the ammo to fight for our case."

Anya nodded. "This makes sense. I could talk with the attorney general and make her understand what we want to do."

Gwynn chuckled. "Yeah, I don't think that's a great plan, but it would be fun to watch. I'm sure Agent White can handle it."

* * *

At 8:45 the following morning, SSA White stepped into the outer office of the U.S. Attorney General to find a pair of men in cheap suits who looked like they should be jogging alongside the presidential limousine. The first of the two men stepped toward him, and Ray stopped in his tracks.

The man said, "Good morning, Agent White. I'm Agent McLennon. Please surrender your weapon and cell phones."

White lowered his chin. "That's not happening. What's going on here?"

The man held his expression. "I'm afraid I must insist that you surrender your sidearm and cell phones."

"I'm afraid I must insist that you're not getting my gun and phone until you tell me what's going on."

The AG stepped through the inner door. "For God's sake, Ray. Just give the man your gun and cell phones. He's on our side."

"Our side of what, General?"

"Just do what he says, or I'll shoot you myself. We're going downstairs to the SCIF."

White pulled his pair of phones from his pocket and slammed them onto the man's waiting palm. "Fine. You can have my phones, but you're not getting my gun."

The agent said, "Again, sir, I must insist."

"Insist all you want, but you're not getting my gun."

The AG said, "Forget it, Agent McLennon. He can keep his weapon."

The agent said, "With all due respect, ma'am . . ."

The AG took a step toward the agent. "I don't think you have any understanding of the amount of respect I am due in this office. Supervisory Special Agent White may keep his weapon. Now, let's go."

The agent wisely obeyed and terminated his endeavor. The two agents flanked Ray and the attorney general, shuffling them toward the elevator. The AG scanned her ID card through the reader inside the elevator, and the car descended smoothly into the bowels of the Robert F. Kennedy Building. When they stepped from the elevator, the two agents led Ray and the AG through three sets of secure doors and into the sensitive compartmented information facility, where two men waited with binders on the table in front of them.

The two agents who'd escorted them to the SCIF stepped from the room and secured the doors behind them.

The AG motioned toward a chair. "Have a seat, Ray. These gentlemen are Mike and Chris. Mike is with the FBI, and Chris is from Langley."

White studied the two men, neither of whom offered a hand. "Let me guess. You're with Hostage Rescue or Counterterrorism, and you're from CIA Clandestine Service. How'd I do?"

Neither man spoke, but the AG did. "These gentlemen are with a joint special missions task force called Violence Against Americans Abroad, or V triple A, as they prefer to be called."

White repositioned in his chair as his brain spun out of control. "You'll have to forgive me, but I've apparently been out of the loop. I've never heard of V triple A."

"Almost no one has," the AG said. "The very existence of the task force is classified top secret, and the operations are TS-SCI."

White turned to his boss. "Sensitive compartmented information? I don't have—"

She glared at him. "You do not, so listen and answer their questions."

"Questions?" White said. "Wait a minute. Am I being questioned as a subject matter expert or as a suspect of some kind?"

Mike pulled off his glasses and stared at White. "Have you done something to make you a suspect of some kind, Mr. White?"

He didn't flinch. "It's Supervisory Special Agent White, Mikey."

The two bulls continued pawing at the ground and snorting until the AG said, "That's enough, boys. Play nice. We're all on the same team here."

Chris claimed the floor. "Let me see if I can defuse this situation a little. Agent White, you are under no suspicion of any kind. You are here at the behest of the AG as a federal agent with information that may be actionable by our organization."

White turned his attention to Chris, and the man extended a hand and rose from his seat. "My name is Christopher Parks, and yes, that's my real name. Like you, I'm a servant of the people."

White glanced at his boss and back at Chris and shook the offered hand. "Ray White. I'm afraid I find myself at a distinct disadvantage here, and if you two wouldn't mind, I'd like to speak with my attorney alone before we go any further."

Chris said, "I'm sorry, Ray, but this isn't that kind of meeting. No one can be permitted in this room during this discussion."

White pointed toward the AG. "She's my attorney."

Mike cleared his throat and started to speak, but the attorney general halted him. "Step outside, gentlemen. We'll call you back in when we're ready."

Mike huffed. "I'm afraid that isn't—"

The AG said, "I'm sorry to hear that you're afraid, Mike, but be afraid outside while Agent White and I have a conference."

Mike made no effort to vacate his position until Chris slid a hand beneath his arm. "Let's step outside. We've gotten off on the wrong foot. Let's reset and restart."

The two men stepped through the door and sealed it behind them. Almost before the door closed, the AG said, "Ray, I'm sorry for throwing you directly into the fire. Here's what's going to happen. We're going to surrender this case to the FBI and CIA. They're equipped to deal with the problem."

White spoke in the calmest tone he could muster. "Are you assigning Agents Davis and Fulton to the V triple A task force?"

"No, I have no intention of doing that."

White nodded. "Then the task force isn't equipped to deal with the problem, Judy."

She raised an eyebrow. "Judy? Are we buddies now?"

White sighed. "This thing has gotten so far out of bounds that it doesn't matter what either of us calls the other. We might as well crawl into the same foxhole and help each other reload. If you give this investigation away to the feebs and spooks, it'll turn into a fiasco like nothing you've ever seen, and your boss will be looking for somebody to blame. When heads start rolling, I don't want one of them to be yours, ma'am."

She slumped in her chair. "You know something, Ray. You're far more politically savvy than most of the department heads at Justice. Somedays, I'd like to have two dozen just like you, but most days, I'd like to have one less."

Ray made no effort to stifle his smile. "Good generals know when to fight the battle before them. Don't give this one away, ma'am. The angels and I will keep your head right where it belongs . . . if you'll let us."

The AG closed her eyes and allowed herself a rare silent moment. When she finally reopened them, she stood and dragged a hand across Ray's shoulders on her way to the door. "The meeting is yours, Supervisory Special Agent White. I'll send the boys back in and see you back upstairs when you're finished. A good general knows when she can walk off the battlefield and leave the fight in competent, capable hands."

16

Ty Nikogda Ne Promakhnesh'sya
(You Never Miss)

Far sooner than the attorney general expected, SSA Ray White strolled through her door and planted himself in one of the two matching wing-backs. "Come on in and make yourself at home. Can I get you anything?"

White waved a hand. "Nah, I'm good. Thanks."

The AG glared at him. "Well?"

"Ah, you know me. I've been winning friends and influencing people."

"How about a few specifics?" she said.

"Specifically, they're going to keep their collective noses out of our business."

"Is that so?"

"It is, and officially, I'll take those ninety days you gave me to wrap up the task force and file all the necessary reports before I turn in my badge and collect my pension."

The AG shook her head. "I'm not going to like the answer to my next question, am I?"

"No, ma'am, you're not, so it'd be best if you didn't ask it."

"You know I have to ask, Ray."

"No, you don't. I'll bring you up to date on everything you need to know."

"Oh, so now you're making the decisions concerning what I *need* to know."

"In this case," he said, "I am, and here it is. I'll officially apply for retirement this afternoon, with my projected date being three months out. Special Agent Ana Fulton has tendered her resignation, and I have her badge and credentials. Special Agent Davis has requested, and I have approved, a ninety-day leave of absence to care for her friend who is recovering from surgery."

"You didn't brief Mike and Chris, did you?"

"Oh, I briefed them, but since I hadn't personally confirmed their appropriate level of clearance, their official need to know, and of course, their signed nondisclosure agreements, my hands were tied. I could only tell them so much."

"Oh, your hands were tied, were they?"

"Yes, ma'am, they were. And it took all my strength to finally wrestle them free on my way up here."

The AG pulled off her glasses and ran a hand through her hair. "Listen to me, Ray, and hear me well. If Davis does anything—absolutely anything —illegal, she's not coming back from that leave of absence. So help me God, if she gets so much as a jaywalking ticket, she'd better hope that little Russian sparrow of yours can teach her how to survive on the street."

White grabbed his chest. "I'm crushed that you'd think Special Agent Davis would do anything outside the law while she's caring for her dear friend."

"And let me guess. You're not going to tell me this *friend's* name."

White said, "I didn't ask."

"Of course you didn't. Listen to me, Ray. If I get any of this on me, you're going to prison. I've worked too hard and kissed too many asses to make this office mine, and you're not going to destroy what I've built."

White pulled an envelope from an interior pocket of his jacket and slid it across the desk. "I would expect nothing less, Madam Attorney General. In fact, if it makes you feel any better, this is a copy of Agent Davis's letter of resignation. I recommend tucking it away somewhere nice and safe for three months or so. If your office needs to disavow any knowledge of anything she might do, that letter makes a pretty nice security blanket for you. If, after ninety days, Davis's friend is healed and back on his or her feet, you can shred that security blanket and reassign that brilliant young agent to another task force that needs a fearless, devoted door-kicker."

The AG slid the envelope into a drawer and waved toward the door with the back of her hand. "You're a pain in my ass, Ray, but I'm going to miss you."

White rose and gave his boss a wink. "I've seen you shoot, General. You never miss."

* * *

Gwynn Davis answered within seconds of Ray pressing the send button. "How'd it go?"

"Better than expected," he said. "Is your sidekick there?"

"She's right here, and you're on speaker."

"Good. Here's what happened. The boss threw me in a room with an FBI agent and a CIA operative who claim to be part of a classified joint task force that resolves problems with Americans who become victims overseas."

Gwynn said, "I didn't know anything like that existed."

"Yeah, the whole thing is classified at the highest levels."

Anya spoke up. "This program is called Violence Against Americans Abroad, or sometimes Task Force V triple A, for short."

White said, "How could you possibly know that?"

The Russian offered nothing more than a silent smile as if White could see it through the cell phone two thousand miles away.

Davis said, "So, does that mean it's not our case anymore?"

White asked, "What case?"

Anya and Gwynn exchanged a knowing glance, and White said. "As far as the attorney general's office is concerned, the investigation has been terminated, and no further official operations will occur in relation to that former investigation."

Gwynn asked, "And you didn't tell the task force guys anything?"

"I hadn't officially verified their qualifications to have access to the case information, so it would've been criminal of me to share classified data with individuals who may not have the proper credentials."

"You're good, Agent White."

"I've been doing this a long time," he said. "Even a public-school graduate can learn to play the game if he's given enough time."

"So, what now?" Gwynn asked.

"You're on a ninety-day leave of absence to take care of your recuperating friend, so take care of her."

A moment of silence hung in the air until Anya asked, "How much do you want to know?"

"I want to know the two of you are alive and well as often as possible."

When the call ended, the battle inside Gwynn's gut began. "Are you scared?"

Anya tilted her head. "Scared? No. Why would I be scared?"

"I don't know. It feels strange. Until right now, I guess I always knew the weight of the whole federal government was behind me and everything I did, but now, that's all gone."

Anya said, "I have taught you how to stay alive when it feels like whole world is trying to kill you. There is nothing more important than staying alive. Think first about that. Everything else is second."

"I know all that, but it's going to be strange working unsupported."

"We will not be unsupported. I have plan."

Gwynn lowered her gaze. "You're going to call Chase, aren't you?"

"No. I am going to call someone better."

"Better than Chase?"

Anya smiled. "Well, she is better at some things than Chase."

The Russian dialed the phone, and Elizabeth "Skipper" Woodley answered in coastal Georgia. "Op center."

"Is Anya Burinkova, and I need your help.

"Hello, Anya," came Skipper's pleasant response to the unexpected call. "How are you?"

"I am finished with surgery for face and is healing quickly, but this is not reason I need your help."

"Are you okay?" Skipper asked.

"I have mission in Dominican Republic . . ."

Skipper listened carefully as Anya laid out the facts, then they walked through a few theories and suppositions.

When the discussion was over, Skipper said. "Okay, I get it. These are bad dudes who have to be stopped. Of course, I can't authorize assets without Chase's approval, but he'll never say no to you."

Anya said, "This depends on question I ask him. He is very good at saying no to me when no is correct response."

"Well, there is that," Skipper said, "but something tells me you're not asking to move in, so what do you need?"

The Russian covered the phone and whispered to Gwynn, "I told you she would help." With the phone uncovered, she said, "I need analyst and maybe airplane. You can do this, yes?"

"The analyst part is easy. I don't have anything on my plate at the moment, so I'm all yours for a few days. The airplane part is outside my purview. You'll have to talk to Chase about that one. On second thought, maybe I should talk to him about it. Penny might not love you calling him."

"I am no threat for Penny, and she knows this, but if you will discuss with Chase, I will be thankful to you."

"Thankful to me . . . That sounds odd," Skipper said.

"I could not think of correct English phrase. In Russian, word is *tsenit*."

"That doesn't help much, but I get the point. I'll talk to Chase and call you back. Should I use this number or your cell?"

"Either is perfect. I will wait for call from you. And I want you to know . . ." She paused for a long moment before saying, "Maybe best words are just, thank you."

"Don't thank me yet," Skipper said. "I haven't done anything. I'll call you back after I talk with Chase."

Anya pocketed her phone, and Gwynn said, "We're really doing this, aren't we?"

"We really are."

Before the conversation had time to go any further, Anya's phone chirped. She didn't recognize the number on the screen but thumbed the answer button. "*Privet, en Anya.*"

"Hello, Anya. It's Penny."

"Oh, Penny, hello. I was not expecting—"

"I'm sure you weren't. Nonetheless, you have me now, and I have some things I need to tell you."

The apprehension Gwynn had felt found its way into Anya's gut. "Okay. I am listening."

"I don't really know how to say this adequately," Penny began, "but I need you to know how much it means to Chase and me that you gave me part of your liver. That's the most generous thing anyone could've done for me, and I'll never forget it."

Anya swallowed the lump in her throat. "Chase will always be very special to me, and you are woman he loves. I would give to him anything he needed, and you are extension of him inside my mind."

Penny said, "Regardless of the reason, you saved my life, and you didn't have to do that. I know how you feel about Chase, and I believe most women in your position would've let me die so they could have my husband. Why didn't you let me die, Anya?"

The Russian didn't hesitate. "If you died, this would destroy Chase. I could never do this to him. We love same man, Penny, but we do not love him same way. I will never hurt him, and I know you feel same."

"Yes, I know that, but there's one more thing I need to tell you."

"I am listening."

Penny cleared her throat. "I know what happened to you in Bulgaria, and it's our fault. We're responsible, so we will pay for any medical procedures you need or want because of the . . . violence."

"This is not necessary. All of surgery is finished, and someone else paid for this."

"Someone else?" Penny asked.

"Yes, you may not know that I work for—wait, this is not true. I *worked* for government, and they paid for doctors."

"Oh, that's interesting. I didn't know, but anyway, Skipper said you needed her help and maybe the use of one of the airplanes."

"Yes, this is true. We have mission in Dominican Republic."

"We?"

Anya didn't hesitate. "Yes, my partner Gwynn and I have mission."

Penny stopped her. "I don't want to know anymore. Just know this. Whatever you need, you'll have. Skipper has the checkbook and free rein to provide whatever you need."

"Thank you, and you are welcome for liver. But I now have something I must tell to you . . . If it had been your heart instead of liver, I would have given mine for you."

17

Chto Moglo Byt'
(What Might Have Been)

Four hours later, a Gulfstream IV, *Grey Ghost*, touched down at Burbank Airport and taxied to the ramp, where Anya and Gwynn stood enjoying the afternoon sun.

Gwynn watched the plane roll to a stop. "That belongs to Chase?"

The answer came in the form of a stroll up the boarding stairs.

As they stepped aboard, a man emerged from the cockpit, towering over both women, and extended a hand. "You must be Special Agent Davis. It's a pleasure to meet you. I'm Chase Fulton."

Gwynn took his hand, grinned, and shot Anya a look.

The Russian said, "I told you he is beautiful."

With the handshake complete, she said, "I'm just Gwynn. I'm pretty sure"—she nodded toward Anya—"she got me fired."

Chase glanced at the woman he'd once adored. "She does that. Make yourself at home. We'll take on a little fuel and have you in St. Marys before you know it."

"It's really nice to finally meet you, Chase."

"The pleasure's all mine," he said as he bounded down the stairs.

The pair settled into plush leather seats, and Gwynn leaned toward her partner. "Oh my God, girl. He's gorgeous, *and* he owns a Gulfstream."

Anya said, "Ah, he is all right, and he owns many airplanes. This is biggest one."

"Where's St. Marys?" Gwynn asked.

"Is in Georgia. American Georgia. This is where we are first going. We must have equipment for mission, and this is where equipment is stored."

Gwynn lowered her voice. "Is Penny going to be there?"

"Probably. Why do you ask?"

Gwynn huffed. "I've got to see the woman he picked over you."

Anya cast her eyes to the floor. "She is very beautiful and also very kind. You will like her."

The three-and-a-half-hour flight ended with the wheels chirping onto the concrete of the private airfield adjacent to Naval Submarine Base Kings Bay in St. Marys, Georgia. A few minutes after taxiing to a stop, Chase emerged from the cockpit again, but this time, he was followed by an older, smaller man.

Anya leapt to her feet. "Hello to you, Disco. This is friend Gwynn."

Disco said, "It's nice to see you, Anya, and it's very nice to meet you, Ms. Gwynn."

She rose. "It's just Gwynn. Did she say your name was Disco?"

"That's not what my mother named me, but in this crowd, everybody's got a nickname."

Gwynn glanced at Anya. "What's yours?"

"I do not have nickname. Everyone is afraid of me, so I get only respect."

Chase said, "Oh, we call you a lot of things, but rarely to your face. And you're right. We're all a little scared of you."

They descended the stairs, and introductions continued until Chase pulled from the hangar in an ancient brown VW Microbus.

Anya beamed. "This was my father's car!"

The five-minute drive to Bonaventure Plantation, where Chase and his team lived, trained, worked, and played, was barely long enough for Anya to tell the story of meeting her father, Dr. Robert Richter, so many years before.

Chase motioned for them to follow him up the steps and into the house. "I imagine you two would like to use the restroom and grab something to drink before we start packing."

Ten minutes later, Anya led Gwynn through the kitchen and to the backyard facing the North River. "This was property in Chase's family since early eighteen hundreds. Is beautiful, yes?"

"Yeah," Gwynn said. "It's really nice."

As they turned back toward the house, a young lady came bouncing down the steps with her arms open wide. "Anya! It's good to see you."

They hugged, and Anya said, "This is friend Gwynn, and she is Skipper."

Gwynn extended a hand, but Skipper stepped in. "You're in the South now. We're huggers."

Gwynn suddenly wished she'd known about the hugging ritual when she met the other team members at the airport. She said, "It's like a movie around here. Everybody's beautiful and genuinely sweet. It's weird for a girl from New York."

Skipper said, "You'll get used to it. It just takes a little time. We'll turn you into a Southern belle before you know it."

Gwynn said, "I don't know about that, but seriously though, thanks for all you're doing for us. I'm a bit of a fish out of water on this one."

The analyst said, "Don't worry. You'll get the hang of it. It's just like your real job, except there are no rules. I've got a mountain of data on the clinic for you. After you get geared up, have Chase bring you up to the op center, and I'll bring you up to speed."

Anya steered her partner toward the basement armory beneath the three-story brick house that looked—at least from the outside—a lot like it did when it was first built over a century before.

They found Chase holding a clipboard when they reached the bottom of the stairs. "There you are. I was afraid I'd lost you."

Anya said, "Never."

Gwynn rolled her eyes. "Anyway, thank you for doing this for us. I know you don't have to, but we really appreciate it."

"Don't mention it," he said. "The world is better with the two of you in it, so we'll do our best to keep you alive."

Gwynn furrowed her brow. "Does that mean you're coming with us to the Dominican Republic?"

Chase froze in place. "Do you need us?"

Gwynn shot her gaze to Anya, and the Russian considered the question before saying, "Perhaps."

Chase bounced the clipboard against his knuckles. "We're between assignments, and everybody's itching for something to do, so we're here if you need us."

"We will see," Anya said, and she reached for the clipboard.

Chase let it slip from his fingers and into hers. "Take anything and everything you want or need. Just write everything down so we can replace it if it doesn't come back."

Gwynn scanned the massive armory with weapons and tactical equipment neatly arranged in every inch of the space that would've been heaven for any doomsday prepper. "Seriously? Anything we want? Who's going to pay for all of this?"

Chase motioned toward Anya with his chin. "We owe her a few hundred thousand favors, so maybe she'll deduct this from our running tab."

Anya took a step toward him. "You owe me nothing, Chasechka, but thank you."

Gwynn studied the look between Chase and her partner and recognized it immediately as the gaze of what might have been.

They spent the next half hour selecting weapons, communication radios, surveillance equipment, and everything they could possibly need for the operation that shouldn't require a single bullet or blade.

When they were finished, Anya handed the clipboard to Chase.

He glanced over the list. "Are you sure this is all you need?"

"Yes, we are only two people, so we do not have to equip whole team. Also, mission should be mostly safe. I chose weapons only to protect ourselves from locals who might see us as easy targets."

Chase laughed. "That would be a mistake on their part."

"A mistake for which we will make them pay," Anya said. "Speaking of making pay, you should see Gwynn fight. She is brilliant and faster than eyes can see. She is like ferocious cat."

"Stop it, Anya. You're embarrassing me. Besides, I'm not that good."

Anya huffed. "This is not true. You are wonderful fighter. I would not want to fight you in dark alley."

Gwynn shook her head. "Let's just say I had a very good teacher and leave it at that."

Chase said, "I'll grab a couple of guys, and we'll pack up your gear. Why don't you take Gwynn out to the shooting range and make sure the weapons are zeroed to your liking?"

On the range, Gwynn demonstrated just how good the instructors at the Federal Law Enforcement Training Center had been. Her pistol work was even more impressive than the rounds she sent downrange from either of the two rifles she chose.

"You are very good with gun," Anya said.

Gwynn said, "Yeah, well, I'll never be as good with a blade as you, but I guess I can hold my own with a pistol."

They added their weapons of choice to the pallet sitting just outside the armory and headed upstairs to the op center.

To Anya's surprise, the door was cracked open, and she pulled the knob, peering inside. "May we come inside?"

Skipper answered, "Oh, good. You're here. Close the door behind you and pull up a chair."

Anya did as she was told, but Gwynn stood in wide-eyed amazement of the room. "This is amazing."

Skipper smiled. "Thank you. I designed most of it. We're soundproof up to five hundred decibels, shielded against electromagnetic pulse, and the room also qualifies as a SCIF, so if either of you have your cell phones on you, we'll toss them outside before we talk about anything classified."

Gwynn finally found a chair and rolled beside her partner as Skipper started the briefing.

"Okay, so here's the Clínica de Belleza in Punta Cana." Several aerial photos filled the screens in front of them. "These shots are a few months old, but I'll have access to an NRO satellite that'll be overhead in about thirty minutes. I'll snatch some up-to-date pictures then."

Gwynn said, "You have access to National Reconnaissance Office satellites?"

"Doesn't everybody?" Skipper said.

"Uh, no. At least the DOJ didn't." Almost before Gwynn finished lamenting her previous lack of recon assets, an alarm sounded.

Skipper glanced up and smiled. "I think someone's here to see you."

Anya spun, expecting Penny to waltz through the door, but instead, Dr. Celeste Mankiller bounced into the op center. She and Gwynn squealed and wrapped each other in a long, overdue hug.

When they pulled themselves apart, Gwynn said, "It's great to see you, but we're right in the middle of a briefing. We'll catch up as soon as we're finished here."

Skipper looked up. "Hey, Celeste. You can join us if you'd like. You may have a gadget or two that might come in handy on this one."

The tech wizard slid herself onto a chair and joined the party as Skipper resumed the briefing.

She brought up a photograph of a dark-haired man who appeared to be in his fifties. "This appears to be our guy. I think his name is Mikhail Kuznetsov, and if I'm right, his father was a former KGB officer turned bigwig in the Communist Party before the fall of the wall."

Anya said, "I do not know if you are correct about this being Mikhail because I have never heard of him. But I knew person named Colonel Greggory Kuznetsov. He was senior advisor to Mikhail Gorbachev."

"That's the one," Skipper said. "I'm running some research in the background that should yield a solid ID on this guy, but I'm ninety-percent confident I've got it right."

Gwynn asked, "Why do you say this Mikhail Kuznetsov is our guy?"

Skipper said, "He has an impressive criminal record and a not-so-squeaky-clean reputation in the Dominican Republic as a racketeer. He's also one of the registered owners of Clínica de Belleza, but that's not even the best part. You're going to love this. He has a younger half brother from a different father."

She paused, and Anya asked, "Why should we love this?"

Skipper grinned. "Because his brother's name is Dr. Maxim Bortsov, the same guy who performed your facial reconstruction."

18

Obychnyye Lyudi
(Regular People)

Anya grabbed Gwynn's arm. "You must report this to Ray. He has to know."

Gwynn laid a hand on top of Anya's. "Agent White isn't our boss anymore. We're on our own, remember?"

"But perhaps this information will change that. Maybe this will make again jurisdiction for us."

"It doesn't work that way," Gwynn said. "It doesn't matter if the president's brother owns the clinic. It's still in another country, where we don't have the authority to conduct an investigation."

Anya considered Gwynn's resistance. "Then I will call him."

Before Gwynn could stop her, Anya had the phone pressed to her ear.

Ray White watched the number fill the screen of his phone and thumbed the answer button. "Please don't tell me you're already in prison in the DR."

"Is Anya Burinkova. No, we are still inside America, and we have important information. You will never believe what Skipper discovered about clinic."

Ray said, "Stop talking, Anya. I don't want to know. The more I know, the more I'll be responsible when this thing ends up as a congressional inquiry."

Anya didn't slow down. "Owner of clinic in Dominican Republic is brother of Maxim Bortsov in California."

Silence filled the phone, and Anya wondered if White had disconnected the call.

Finally, he said, "Are you certain he's Bortsov's brother?"

"Is only half brother, but is same mother."

"You're one hundred percent sure of this information?"

Anya pressed the speaker button and leaned toward Skipper. "Agent White does not believe you are correct."

"I didn't say that," White growled. "I simply asked if you were completely certain about Bortsov and the clinic owner in the DR being half brothers."

Skipper eyed Anya as if asking permission to speak, and the Russian said, "Tell him."

Skipper slid the phone closer. "Special Agent White, this is Elizabeth Woodley. I'm an intelligence analyst, and I never disseminate information I haven't personally verified through every available means."

White said, "I wasn't questioning your information—"

Skipper interrupted. "Yes, you were, and that's perfectly fine. Intel should be questioned, but you can rest assured that I'm not wrong. The man's name is . . ." She paused and glanced back at Gwynn. "Am I free to discuss this with him?"

Gwynn said, "If he wants to hear it, go for it."

Skipper nodded. "Agent White, do you want to hear the information I have?"

White groaned. "The reasonable, rational part of me has absolutely no interest in knowing any of this, but the masochistic part can't wait. So, let's have it."

Skipper said, "The clinic, as you probably know, is the Clínica de Belleza. It is owned by a conglomerate, of which the principal owners are a shell corporation in Georgia—the country, not the state—and a man named Mikhail Kuznetsov. His mother is now Daria Bortsova, wife of Alexei Bortsov, and they live in Kiev, in the house she inherited when her former husband, Miroslav Kuznetsov, was killed."

White said, "This is getting a little complicated. You're telling me they're Russians, but they live in Kiev in Ukraine. Is that right?"

Skipper said, "I've not done enough research on Kuznetsov to know for sure that he was Russian. He could have been Ukrainian, but does it really matter?"

White ignored the question. "How was he killed?"

Skipper sighed. "I'm four thousand dollars an hour. Where should I send the invoice?"

White said, "Okay, I get it. The intel is solid. Davis, are you there?"

Gwynn said, "I'm here."

"Explain to your partner that I'm not the boss anymore."

"I tried, Agent White, but she didn't seem to care. I also tried to explain to her that this new information doesn't give us jurisdiction in the DR."

White sighed. "Anya, listen to Davis. She knows what she's talking about."

"So, you do not want information from us?" Anya asked.

"I really don't," he said. "The less I know, the better."

"As you wish. Oh, before saying goodbye, you will be pleased to know we have everything we need thanks to—"

Skipper slid her palm over the phone resting on the console and mouthed, "The less he knows, the better."

Anya frowned. "Goodbye, Ray."

"Goodbye, Anya. Please don't get Davis killed."

Anya ended the call and pocketed the phone. "All of this is very strange to me. First, we are lawyers with guns and badges. Now, we are only regular people with no badges, but still with guns."

Skipper glanced at Davis, and the agent said, "Don't ask. What else can you tell us?"

Skipper turned back to her keyboard. "What else do you want to know?"

Anya spoke up. "I want to know about local police."

Skipper asked, "Local here, or local in the Dominican Republic?"

Anya gave her the disappointed look, and Skipper threw up her hands. "I never know with you. You ask some bizarre questions sometimes."

Gwynn chuckled. "Sometimes?"

"Enough," Anya said. "Tell to me about police in Punta Cana."

Skipper shrugged. "They're just like most of the cops in third-world banana republics. They're all for sale."

"This is very good and also very bad for us. Mikhail Kuznetsov will have already police inside pocket. We have only two options. We can pay more to police than him, or we can think of police as part of problem."

Skipper let out a low whistle. "It might be tough to outspend him. According to what I can find, the clinic took in over fifty million bucks last year, and that's just the income they reported. It's likely that they made at least twice that amount."

Anya said, "Then we must fight also police. We cannot afford to be competition for Kuznetsov. We can buy maybe one or two police officers, but not all of them."

Gwynn said, "You'll have to forgive me, but I'm a GS-twelve on an unpaid leave of absence. If you're thinking I can contribute to the buy-a-dirty-cop fund, you're out of luck."

"I have money," Anya said.

Gwynn said, "I know it's none of my business, but someday, you'll have to tell me how you made your money."

"Is not secret. Chase gave to me money a long time ago."

Gwynn's eyes widened. "What?"

Skipper said, "That's not exactly how it happened. Chase just delivered money that was already yours."

Gwynn said, "Now, I'm really confused."

"Do not be confused," Anya said. "My father gave to Chase two million dollars when he died because he loved him like son. Chase said to me I should have money because he was my father. I do not agree with this, but Chase is difficult man with head of stone sometimes."

Gwynn leaned in. "So, you inherited two million dollars a long time ago, but you had to spend a lot of that buying the company in Bonaire."

"This is true," Anya said. "But company makes money, and I am very good investor."

Skipper grabbed her phone and fired off a text message.

Chase, they need cash for the DR op.

The reply came almost immediately.

I told you to give them whatever they need. Take what they want/need from the safe, and replenish the stash.

Skipper passed the phone to Gwynn, who read the messages and said, "I need to get some friends like you."

Skipper whispered, "Look around. You've already got us." She turned back to Anya. "How much do you need?"

Without hesitation, she said, "One hundred fifty thousand."

Skipper thumbed open the safe beside her workstation and stacked the cash into a leather bag.

Anya accepted the bag and said, "Thank you. I will bring back to you."

Skipper glanced at Gwynn for an instant and said, "Just make sure your partner gets paid."

"You are very kind," Anya said. "What else do you have for us?"

Skipper spun back to her keyboard. "That depends on what you want. If you want to go alone, I'll book a nice, safe place for you, and I'll arrange for whatever transportation you need."

"I think maybe this is not really what you are asking from me."

"You know what I'm asking," Skipper said.

Gwynn and Dr. Mankiller stared at each other in obvious confusion, but Anya clearly knew what was on the verge of happening. She asked, "Who?"

Skipper said, "Whoever you want."

Gwynn asked, "What's happening right now?"

She didn't look away from Skipper, but the Russian said, "We do not have to do this alone if we want to take Chase's team with us."

Gwynn gasped. "Oh. Is it . . . Do you think we . . ."

Anya said, "Thank you for offer, but is not necessary."

Gwynn said, "Hold on. Maybe you could have a couple of guys on standby if we get in over our heads down there."

Skipper shrugged. "Whatever you need. When we offer, we mean it."

Anya stared at the ceiling for a moment. "We will have Mongo and someone who speaks also Spanish."

Skipper said, "That narrows it down to three—Kodiak, Hunter, or Chase."

"Not Chase," Anya said. "I think Kodiak."

Skipper scowled. "Not Chase? Why not?"

Anya looked away before saying, "Is better for me if he is not there. Mission should be simple, but last time I was on mission with Chase"—she motioned to her face—"this happened because I was not focused. And also other reason. Penny should not have to think about Chase and me in other country together. She is good person, and I do not want her to have reason to mistrust her husband."

"That came off a little cocky," Skipper said. "But it's cool of you to think about Penny's feelings in all of this."

"I am learning to be better person."

Skipper pushed herself away from the console. "I can see that, but you will have Chase for at least a few hours during the mission. The *Grey Ghost* requires two pilots, so Disco can't do it alone. That leaves you with either Clark or Chase in the right seat, and Clark is on an extended vacation."

"When can we leave?" Gwynn asked.

Skipper dialed the phone.

"Hello, this is Chase."

"Hey. What's your ETD?"

Chase said, "We're ready whenever Anya and Gwynn say the word."

"They're ready now," Skipper said. "And they want Mongo and Kodiak to ride shotgun."

"That's who I thought they'd pick. They're geared up and waiting at the hangar. The *Ghost* is fueled and ready. All we need is a couple of high-speed federal agents, and we'll head south."

Skipper said, "They'll be there in less than half an hour." She turned to her audience. "They're ready and waiting. Do you need anything else from me?"

Anya said, "You will send to us live photographs from satellite, yes?"

"Yes, of course." Skipper snapped her fingers. "And that reminds me . . ." She pulled a pair of tablets from beneath her console and handed them to Anya and Gwynn. "We can communicate through these. They're encrypted and secure. I'll shoot everything from maps to aerial photos to local restaurant menus whenever you need them. Anything else?"

Anya stood. "Thank you for all of this. I owe now to you favor."

Skipper stood and hugged the Russian. "We're not keeping score, and we're all on the same team. Be safe, and have fun."

Gwynn tucked her new tablet into her bag and turned for the door. "I guess this means it's time to go to work."

19

DIPLOMATICHESKIY IMMUNITET
(DIPLOMATIC IMMUNITY)

The bearded man offered his right hand. "We met earlier, but you've met a lot of people today, so I should probably reintroduce myself."

Gwynn said, "Oh, I remember those green eyes. You're Kodiak. How could I forget?"

The giant already seated behind Anya gave Gwynn a shy wave. "I'm pretty sure you remember that I'm Mongo."

"Both of you are unforgettable. Thank you for doing this. I know it's not what you normally do, so it means a lot to us."

Mongo chuckled. "Ma'am, this is so much better than what we normally do that we should pay you for the privilege of tagging along."

Gwynn said, "Chasing down a murderous Russian mafia boss on an island full of corruption and gangs is better than what you normally do?"

"Yes, ma'am. I don't remember the last time we deployed and didn't get shot at." The big man motioned toward Anya. "She was there for the last one, so she knows. This one's a walk in the park."

Anya looked up. "I would not say walk in park, but is unlikely anyone will shoot at us."

Gwynn said, "You guys live in a world I'll never understand."

Kodiak smiled through his beard. "So do you, ma'am."

Chase leaned into the aisle from the cockpit's right seat. "This is your captain speaking. Please take your seats and fasten your safety belts for departure."

Anya wadded the napkin resting on her leg into a tight ball and threw it into the cockpit. "You are not captain. Captain sits on left side. You are only copilot and not important, so leave us alone and fly airplane."

Mongo chuckled. "You know you're the only person on Earth who's brave enough to talk to the boss that way, right?"

"He is not my boss. Today, he is my driver, and I am boss."

"I heard that!" came Chase's admonishment from the cockpit.

Anya leaned into the aisle. "Good. Now drive, boy."

That garnered a raucous round of laughter from the cabin of the Gulfstream IV, *Grey Ghost*, but that's not all it garnered. Disco's hand appeared from the captain's side and shoved Chase back upright.

They blasted off into the afternoon sky and pierced a layer of cumulous clouds as they climbed into the flight levels seven miles above the Atlantic Ocean. The *Grey Ghost* put a thousand nautical miles behind them in just over two hours before touching down at the Punta Cana International Airport at the eastern extreme of the Dominican Republic.

As they taxied the Gulfstream to the ramp, Disco leaned into the aisle. "This really is your captain speaking, and I'd like to welcome you to the deceptively beautiful island paradise of the Dominican Republic. We'll have the door open in just a few minutes, and the customs officer will come aboard."

Gwynn panicked. "Customs? But what about the weapons? They won't let us into the country with that pallet of gear back there."

Kodiak gave her a wink and produced a wad of American cash from his backpack. "Just hand over your passports, and I'll take care of everything else."

Gwynn grabbed Anya's arm. "Is that really going to work?"

The Russian smiled. "It always does."

They produced their passports, and Chase opened the door. The uniformed customs officer climbed aboard and never glanced beyond Kodiak standing by the coffee maker just inside the doorway. Passports were stamped, pockets were lined, and the team was legally inside the DR with a thousand pounds of guns and bullets strapped to the deck behind them.

Anya and Gwynn unbuckled and stood, but Kodiak held up a hand. "Hang on a minute. We've got special handling."

He pulled the door closed, and a motorized tug attached itself to the *Ghost*'s nose gear. A few minutes later, they arrived inside an enormous hangar with two other business jets with American registrations resting safely inside.

Gwynn whispered, "I feel like such a rookie right now. I have no idea what's going on."

"This is hangar belonging to United States embassy. We have diplomatic immunity against every law on island as long as we are inside hangar. Rules change when we go through door, but is nice for unloading equipment."

They descended the stairs to find a pair of Toyota 4Runners sitting near the tail of the plane.

Anya eyed the vehicles and headed for the brown one with one headlight missing and a rust-covered dent in the front fender. "Is perfect!"

Gwynn recoiled. "Perfect? It's a junker."

Anya tossed her backpack into the driver-side window. "Yes, this is why car is perfect. You will see."

The six of them offloaded the gear from the *Grey Ghost* and into the waiting SUVs in fifteen minutes.

Chase motioned for Anya to follow him, and he led her into a small office near the back of the hangar. "Disco and I are headed back to St. Marys, but we're just a phone call away if you need us. I'm not sure what your mission is down here, but if things get sticky, we're pretty good at breaking up bar fights if you get in over your heads."

"Thank you, my Chasechka. I cannot say to you enough thank you."

"You don't have to thank me. You've always come running every time I've asked for your help. It's nice to be able to return the favor."

"Is okay for me to hug you, yes?"

He smiled, opened his arms, and stepped toward her. As they parted, she quickly wiped the first hint of a tear from her eye and stepped behind the man she'd always love.

By the time they made their way back to the 4Runners, the plane's cargo door was closed, and the fuel truck was pumping jet fuel into the tanks. Chase took a minute talking with Kodiak and Mongo as Gwynn looked on.

She stepped beside Anya. "What do you think they're talking about?"

"He is telling them to watch over us, even if we tell to them do not. Chase is very protective of people he cares about."

Gwynn smiled. "And it's obvious he cares about you."

"Yes, and for now, this is enough for me."

The tug reappeared, and the *Grey Ghost* began her slow journey from the hangar back into the humid evening air.

Mongo said, "You took the better truck."

Anya nodded. "Yes, because we will be working while you and Kodiak are lying beside ocean in sun."

"I hope you're right," the big man said. "But Chase handed down our marching orders. You know how he gets."

"He is worried about us," Anya said, "but this is not necessary."

Mongo said, "He's not worried about you. He's worried about that partner of yours."

"She is strong and fierce. You will see. I am not worried about her at all."

"I hope you're right," Mongo said. "This is no place to show weakness."

"I know, and Gwynn will soon learn this."

Mongo sighed. "Are you going to make this difficult for us?"

Anya smiled. "Do you want me to?"

"Please don't."

She shrugged. "Then I will let you follow us, but I am in charge always."

"Isn't that always the rule?"

"It should be," she said. "Skipper made for us reservations at different places, but if you insist on watching us, we can make room for you."

Mongo examined the ceiling of the hangar fifty feet above his head. "Skipper wasn't completely honest with you about our digs. We're staying next door, so we'll already be in your hip pocket without you having to hear Kodiak snore."

"We will meet you at our house, but first, I will go for drive with Gwynn so she can learn city."

Mongo nodded and climbed aboard his much cleaner, much newer 4Runner.

Anya gave Gwynn a playful shove toward the left side of the vehicle. "You will drive. I will be passenger."

"That's a terrible idea," Gwynn said. "I don't even know which side of the road to drive on."

Anya pulled her door closed. "Drive on top side of road. Is much easier than bottom side."

"Oh, that's real funny now, but just wait. I'm a terrible driver."

Gwynn was less than truthful concerning her skill behind the wheel. Before they turned onto the road leading away from the airport, Gwynn had already learned to keep right, just like back home. They drove past posh luxury homes for a mile before the cityscape gave way to the third-world truth about the Dominican part of the island. Paved roads became sandy, pitted lanes that could've passed for livestock paths, and probably were at times.

As Gwynn white-knuckled the wheel and bounced in her seat, she said, "They don't put this half of the island on the tourism brochures." The vibrato of her tone punctuated the statement perfectly.

Anya pressed her feet against the floorboard and gripped the handle above her door. "Show to me clean, undamaged car."

Gwynn slowed the 4Runner, softening the blows. "I get it now. You were right. You're always right."

"Not always," Anya said. "But I have been to many of the islands inside Caribbean Sea, and most are similar to this when outside of tourist resort."

Gwynn said, "Did Skipper provide an address for the clinic?"

"Yes, is on tablet. Turn left and left again at next cross street."

Gwynn did as Anya directed, and they were soon back on relatively smooth, concrete roads.

Five minutes later, Anya motioned through the windshield. "There it is."

Gwynn slowed as they passed the clinic. "It doesn't look like a fifty-million-dollar business."

"Not from outside, but we will see how it looks from other side of doors."

"Do we have an address for Mikhail Kuznetsov?"

"Turn to right in four blocks. If Skipper is right, Kuznetsov's house will be just around corner."

Gwynn followed the directions. "I get the feeling Skipper isn't wrong very often."

"She is very smart."

As they turned right, Gwynn said, "Wow. These are nice places."

"Yes, almost like place where someone who owns fifty-million-dollar business would live." The Russian leaned forward, peering outside the vehicle as they passed each address. "This one is his."

Gwynn pulled her foot from the accelerator and coasted by the house. "Nice security fence."

Anya scoffed. "Do not worry about fence. There is no such thing as security. There is only perceived security."

"That's kinda deep."

"Is true. I will show you. Make circle behind houses."

Gwynn turned down a narrow alley and then turned again on the walled street only wide enough for one car.

Anya pointed at the back of Kuznetsov's house. "His wall is high, but only one meter higher than top of our truck. We can be inside wall in five seconds."

"Yeah, but he's probably got security cameras everywhere."

"This is also no problem. We have Skipper, and she can make us invisible."

"This is a strange new world for me. I've never worked outside the bounds of the federal government, so it's going to take some time for this covert-ops stuff to sink in. What if we get busted and go to jail down here?"

Anya grinned. "We brought with us giant man who can tear bars from windows with only pinky fingers. Do not worry. You will like this strange new world. Rules are not same as government. We are free to do what is necessary instead of what is legal."

20

Nazemnyy Kontrol'
(Ground Control)

Anya, Gwynn, Mongo, and Kodiak ate steamed shrimp and Caribbean lobster, rice, and plantains at Fiesta del Mar, a tourist trap of a restaurant that tried to pass itself off as authentic.

Mongo looked up at Gwynn with lobster juice dripping from his beard. "Do I have something on my face?"

Gwynn blushed and redirected her gaze. "No . . . Well, you do have a little something in your beard."

The big man wiped his beard with the remains of a shredded napkin. "Did I get it?"

Gwynn giggled. "Yes, you got it. I'm sorry for staring."

Mongo went back to work on his platter. "Don't be sorry. I don't get a lot of attention from women as beautiful as you. When they do stare, it usually means they're scared of me."

"Oh, I'm not scared. I was just thinking that I've never seen anyone as big as you. It has to be hard to buy clothes."

Mongo chuckled. "It's not easy. I have to special-order most of my threads from Baby Gap."

Anya rescued her partner. "I have plan. You would like to hear it, yes?"

Heads nodded, but Mongo didn't slow his assault on the mound of seafood in front of him.

"We must probe for security," Anya said.

Kodiak grinned from ear to ear. "Oh, yeah! Put me in, coach."

Anya froze. "I do not know what this means."

Mongo paused his seafood aggression long enough to let out a chuckle. "I think it means he wants to do the probing."

"Yeah, I do," Kodiak said. "I'll go over that wall in a heartbeat."

Anya leaned forward. "Do not be so loud. There are too many people who will maybe hear you."

Kodiak grimaced. "Sorry. I didn't mean to get so excited. I haven't had the chance to stick my nose where it doesn't belong for a while, and I've got the itch."

"I understand," Anya said. "I have also this itch, but you are here to help if our head becomes under what we are in."

That halted Mongo completely. "What?"

Gwynn rolled her eyes. "She's pretending that she doesn't speak English today. She means you're here to pluck us out if we get in over our heads."

Anya huffed. "This is exactly what I said."

Kodiak said, "I'm not sure where that directive came from, but we're here to do whatever you want."

Gwynn raised an eyebrow. "Oh, really? I think I like the sound of that."

"Do not do that!" Anya barked. "Captain Tom would not approve."

"Don't do what?" Gwynn said.

"Flirt with other people when you are away from Tom."

Gwynn lowered her head. "Yeah, about that . . . There is no Captain Tom anymore."

Anya grabbed her partner's hands. "Oh, no. What happened to him?"

"He got promoted to major and sent to Germany on an assignment he said he's wanted his whole career."

"And he was killed?"

Gwynn recoiled. "What? No! He's not dead. He just broke it off with me because I wouldn't go to Germany with him."

Anya relaxed. "Oh, I thought you meant he was dead, but is only that he is no longer boyfriend?"

"Well, yeah, that. And it turns out I wasn't his only girlfriend."

"This is terrible. I will find him and do terrible things to him if you want."

Gwynn smiled. "I know you would. That's why you're my best friend. But it's okay. It's his decision, and if I'm not a man's first choice, then I'm not going to be an option for him."

Kodiak and Mongo dived back into their platters as if the two women weren't even there.

Gwynn reached across the table and laid a hand on Kodiak's arm. "Relax. I'm not freaking out. I'm not that kind of woman."

Kodiak shoved a forkful of rice into his mouth, but Gwynn wasn't going to let him off that easy.

"Oh, no, you don't. I'm on to you, big boy. You can swallow that mouthful or spit it out, but either way, this isn't over. You're way too cute to run and hide."

Kodiak stomached the rice, wiped his mouth, and said, "Forgive me, but I can't stop singing 'Ground Control to Major Tom.'"

Gwynn laughed in spite of her desire to punch Kodiak in the nose, and Mongo followed suit.

Anya wore the look of the lost. "I do not understand. Why is this funny?"

Kodiak gathered himself and said, "Never mind. Let's hear your plan for probing security."

Anya pushed her plate away. "I think we should aim small cameras at every door and begin keeping log of who comes and goes from these doors. This is step number one. After this, we should get inside and memorize as much of building as possible. With this information, we can calculate best time to go inside to capture information from computers."

"I like it," Mongo said, "but it surprises me that you want to be so cautious. You'd normally set your hair on fire and crash through a window. Is this the kinder, gentler Anya?"

She said, "This is older, wiser Anya. I am no longer twenty years old and unbreakable."

Kodiak shrugged. "I think I liked the old Anya better. Anybody can plant cameras and sneak inside, but I'm a big fan of breaking stuff, pillaging, and taking what I want." With that, he eyed Gwynn. "If you know what I mean."

Her silent smile said far more than any words she could muster.

Anya said, "Good. Is plan, and we will do tonight. Thank you for offering to go with me, Kodiak, but I will take Gwynn. She is my partner, and we move together in darkness like we are one person. She's very dangerous inside darkness."

Kodiak studied the federal agent as if seeing her for the first time, and Gwynn didn't let his gaze diminish hers.

Mongo said, "If we're just placing cameras, we can do that in two teams of two and cut the window of time we're vulnerable in half."

The meal ended when Mongo finally surrendered, and the four returned to their rented houses located diagonally across the street from one other. From each house, the front and one side of the other were clearly visible, making their positions tactically advantageous. Assaulting both houses from one vehicle simultaneously would be all but impossible. That became the basis of their preliminary security plan, and Gwynn nudged that plan into action.

"We have plenty of cameras, so let's start at home. I think we should cover the sides and rear of each of our houses with at least two cameras. It shouldn't take any more than six at the clinic, so that leaves enough in reserve to give us a comfortable cushion."

Anya said, "You are thinking like covert operator already. This is very good."

They spent twenty minutes carefully placing the cameras for optimal coverage while keeping them hidden as much as possible. The satellite cameras worked like a sat-phone but transmitted video instead of audio.

With the cameras installed, tested, and running at peak efficiency, Mongo said, "We should check in with the op center."

Anya cocked her head. "Is easy for me to forget we have op center."

Skipper answered almost before the phone rang. "Ops."

Mongo said, "Hey, Skipper. We're in-country, and preliminary recon is complete. We have six sat-com cameras in place at the residences."

Skipper said, "I've already got the video feeds up and running here, but I don't have any feeds for the front of either house. Are the cameras in the front malfunctioning?"

He said, "We have good visibility between houses to cover the fronts."

Skipper said, "Maybe so, but if you'll plant the cameras, we can monitor every angle around the clock from here and ping your sat-phones if we see something we don't like."

Mongo glanced at Anya. Even though no formal rank structure had been established, she was the logical element commander and gave Mongo a silent nod.

He said, "We'll set up the cameras out front as soon as we finish this call. We're planning to do the same thing at the clinic and start a log of who's coming and going."

Skipper said, "Perfect. Get the cameras in place, and we'll take care of the monitoring from here. I can run everybody through facial recognition and put together your head count and ID list a lot quicker than you can on the ground."

Anya leaned toward the phone. "I am grateful for your help, but why are you doing all of this for us? This is not assignment for team."

Skipper cleared her throat. "Do you not remember Bulgaria?"

"Yes, of course I remember. This is where I was captured, and you rescued me."

"It was a little more than that," Skipper said. "Just like Chase said, you volunteered to work an op with us, and you almost died. We don't walk away from operations like that and never look back. We fought and bled and ultimately won as a team on that mission. That makes you one of us, and we don't let our family hang themselves out on a limb. We're a team. We're a family."

"But this is not your mission. This is mission for friend Gwynn and me."

Skipper said, "We don't care about the mission. We care about the people. Now, shut up and get those cameras fired up. We've already worked out a twenty-four-hour schedule for the op center. You're not alone. We're in this together."

"This is very kind of you," the Russian said as a wave of emotion washed over her. "I cannot tell to you how much this means to me."

"You're welcome, but you don't have to thank us. Remember, to us, there's no difference between team and family. Oh, that reminds me. Chase has the Gulfstream loaded with gear, and the rest of the team is on recall to back us up if things go south down there."

Anya said, "I do not think this is necessary. What we are doing is only slightly dangerous, so I do not understand why all of you are being so, what is word? Maybe *protective*."

Kodiak and Mongo shared a glance, and the big man said, "We all know what you went through when you were a little girl in the Soviet Union. You were turned into a one-person killing machine. That's a very different experience than how the rest of us learned to fight and stay alive. Well over ninety percent of our training and experience involves at least one other person, so our whole understanding of combat is a team concept. The core of that team mentality is loyalty. I think I speak for all of us when I say that once I lay in the mud or blood-soaked sand and fought for my life and for the life of the man beside me, I felt a loyalty to him that can't be described in words. It's a primal instinct . . . at least it is in me."

Kodiak nodded with enthusiasm. "Absolutely. Mongo's exactly right. And when you lay in the dirt and bled beside us in Bulgaria, you became part of that indescribable family in the mind of every person on the team.

That's why we're here, and that's why Chase is chomping at the bit to haul two tons of guns, bullets, and grenades down here to back you up. To us, you're not a Russian anymore. You're not the Lone Ranger. You're our American teammate and family member."

Anya squeezed her eyelids closed and choked back the coming emotion while Gwynn sat in wide-eyed wonder at the scene unfolding in front of her.

21

URODLIVAYA PRAVDA
(THE UGLY TRUTH)

Anya stood from the table, determined to do anything other than melt in the outpouring of admiration, respect, and loyalty. "We must now work."

The remaining three rose, and Mongo knocked the table with an enormous knuckle. "Work, indeed."

They spent half an hour setting up the additional cameras to monitor the front of each of their rented houses so Skipper, and whoever she recruited to stand watch in the op center a thousand miles away, could see every inch of the properties.

Mongo checked the signals from each of the cameras and called St Marys. "Are you receiving the video feeds?"

Skipper said, "I have them all, and they're crystal clear. Are you headed to the clinic next?"

"We are," Mongo said. "Will you be in the op center overnight?"

She said, "No, Celeste is working the overnight, but I'll be back in the morning."

"Sounds good. We'll check in as soon as we get the cams installed at the clinic."

"Do you need anything else from here?" Skipper asked.

"Not for now, but we'll check in every two hours."

They drove to the clinic in separate vehicles and arrived simultaneously at opposite corners of the facility. Darkness mostly shielded them from prying eyes, but a few young men lingered about with an unwanted interest in what the team was doing.

The open-channel satellite communications the team wore tucked beneath their shirts allowed the four to talk as though they were side by side without the necessity of push-to-talk buttons.

Anya said, "Four boys along western side of wall are watching us. We must move to eastern side to cross wall."

Mongo answered. "I saw them, too. I can discourage them from sticking around if you'd like."

Anya said, "This would be fun to watch, but is better if we do not give them reason to remember us."

"You never let me have any fun," the big man said.

Anya chuckled in spite of the necessity to remain focused on the mission. "I promise I will find someone for you to punch before this is over."

Mongo and Kodiak parked near the southeast corner of the clinic's security wall while Anya and Gwynn drove behind a pair of delivery trucks parked a hundred yards from the northeast corner. The four moved through the darkness like shadows drifting almost silently across the hardscrabble road. Mongo planted an enormous boot at the base of the wall and knelt an instant before Kodiak stepped on his partner's bent knee and bounded across the wall. In one motion, Mongo leapt and grabbed the top edge of the concrete block barricade, pulling himself across with far more agility than a man of his size should possess. They landed with as little noise as possible and immediately scanned the area inside the wall for both personnel and cameras. They could deal with guards, but cameras never ceased being a silent, electronic threat.

"We're in," Gwynn said.

Kodiak whispered, "Us, too. South perimeter, clear."

Gwynn hesitated and then scanned. "East and north perimeter, clear."

"Cameras?" Kodiak asked.

"Negative," came Gwynn's reply.

Kodiak said, "We're moving to the southwest to work north."

Gwynn glanced at her partner, and the Russian gave her a nod. "Roger. We'll work south. Report any contact."

Anya stared into the darkness, scanning every inch of the area for signs of life or electronic surveillance, while Gwynn placed the miniature cameras in crevasses within the block wall. Four minutes later, the cameras were in position and relaying imagery straight up, miles above the island nation, to satellites silently slipping through the vast darkness above, and Skipper's voice coursed through those same satellites. "I have eight camera feeds operational."

Gwynn said, "We placed four on the east and south walls."

Kodiak didn't report their success. Instead, he whispered, "Contact. Two personnel. Northwestern corner."

"I've got 'em," Skipper said. "Hold position."

Kodiak and Mongo froze and never took their eyes off the two men who'd just come through a side door. Their night-vision monoculars gave them the advantage of seeing what the two unknown contacts could not, but that advantage would diminish with every passing second as the two men's vision adjusted to the darkness. The night-vision capability of the cameras was inferior to the monoculars the team carried. The batteries required to power night-vision cameras would more than double the size of the devices, making them far more challenging to hide.

Skipper said, "I've got a light source reflecting into the lens of the closest camera, but the two men appear to be holding position."

Kodiak clicked his tongue against his teeth, barely loud enough for Skipper and the rest of the team to hear.

A small flame flickered, lighting up the face of the man standing closer to the doorway. His cigarette glowed orange before he passed the lighter to the second man, who repeated his smoking partner's performance, and Kodiak and Mongo exhaled nearly identical sighs of relief.

Skipper's reassurance eased the whole team's concern. "Hold positions. They're just a pair of smokers. I guess smoking inside is a no-no, even down there in the tropics."

Anya said, "Are we safe to go back over wall?"

Skipper said, "Affirmative, but the boys need to stay frozen until the smoke brothers are finished destroying their lungs."

Anya offered Gwynn a knee, and they were over the wall in seconds. Mongo and Kodiak continued their motionless scan of the western side of the building as the second hand slowly ticked away.

"*¡Levántense las manos y pónganse de rodilla!*"

Gwynn and Anya threw their hands into the air and hit their knees exactly as *la policía* ordered.

"We're busted," Gwynn said softly into her mic.

"Not yet," Anya whispered. "Do not let him see your face. He will not shoot two women."

The officer approached the compliant twosome just as he'd been trained, believing them to be a potentially lethal threat, but he had no way of knowing just how lethal his would-be prisoners could be. As he grew ever closer, his tone softened, along with his previously measured caution.

In rapid Spanish, he asked, "What were you doing on the clinic property?"

"Pretend you don't understand," Anya whispered.

Gwynn let her voice tremble with the perfection of a Broadway actress. "Uh . . . *no hablo* . . . uh, sorry."

The officer repeated his question in English, and Gwynn froze. It was time for Anya's performance of the night. "*My ne govorim po-ispanski.*"

The officer may have been multilingual, but Russian wasn't in his repertoire. Instead of recognizing the trap before him, he took the final stride of the encounter, landing a booted foot only inches behind Gwynn.

Anya said, "Go!"

Gwynn swept the officer's feet, sending him crashing to the ground on his side. Anya leapt to her feet, spun, and sent a punishing kick to the man's face. She followed up the kick by planting a knee on his throat and grinding a handful of sand, gravel, and crushed shells into his eyes. As his hands came to his face, Gwynn thrust one of the rings of the officer's stainless-steel handcuffs onto his left wrist, and as if they'd practiced the maneuver countless times before that night, Anya rolled the man onto his stomach as Gwynn yanked the cuffs between his kicking legs. The Russian pinned the defeated man's right hand to his butt so her partner could apply the remaining cuffs. The treatment rendered both the man's hands, as well as his eyes, useless.

Anya sent one final crushing blow to the base of the officer's skull, giving his brain the rest it so desperately longed to find.

"What's going on?" Skipper asked with anticipation in her voice.

Anya answered before Gwynn could. "A policeman tried to arrest us. He is unconscious and handcuffed."

"Oh, that's not good," the analyst hissed from a thousand miles away.

"Is okay," Anya said. "It changes mission, but maybe is best. Help me take him to car."

"Our car or his?" Gwynn asked.

"His."

"Wouldn't it be easier to bring his car to him instead of carrying him?"

"This is good plan," Anya said. "You will bring car. I will set him up."

Gwynn sprinted across the rugged earth and slid onto the driver's seat of the twenty-year-old police car. She yanked the shifter into drive and threw gravel into the air.

The instant the car slid to a stop, Anya jerked open the rear door and dragged the limp body of the officer into his own back seat.

"Are we just going to leave him here?" Gwynn asked as a pair of boots thundered toward them.

Both women jerked their heads up, preparing for another fight as Kodiak slid to a stop beside the open door of the car. "What's going on here?"

Anya reached for his hand. "Help me out of here, quickly!"

Kodiak locked his grip around her wrist and yanked her across the officer's body. Anya scampered to her feet and spun into the front of the car. The engine revved when she jammed a nightstick between the seat and accelerator, then she wrenched the car into gear and dived from the seat and onto the ground as the car careened toward the street, doors slamming with the momentum.

Anya raced toward her 4Runner and yelled, "We must go!"

Like Lot's wife when Sodom and Gomorrah burned beneath God's fury behind her, Gwynn couldn't deny the beckoning call of the police car speeding into the darkness. As the other three ran toward their waiting vehicles, Gwynn stood in stark disbelief at what they'd just done. An innocent man, who was only doing his job, lay cuffed, blinded, and unconscious in the back seat of his own car as it thundered toward an unpredictable end that could've been a row of welcoming shrubbery, a killing concrete wall, or a collision with another car filled with equally innocent lives.

The quivering breath inside Gwynn's lungs exploded from her lips as Mongo wrapped her in a massive sweeping arm and lifted her from her feet. He thrust her into the back seat of Anya's 4Runner and slammed the door behind her before jumping into the vehicle with Kodiak.

Gwynn drove her palms into the floorboard and seat, twisting her body to refocus on the out-of-control police car growing smaller with every passing second. "Anya! He's going to crash!"

The Russian never lifted her foot from the accelerator until two turns and a full city block lay between them and the clinic. With time and distance on their side, both Anya and Kodiak slowed to blend with what little traffic traversed the crumbling streets of Punta Cana.

Gwynn grabbed the edge of the driver's seat and shook it. "What are we going to do about that officer? What if he gets killed in the wreck?"

"We will talk of this when we are inside house. Is very different from working inside law with Department of Justice and Ray White."

Gwynn couldn't force her eyes from the direction they'd come, hoping against hope that she wouldn't watch a rising ball of fire escape into the night sky.

The men followed Anya and Gwynn through the door of their rented house. Mongo passed out bottles of water, but Gwynn refused.

"No! I don't want it. What we just did is *not* okay. We probably killed that police officer. We can't do that!"

Mongo, Kodiak, and Anya exchanged glances as if voting who would dispense the ugly truth.

Anya silently volunteered and slid onto the couch beside her partner. "Listen to me. You must understand something that will be difficult for you." She lifted the bottle of water from the end table and placed it in Gwynn's hands. "You must drink and listen to me."

Gwynn took the bottle from Anya with her trembling hand and clumsily twisted the top. She sipped the water, but every drop felt like razor blades being forced down her throat.

Anya said, "You remember our first mission together, yes?"

Gwynn nodded without a word, and Anya continued. "You killed man called Leo before he could kill me, yes?"

"Yeah, but he was going to kill you. I had no choice."

"There is always choice," Anya said. "You could have missed, you could have failed, and I would have died." Anya squeezed her partner's hands inside hers. "You did not miss, and because of this, I did not die. Same thing happened tonight. We do things no one should ever have to do to save lives of others."

"But that cop wasn't going to kill any of us."

"No, he would not have killed us tonight, but if he had taken us to jail, Mikhail Kuznetsov would know of this before morning, and our mission to stop him from killing patients and stealing organs inside them would have failed, and many more people would die."

"But it's still not right," Gwynn said.

"Tell to family of patients who will be killed inside clinic that we made decision to not stop Kuznetsov because it was not right."

22

PERVOYE UBIYSTVO
(FIRST KILL)

Mongo slapped his knee and stood. "If we don't have any more pillaging to do tonight, I need some rest."

Anya glanced up at him. "Thank you for coming here with us. Tonight would have been difficult without you, but what happened tonight makes this very different from original plan. If you and Kodiak want to go home, I understand."

Kodiak laughed. "Go home? That's crazy talk. It's just getting good. I thought we were coming down here to sit on our butts and play quick reaction force in case you got in trouble. I love being on the starting lineup. We wouldn't miss this for the world, but we do need to let Chase know that things are accelerating."

She said, "I am certain Skipper will brief him. He will probably offer to come, but just the four of us is perfect. We do not need bigger team."

"You're probably right," Kodiak said. "Chase hates to miss a fight."

"He would not like this fight. Is going to be terrible."

Gwynn raised an eyebrow. "Terrible? How does it get more terrible than what you and I've already seen?"

Anya turned to her friend. "Get some sleep. There is nothing we can do tonight, but tomorrow will be busy day." She kissed Gwynn's cheek and gave her a smile that could've been laced with the dread of what she would ask her partner to do in the coming days.

Anya brushed Mongo's arm as she passed. "Thank you again. Is nice having you to help with this."

The big man gave her a nod and eyed Kodiak. "You coming?"

The former Green Beret and combat-hardened warrior said, "Go ahead. I'll be there in a bit. I want to talk with Gwynn for a few minutes."

Mongo glanced at the fed as if asking if it were okay for his partner to stay with her, and she said, "Goodnight, Mongo. Thank you for scooping me up out there. I kind of froze. It won't happen again."

He showed no reaction and stepped through the door and into the night.

Almost before the door came to rest in its jamb, Kodiak asked, "Are you okay?"

Gwynn sighed. "Would you like something to drink?"

"Yeah, that'd be nice. Thanks."

She poured two glasses of wine and returned to the couch.

"Thanks," Kodiak said. "Now, back to my question. Are you okay?"

Gwynn took a sip and pulled off her boots. "I was a federal agent . . . Well, I guess I still am, but what I meant was, before I met Anya, I was a decent fed. I didn't break the rules. I had a good career in front of me."

"Do you think she screwed that up for you?"

She took another sip. "Probably, but I don't care. I've been a good girl my whole life. Law Review, top of my class, great scores at the academy. You know the drill."

Kodiak chuckled. "No, not really. I sucked at school, barely graduated high school, and would've ended up in prison if it wasn't for the local cop in the little town I grew up in. He beat the crap out of me after he caught me sticking m-eighties in mailboxes and watching them blow sky-high."

Gwynn turned to face him and pulled her feet beneath herself. "Are you serious?"

Kodiak took a sip. "Yeah, dead serious. He told me I had two choices. Option one was for him to lock me up. Number two was to meet him in front of the Army recruiter's office at eight o'clock the next morning."

"Let me guess. You picked the recruiter's office."

"No way," he said. "That's what he wanted me to do, and I didn't give a rip about what anybody else wanted back then. He threw my hoodlum butt in jail, right where I belonged."

"Really?"

"Yes, ma'am. Really."

"So, how'd you end up doing this?"

"While spending three nights in jail awaiting arraignment over the weekend, I started looking around at the people I was surrounded by. Drug dealers, pimps, wife beaters, drunks, addicts, and even a guy who was in there for unlawfully handling a corpse . . . whatever that means."

Gwynn almost gave a quick legal briefing, but she stopped herself. "Go on."

"I made a decision over a cardboard bowl of what was supposed to be grits and eggs. I was looking all fly in my orange jumpsuit and head of crazy hair I hadn't washed in a week."

She stuck her fingers through the hair on top of his head and gave it a shake. "I'd say it's still crazy, but at least it's clean."

He laughed. "Yeah, I don't mind getting dirty, but I don't like staying dirty. Anyway, I decided I didn't want to spend my life around people like that. I finally got my thirty seconds in front of the judge on Monday morning. He rattled off some legal gibberish I didn't understand and waved me away with the back of his hand. I guess I was supposed to waddle back to my cell with the rest of my inmate buddies, but I didn't go away. I said, 'I want to go see the Army guy.' The judge looked down at me from his lofty little perch and said, 'What did you say?'"

He paused, took a drink, and noticed Gwynn hanging on every word. "So, I said it again, and he said, 'What Army guy?' I said, 'I don't know, the recruiter guy.'"

"Did that work?" Gwynn asked.

"I guess. I've never been back inside a courtroom, but just short of three years after that, I was an Airborne Ranger who'd just earned his Green Beret. It turned out that I just needed the right environment, and the Army gave it to me."

"What a great story," Gwynn said. "How long were you in the Army?"

"Until they medically retired me after one too many broken bones and close proximity to too many explosions. All in all, it was almost fifteen years. I hooked up with Chase and those guys a couple years ago, and I've never looked back."

Gwynn stared into her wineglass. "If this is your way of getting to know each other or whatever . . . I mean, if you're going to ask me out . . ."

Kodiak held up a palm. "Relax. That's not what this is about, although I'm open to the idea when we wrap up this mission. But I wanted to talk to you about what happened tonight. Are you okay with that?"

"Sure."

He said, "It's pretty obvious this is your first black-ops mission."

She looked away. "Is it that obvious that I'm an idiot?"

"Hey, don't do that to yourself. You've got skills. You're quick, sharp, strong, and I see a warrior behind those eyes. This kind of thing is a whole different world than the one you grew up in. There are a few definitive black-and-whites in this world, but we live in the greys between those two. That cop tonight may have been a solid family guy just doing his job, but that's not likely the case. The reality in the third world is that far more officials are corrupt than clean, and us staying alive and without handcuffs on our wrists are the two most essential elements in mission completion."

"I get that," she said. "I do. It's just—"

"Let me finish," he said. "I already told you that I grew up being a jerk. I never really hurt anybody, though. I got in some kid fights, but nothing serious, so when I saw my first real fight, it changed who I am inside."

He paused and took another drink, but Gwynn was frozen in place. After gently placing his glass on the end table, he cleared his throat. "It was a long way from home, in a town I can't spell, in a country I couldn't find on a map at the time. We were clearing houses in four-man teams, and I was the number-three man through the door. I'd done a thousand CQB drills, so I thought I knew everything there was to know about working inside a building. We cleared the front door without a single shot, and the next three rooms were the same, so I relaxed, thinking the rest of the structure was going to be empty. I couldn't have been more wrong. When we went through the fourth door, the world stopped turning. Men were everywhere. Women were screaming. Children were screaming. And I was terrified."

He stopped talking and replayed the night through his head as Gwynn stared. "Anyway, I had my rifle at the high ready. You know what that is, right?" She nodded, and he continued. "A dude popped up in front of me and grabbed the barrel of my rifle, shoving it toward the ceiling. I yanked and pulled for all I was worth to get my rifle back, but if there was anybody on Earth more scared than me at that moment, it was the guy with my muzzle clasped in his hand. At that moment, his buddy hit me from the right with a shoulder to the ribs, but I didn't go down. Now I was fighting two guys in the dark, and I couldn't get my rifle on either of them. Worst of all, though, I couldn't get to my pistol in the holster on my right hip."

"What did you do?" Gwynn blurted out.

"I drew my knife with my left hand and sent the blade through the guy's stomach and into his heart. I couldn't believe how easily the blade went in. It was like he was made out of paper or something. When he fell, the other guy, who was still under my right arm trying to wrestle me, grabbed my pistol, and I shoved him away and stuck my rifle under his chin. I hesitated for an instant, and the number-four man who'd come through the door behind me put two rounds in the guy's left ear."

Silence filled the room as Kodiak wished he'd never begun the story, but Gwynn beckoned for more.

He settled himself and continued. "When we finished clearing that building and got back outside, my teammate grabbed me by my vest and shook me more violently than I thought possible. He screamed in my face,

'If you ever hesitate like that again, you're going to get one of us killed. You got me, soldier?' My hesitation had been less than a second, but that fraction of an instant can be the difference between the bad guys winning and the good guys dying."

Gwynn swallowed hard. "I froze up out there tonight, and that could've put you in danger. I'm sorry. I've never been a soldier. I didn't . . ."

He reached for her hand, and she let him take it. He squeezed and gave it a shake. "I'm not going to throw you around like Sergeant Kingsly did to me, but don't ever forget that you're putting your team in danger every time you hesitate."

She bit her lip and begged for the words to make him believe it would never happen again, but before they could come, Kodiak raised his hand to his lips and gently kissed the back of her hand. "Good night, soldier. I'll see you in the morning."

23

POLITSEYSKIY NE BYL POLITSEYSKIM
(THE COP WASN'T A COP)

Just as Gwynn's eyelids succumbed to the exhaustion her body and mind felt from the night she'd never forget, Anya stepped through her bedroom door. "Gwynn, you must wake up."

Suddenly, the exhaustion morphed into anticipation. "What is it?"

Anya punched the speaker button on her phone. "Say all of that again."

From behind the secured doors of the operation center in St Marys, Georgia, Dr. Celeste Mankiller said, "The cop wasn't a cop."

Gwynn sat up and swung her legs over the edge of the bed. "What?"

Celeste said, "The guy you thought was a cop at the clinic a few hours ago wasn't a cop."

"He was dressed like a cop, and he had a cop car," Gwynn said.

"Describe what the Policía Nacional cars in Punta Cana look like," Celeste said.

Gwynn wiped her eyes. "Well, his car was—"

Celeste cut her off. "I don't care what *his* car looked like. Tell me what the police cars in Punta Cana look like."

Gwynn considered the question for a long moment. "I guess I don't know, but why does that matter? You wouldn't have called just to tell us that guy wasn't a cop."

"I called because that guy was private security for somebody important."

Gwynn grabbed the phone. "Who?"

"We don't know who, but we know it was somebody who needed private security. Two of the cameras you planted picked up the arrival of somebody in a big SUV that we couldn't identify, but he wasn't there for cosmetic surgery."

Gwynn eyed her partner. "Okay, so keep talking."

Celeste cleared her throat. "Whoever he was, he was in bad shape. He looked more like he needed to be headed to a hospital. The video isn't clear enough to run facial recognition, but he was around six feet tall and a hundred fifty pounds."

"Six feet and one-fifty?"

"Exactly, and he moved as if it was all he could do to lift his feet."

Anya stepped into the conversation. "Maybe clinic provides medical care for locals who cannot afford regular hospital."

Celeste said, "Uh, no. The SUV was nice, and the guy had an entourage, including more security."

"Nothing about this is adding up," Gwynn said. "Do you have any theories?"

"Skipper's on her way in, but I don't know what to make of it."

"Can you send us the video?" Gwynn asked.

"It's already on your tablets."

Gwynn pulled her tablet from the nightstand and brought up the video of the SUV arriving and the clearly decrepit man struggling to make his way into the clinic. "I see what you mean. That guy's in bad shape."

"Yeah, he is," Celeste said. "Got any guesses on what's going on?"

"My special agent brain has a few potential theories, but I'd like to hear Skipper's first."

"That's not fair," Celeste said. "You've got training I don't have. Can you give me a hint about what you're thinking?"

Gwynn sighed. "Okay, but don't tell Skipper. I don't want to influence her thinking. I think they're doing more than just harvesting organs in that building. I think they may be conducting assisted suicides. You remember Dr. Kevorkian, right?"

"Ooh, you may be on to something. Maybe they're doing all sorts of procedures in there that would be illegal in the States. You need to get inside that place and find out what's going on."

"That was the plan for tomorrow night, but that was before we realized they were a twenty-four-hour operation."

"Oh, hey. Skipper's on her way up. She just came through the door downstairs. Hang on. She'll be up to speed and in charge before you know it."

Gwynn glanced up at Anya, and the Russian said, "She is very smart, and she will know more than all of us in very short time."

Skipper joined the conversation, and there was little doubt she'd been sound asleep only minutes before. "Hey, guys. What's going on?"

Celeste spent three minutes bringing Skipper up to speed and walking her through the video, and with that, the grogginess was gone and the elite analyst was back in command of not only her faculties, but also the situation at hand.

"It's clear what's going on here," Skipper said. "I need you to scour the video over the twenty-four-hour period after they brought in the dying guy, whoever he is."

"What am I looking for?" Celeste asked.

"You're looking for the dead body and the surgeons."

That sucked Gwynn back into the discussion. "Dead body and surgeons?"

Skipper said, "Yeah, it's simple. There's somebody inside that clinic with the organ that dying guy needs, but that's not all. There are at least two transplant surgeons in there. Those guys aren't general surgeons like the guys who cut cysts out of you. These guys are specialists. Somebody is harvesting an organ from a patient who thinks she's getting a tummy tuck, and somebody else is implanting it into that guy on the video right now."

Gwynn said, "So, you think they're performing transplant procedures inside the cosmetic surgery clinic?"

"Of course they are," she said. "You don't think they're shipping the organs all over the world, do you? You can't magically have a kidney show up in St. Louis for a wealthy transplant patient. That kind of stuff in the States is regulated out the wazoo. Even the filthy, nasty rich can't get around that in this country. That kind of stuff happens where regulations aren't enforced to, let's say, a reasonable standard."

Anya narrowed her gaze and leaned toward the phone. "If we go inside there right now, we might have time to stop it."

"Sure, you could," Skipper said, "but are you going to wait by the door every night for the next twenty years and stop every one of them?"

"What are you saying?" Anya asked.

"I'm saying we need to find out who the surgeons are, find out who's really running the clinic, and calmly and kindly tell them we'd like them to stop doing that."

Anya smiled. "This is definitely job for me. I am always calm and kind, especially with very sharp knife in my hand."

"Exactly," Skipper said. "Do you have any better cameras with you down there?"

Gwynn looked to Anya, who said, "I do not think so, but we must ask Mongo."

Skipper said, "Wake him up. We need good shots of the surgeons coming out of that clinic when they're finished with the transplant. That's the only way we'll be able to identify them."

Anya dialed Mongo, and he answered after the fourth ring. "Yeah?"

"Is Anya Burinkova. You are awake, yes?"

Mongo rubbed his eyes. "Yeah, I'm awake now. What's up?"

"We must have better camera at clinic. Tell to me you have this."

He groaned. "Better camera?"

"Skipper says we must have better video of faces coming from clinic. Do you have better camera?"

He sat up in his bed. "No, we don't have any other cameras. We used what we had. What's this about?"

"Is not important that you know details. Is important you find for us better camera."

He said, "I can probably make one, but why can't we just use the cameras on our phones? They're pretty good, at least compared to the spotcams we put up."

Anya turned back to the speakerphone with Skipper and Celeste. "I have idea. You will not like, but it will work."

Skipper's voice turned harsh. "Slow down, Anya. Tell me what you're thinking."

"We have no other cameras except our phones. We will be waiting outside clinic, and you will tell to us when surgeons leave."

"You're wrong," Skipper said. "I do like that plan. In fact, I love it. How quickly can you be in position?"

Anya pulled her other phone back to her lips. "How quickly will you and Kodiak—"

Mongo interrupted. "We'll be mounted up and ready to roll in three minutes."

The big man's estimate wasn't accurate. Both vehicles and all four operators were rolling from their rented driveways two minutes later.

Kodiak activated his sat-com. "The boys are in position."

Anya answered, "We will take first car."

Kodiak said, "Roger. We'll hold position for the next one, unless you need reinforcements."

Parked beneath a pair of bent trees forming the perfect stakeout position, Gwynn and Anya settled into their perch for what could've been the remainder of a very long night.

"I think maybe we made mistake," Anya said. "Transplant will not be fast, no matter what organ. I think maybe many hours."

"You're probably right," Gwynn said. "We could take turns getting some sleep."

"This is good idea. You will sleep first."

Gwynn gave her partner a knowing glance. "And you're not going to sleep at all, are you?"

"I will sleep when is necessary."

The night dragged on, and the city beat on as if no one were watching.

"Are you seeing this?" Kodiak asked over the sat-com.

Anya answered. "I see, but we cannot do anything. This is not our mission."

"I know, but that's going to turn ugly, and we could wrap it up in a few seconds."

"You're in charge," Kodiak said. "But are you sure about this one?"

Anya peered through the windshield at the scene unfolding in front of her. Five knife-wielding thugs surrounded two adults and a child who obviously didn't belong on that street at that hour . . . or any hour of the Dominican night. As the knot grew in her stomach, she said, "Skipper, is there movement at clinic?"

"Negative," the analyst said. "It's still dark and quiet."

Anya laid a hand against her partner's arm. "Is time to be awake, Gwynn."

She jerked. "Are they on the move?"

"No," Anya said. "Look on corner of streets. Family is maybe in danger."

Gwynn blinked, bringing the scene into focus. "Ooh, that's not good. We have to do something."

"No," Anya said. "This is wrong pronoun. *We* do not have to do something. *I* have to do something."

Gwynn flipped the switch on the interior light to stop it from coming on when Anya opened the door, and an instant later, the Russian was staggering diagonally across the street toward the potential crime scene. When she fell down the second time, her antics finally drew the attention of both the potential victims and the armed boys who had no idea how quickly they were about to become the actual victims of the night's violence.

The boys stepped from the intersection as a group, leaving the young family behind, and approached their soon-to-be assailant lying restlessly on the edge of the street.

When the thugs were one step closer to Anya than the family, she leapt to her feet and yelled, "Run!"

The family froze in disbelief at the scene unfolding in front of them. Anya threw a blindingly fast shot to the throat of the nearest boy, sending him melting to the ground, and she caught his knife before it could fall to the street. Gripping the knife in the hold she'd perfected over decades of training and street-fighting experience, she advanced toward the remaining boys, daring them to accept her unspoken challenge.

The four remaining would-be fighters raised their knives, and Anya grinned. The first boy lunged forward, and before his brain could decipher the signals racing from his hand, Anya opened a wound from just below his elbow, down his arm, and across the back of his hand, rendering the limb utterly useless. The boy crumbled to the ground beside his fallen friend, and the fight continued.

Two of the three remaining boys thrust toward Anya in the worst decision of their young lives, and she sidestepped the first while catching the second by the elbow and shoulder and driving him into the third fighter, blade first. The redirected boy's knife plunged into the boy's stomach until the point of the double-edge blade contacted his spine.

Her victim's eyes exploded in agony, terror, and disbelief, and he joined the first two on the ground. The assailant she'd sidestepped raised his knife high above his head, and Gwynn grimaced, knowing the coming result seconds before it occurred. Anya moved aside, trapped the raised arm of the thug, and forced it downward until his blade pierced his waiting thigh. She swept his feet, sending him onto his back as he yelled in agony.

The only remaining fighter stood with his eyes darting from one victim to another until Anya stepped within inches of his face, threw a crushing elbow to his jaw, and snatched the weapon from his grip. He staggered backward, and she moved in perfect synchronization with the retreating young man. She threw a powerful punch to his shoulder, spinning him away from her, and laced an arm around his neck from behind.

In Russian-accented Spanish, she hissed, "Look at those people watching me tear you to pieces. If anything happens to them, I will find you, and I will feed pieces of you to sharks in ocean."

He fought against her, jerking and pulling with every ounce of strength he could muster, and growled, "You don't know who I am. You'll never find me."

Anya released her hold around his neck and shoved him onto his back. She planted a knee in the center of his chest and drew the boy's own knife through the air too quickly to see until a deep slash appeared on each of his cheeks and across his forehead. "I think I will not have problem finding you now."

With the bleeding victim still pinned to the ground, she looked back up at the family staring in awe. "Run! Now! And do not come back here in nighttime. Is dangerous place."

24

Pogonya za Dikim Gusem
(Wild Goose Chase)

By the time Anya made it back to the car, four of the boys were on their feet and carrying the fifth into the darkness.

Kodiak came over the sat-com. "Well, that was fun to watch. Are you okay?"

"Yes," Anya said. "I am fine."

Gwynn shook her head. "That was awesome. I'll never have the confidence to pull that off. There were five of them."

Anya chuckled. "Yes, but they were five boys who did not know how to fight."

"Yeah, but you couldn't have known that before you went out there."

Anya scowled. "I have failed to teach you anything."

Gwynn recoiled. "That's not true. You've taught me everything I know about fighting."

"You saw how they were standing and how they were holding knives. They obviously did not know how to fight. They were clumsy and standing in each other's way. I won fight before I stepped out of car."

"You're amazing. You know that?"

Anya nodded. "Yes, of course I know this, but there was nothing challenging about what I did. You could have also done it."

"I've still got a lot to learn," Gwynn said.

Anya cocked her head. "Me, too."

Kodiak said, "I thought we weren't getting involved."

"I am sometimes wrong," Anya said. "This was one of those times. You were right this time."

"Yeah, I'm right occasionally. You could've let us help."

"I did not need help, but thank you for being concerned about me. You are very sweet man."

Gwynn almost blushed and whispered, "He is, isn't he?"

Anya waggled a finger. "Is not good idea."

Her partner shrugged and looked away. "Do you really think the surgeons are going to leave tonight?"

"I do not know, but if we are inside house, we will never catch them. This means we must stay here until they leave."

As if on cue, Skipper said, "We've got movement. Stand by."

No one said a word, but each of them leaned forward, watching for the heavy gate to the clinic compound to swing open.

Seconds ticked by like hours until Skipper said, "Three vehicles. Four people."

"We can only hit two vehicles, so choose carefully," Mongo said.

Before Skipper could make the decision, Anya said, "This is not true. Gwynn is excellent driver. We can hit two."

Skipper said, "How?"

"There are three cars. At least two of these must go in same direction, probably all three," Anya said. "If they go two directions, boys will follow one car, and we will follow two."

"I get that," Skipper said, "but how are you going to hit two cars at once?"

Anya said, "We will make small accident. Do not worry."

"Gate's coming open," Mongo said.

The first car pulled through the narrow opening and turned left. Gwynn and Kodiak pulled their vehicles into gear, and the second car turned right.

"Here we go," Kodiak said. "When the next one makes the turn, we'll take the single."

The third car turned to follow the second, and the team withdrew from their hides.

Kodiak pulled alongside his target vehicle, and Mongo rolled down his window. He extended a massive arm into the space between the two slow-moving cars and waved for the driver's attention. The man behind the wheel ignored him, so Mongo said, "Help me get his attention."

Kodiak didn't hesitate. He swerved to the right, missing the car by mere inches as he lay on the horn. The driver finally reacted, yanking his car off the road. Kodiak pinned him against a pair of trees by stopping the front bumper an inch from the car's fender.

Mongo leapt from the vehicle and grabbed the car door handle. The driver threw an arm across his body and shoved the lock into its cavity. Mongo shook his head and spun a finger in the universal signal to roll down the window. Instead of complying, the driver snatched a cell phone from the seat and drove his thumb against the screen, so the giant yanked his hat from his head and wrapped it around an enormous fist. An instant later, he demolished the driver's window, sending shards of glass into the car. He grabbed the cell phone and crushed it against the steering wheel as he pulled his own phone from a back pocket.

The driver pawed furiously at his seat belt, desperately trying to free himself for escape across the front seat, but Mongo was too fast. He grabbed the man's collar and pulled his head and shoulders through the opening where the glass had been only seconds before. Holding the phone in front of the man's face, Mongo snapped several rapid shots before shoving him back inside the car.

Before the man could process what had just happened, Mongo was back inside the SUV, and Kodiak was putting time and distance between them and the scene.

While Kodiak and Mongo were assaulting the first car, Gwynn and Anya chased their prey onto an even darker road than the one beside the clinic. Gwynn followed at an unthreatening distance until the two cars had just enough space between them for her trap to work perfectly. She accelerated around the rear car, doubling her speed in less than a hundred feet. As soon as her rear bumper was clear of the trail vehicle, she spun the wheel, sending the left front corner of the SUV colliding with the lead car's right rear. The PIT maneuver worked flawlessly, and the car spun out of control, coming to rest facing the wrong direction in the roadside drainage ditch.

Anya leapt from the SUV and sprinted toward the car while Gwynn continued with phase two of the maneuver. The well-trained federal agent spun the heavy SUV like a child's toy in the street until her glaring headlights shined directly into the windshield of the oncoming second car. The driver slammed the brakes, sliding to a stop. Gwynn spun the wheel again and threw crushed shells and gravel into the air behind her SUV until coming to rest behind and beside the car, blocking any avenue of escape.

She threw the vehicle in park and exploded from inside. Before the driver of the car could react, Gwynn forced open the passenger's side door and dived onto the front seat beside the terrified driver. She threw up her cell phone between them and yelled, "Smile!"

Almost before it all began, the two women were back inside the SUV and speeding into the night.

Gwynn caught her breath. "Did you get yours?"

Anya nodded. "Yes, did you?"

"You know it, baby! We're good at this."

"Yes, we are," Anya said before keying her sat-com. "We have photographs of two drivers, and we are clear of scene."

Kodiak answered, "We're clear as well, and Mongo got some great shots. We'll see you back at the house."

They pulled into the driveway of Gwynn's and Anya's house simultaneously and headed inside.

Skipper was back on the speakerphone in minutes. "Nice work, guys. I couldn't see it, but that sounded awesome, and the pics came out great. I've got IDs on two of them, but the third one is a mystery so far. It'll take some time."

"Are they surgeons?" Anya asked.

Skipper said, "One is, but the other is a nobody—probably a technician or something from the clinic. The doctor is one Dima Ivanov, graduate of the Pervyy Moskovskiy gosudarstvennyy meditsinskiy universitet."

Anya said, "This means First Moscow State Medical University. Is oldest and most prestigious medical university in all of Russia."

Skipper continued. "I'm translating what I can find on him, and he's a good candidate for a transplant surgeon. I'll send the details to your tablets."

Celeste's voice sounded from the background. "More movement."

Kodiak grabbed his tablet and brought up the camera array. They watched as three men forced a long black object into the back of a white van.

"That looks a lot like a body bag to me," Mongo said. "I've seen enough of them to be able to pick 'em out. I say we try to catch those guys before they dump the body."

Skipper said, "I'll try to get a satellite track on the van, but it won't be easy. Get going, and I'll let you know if I get it done."

The four loaded up into the rougher of the two SUVs to blend in more easily with the local traffic and headed for the clinic.

A block away, Kodiak shot a finger into the air. "There they are!"

Gwynn stared at the van. "That could be them, but something tells me there's no shortage of white delivery vans running around."

She moved into position behind the van but left enough distance to avoid suspicion. The driver led them through progressively more rural areas toward the interior of the island.

Mongo called the op center. "Any luck on the satellite track? We're following a van, but we're not sure if it's the right one."

Skipper growled. "No. I couldn't get anything up and running. It's like every satellite in orbit hates me this morning."

"We'll keep tracking this one and see where he takes us. Have you had any success with the ID on the third guy?"

"I'm still on it, but I'm hitting roadblocks on that road, too."

"Hang in there," Kodiak said. "If anybody can do it, it's you. We'll let you know how this wild goose chase goes."

They followed the van another half hour, and Gwynn asked, "Anyone else have the feeling that we're going nowhere?"

Before anyone answered, the van turned left and came to a stop in front of a locked iron gate across a sand-covered road barely wider than the vehicle.

"Keep driving past," Kodiak ordered.

Gwynn gave him an eye. "I know what I'm doing."

"Sorry."

She rounded a curve and stopped behind a stand of fruit trees.

Anya said, "This would be very good time for satellite."

Gwynn said, "Hey, we don't need a live satellite to know where that road goes. Any satellite image will do."

In seconds, Mongo had a black-and-white image on the screen of his sat-phone. "It looks like it dead ends about a mile down the road. We'll put eyes on it. Let's go, Kodiak."

Anya pointed through the window toward a rising hill a few hundred yards to the east. "Wait! If is only one mile, we can probably see from there."

Three pairs of eyes followed her finger, and Mongo said, "That's a much better idea than running through bush."

Gwynn drove up a winding trail in four-wheel drive until she reached a clearing near the top of the hill. Anya climbed on top of the SUV as soon as they came to a stop and peered into the distance as the rising sun lit up the sky.

"What do you see?" Gwynn asked.

"Is not good news. Is building with smoking chimney."

A collective sigh rose from the team as the realization of what they'd discovered washed over them.

"I guess that means that was the right van," Kodiak said.

Gwynn said, "That gives us no choice. We have to check it out."

They climbed back into the SUV and made their way down the hill and across what little open ground lay between them and the building.

When they'd gone as far as the vehicle could take them, Mongo said, "It looks like we're on foot from here. Kodiak and I will make the trek and report back."

Anya said, "No, we will go together. If there is trouble, it is better if we are together."

They climbed from the SUV and pressed through the brush and undergrowth of the lush tropical ground, making slower progress than any of them wanted, but before they'd covered the half mile to the building, Kodiak grabbed a handful of Mongo's shirt.

He tapped Mongo's nose with the tip of his finger. "We don't have to go any farther. That place is exactly what we think it is."

Mongo raised his face into the warming morning air and inhaled deeply, then he hung his head and blew out a long breath. "Kodiak's right. There's only one thing that smells like that."

25

NIKOGDA NE BEYTE NYAGKO (NEVER HIT SOFTLY)

The ride back to the rented houses was painfully quiet as the lack of sleep and psychological exhaustion overcame the team.

Gwynn was the first to speak. "They're literally killing people and cremating their bodies to sell and implant organs on the black market. Is there anything worse?"

Anya said, "There are many things worse, but I hope you never have to see them. We will stop these people. This is why we are here."

"How are we going to stop them?"

"We do it by cutting body from snake."

Gwynn glared at her partner. "The saying is cut off the head of the snake."

Anya slowly shook her head. "Yes, I know this, but this time, we are cutting off body from snake. Head of this snake is maybe Kremlin. Do we have any way to cut off that head?"

Gwynn closed her eyes. "I'm too tired to play these word games with you, but I get your point."

Kodiak asked, "Does this mean you've got a plan?"

Anya nodded. "Yes, I have part of plan, but I will need more time to finish plan. I am tired, and my brain needs to sleep. We will have early dinner and discuss plan in a few hours, yes?"

Heads nodded, but no one spoke. Each of them simply parted ways and succumbed to their bodies' demands for rest.

* * *

Sleep took them, and seven hours later, they reconvened with a call to the op center.

Anya began the briefing. "I have first questions and then plan."

Skipper said, "Let's start with the questions."

"First, did you find identity of third person from cars last night?"

"I did," the analyst said. "And you're not going to like it. His name is Gedeon Zhukov, and he's the son of one Alexi Zhukov, former KGB colonel."

Anya interrupted. "This is not correct. Zhukov was colonel in SVR. In KGB, he was only major."

"How do you remember all these guys?" Skipper asked.

Anya's tone grew dark. "You would also not forget name of man who raped you four times."

Leaving Elizabeth "Skipper" Woodley speechless was one step short of impossible, and Anya Burinkova had just taken that step.

Unlike Skipper, Gwynn gasped. "What?"

Anya's stern Russian expression never betrayed her. The look was neither anger nor loathing; it was merely the memory of a time in her life she could never undo and never release. "He was one of men who came to State School Four—sparrow school—during our training and forced himself on those of us who he found to be beautiful. When one of us resisted, she was never seen again, and we were forbidden from speaking of her."

Kodiak lowered his chin. "Then I'll tear his arms off and beat him to death with them."

Anya focused her full attention on the warrior beside her who possessed not only the strength and fortitude to do exactly as he threatened, but also the wherewithal to do it with neither remorse nor regret. "Gedeon Zhukov is not man who did this to me. He is only son of Alexi Zhukov. We cannot punish him for sins of his father."

Kodiak scowled. "Maybe not, but from the looks of things, Gedeon's sins are stacking up, too, so maybe ending the bloodline isn't a bad idea."

"We must focus on mission. There is saying in Russia: Vendetta makes large hole in shield. Please do not cut this hole in your shield."

Skipper cleared her throat. "I don't mean to, you know . . . But we should get back on track."

Anya said, "I am sorry for interrupting briefing."

"No, don't be sorry," Skipper said. "I didn't mean to bring up bad memories. Anyway, I'm sending a bunch of information to your tablets. It should be there any second."

Gwynn opened her tablet and thumbed through the packet. "Wow. You've been busy."

Skipper said, "It's what I do. You should have an incomplete list of the clinic employees, including addresses and telephone numbers. You should also have a satellite photo of the clinic without a roof. That was taken as they rebuilt after a hurricane three years ago. I thought it might come in handy."

Anya leaned to look over Gwynn's shoulder. "This is wonderful information. I still believe we must get inside, but I wish to tell to you plan I made inside mind."

Skipper said, "Let's hear it."

Anya began. "I believe making campaign of terror for everyone inside operation is best way to move forward. We will frighten these people so badly they cannot continue to do their jobs. I believe this should begin at lowest level and move quickly to men at top of organization."

"What kind of terror are you talking about?" Skipper asked.

"Whatever is necessary. Everyone is afraid of something, and it does not take long to determine what this thing is. If we can stop nurse from taking patient into clinic, this will slow progress. Then, if we make surgeon afraid to make transplant, this will further slow them."

Gwynn said, "Won't they just bring in other nurses and other surgeons?"

"Maybe," Anya said, "but this is only beginning of process. Eventually, we will move to people who are getting rich from this, and we will make them pay."

Skipper paused a moment before saying, "I don't know, Anya. This vigilante stuff makes me a little nervous. It's one thing to go after the guys at the top, but I'm not comfortable taking out the nurses, clerks, and technicians. They're doing plenty of bad stuff, and I'm not saying they shouldn't be stopped, but I can't be on board for taking them out."

Anya recoiled. "I am not talking about killing anyone, especially not people you mentioned. I agree with you. I only wish to frighten, not to kill."

"In that case," Skipper said. "Let's get to work. Who do you want to start with?"

Anya said, "I want to have conversation with person we photographed who you said is maybe technician. What do you have on him?"

"He's in your package," Skipper said. "His name is Emilio Parra, and you'll find his address in the packet."

Gwynn scrolled through the list. "I've got him. Do you think he knows what's going on at the clinic?"

Skipper said, "There's only one way to find out, but he left at the same time as one of the surgeons and Gedeon Zhukov, so he probably knows something."

Anya said, "We will start with him. I will smile and flirt with him as distraction, and—"

Gwynn laid a hand on Anya's arm. "Maybe it would be better if I did the flirting."

Anya closed her eyes and subconsciously touched her face. "Yes, of course this is better idea. I forgot . . ."

Kodiak said, "Gwynn is a better idea anyway. She can certainly get Emilio's attention, and we may need Anya as a hitter if the guy gets out of control."

Anya gave him a smile. "This is kind of you to say, but look at Mongo. Do you think I can do anything he cannot?"

Kodiak eyed the big man. "Yeah, he's got skills, but those skills tend to tear down walls. You've got the finesse to be subtle and still deadly."

"This is true," Anya said. "We make good team. Do we know if Emilio lives alone?"

Skipper's fingers turned to a blur above the keys. "I'm working on it. It looks like he's not married, or if he is, there's nothing in the public records. I'm searching for recent satellite photos. Give me a minute."

Thirty seconds later, she said, "Okay, according to the shots I found, two different cars park at his address. It must be a rented place because he's not on the record as being the owner. I can't find anyone else listed at that address on a driver's license, but that's the best I can do in short order."

Anya let her eyes drift to the ceiling for a moment. "This means he probably has roommate or maybe two. We can easily handle three people. I cannot think of reason to wait."

Mongo shrugged. "Me, neither. Let's hit him."

The team climbed aboard the more believable SUV and headed for Emilio Parra's address. Gwynn drove by twice, giving everyone in the vehicle time to memorize every aspect of the low, concrete block house with two cars parked almost touching the front of the building.

"How are we feeling?" Gwynn asked after the second pass.

Mongo said, "Drop me and Kodiak off at the back door. We'll make entry on your command, and we'll flank whoever's inside."

Anya nodded. "Is good plan."

Gwynn eased to a stop a few hundred feet from the back of Emilio's building.

Mongo pushed open the door. "This is perfect. Give us a countdown for entry."

With the men out of the vehicle, Anya said, "Park behind both cars so they cannot run. I will pick lock, and you will be first through door, yes?"

"Good with me," Gwynn said. "How hard are we hitting them?"

Anya pulled out the tiny plastic American flag she'd carried in her front pocket for over a decade and spun it playfully between her thumb and index finger. "I believe it was your President Roosevelt who said, 'Do not hit at all if it can be avoided, but never hit softly.'"

Anya pressed herself against the wall beside the front door and gripped the knob. Gwynn waited in anticipation until her partner shook her head and took a knee in front of the door.

Gwynn keyed her sat-com. "Sitrep?"

Kodiak answered instantly. "Door is free, and we're standing by. No prying eyes in any direction."

Gwynn said, "Front door is secure, and Anya's working on it. Stand by to go."

Anya slipped her pick and tensioner from the knob and glanced up at Gwynn with a nod.

Gwynn slipped her pistol from its holster beneath her shirt and tucked the weapon against her stomach. "On my count. Three . . . two . . . one . . . go!"

Both doors swung inward silently and simultaneously. Gwynn led the front entry while Kodiak led Mongo through the rear door. Pistols came up, and the practiced art of room clearing began.

Anya whispered, "Clear front."

Kodiak said, "Clear rear. Moving to hallway. Motion at the end will be me."

Both entry teams came into sight of each other at the same moment, and no one flinched. Two doors stood closed on the left side of the hallway, while a single door rested in the center of the right wall. Every eye went to the floor and instantly saw the same thing.

Gwynn was first to voice it. "The door closer to you is a bathroom. Everybody, go right."

Instead of answering, everyone nodded, and they crept toward each other with pistols at the ready.

As they came to a stop in front of their respective doors, Kodiak whispered, "Dynamic?"

Gwynn nodded and held up three fingers, then two, then one. The world inside the two rooms turned to absolute chaos in an instant. Kodiak and Mongo poured into their room with pistols raised and boots pounding.

Kodiak roared, "*¡Manos! ¡Manos!*"

The man lying on the bed exploded from beneath his single sheet, wearing nothing but a pair of boxers. Confusion shone in his dark eyes as panic overtook him. Kodiak sent a crushing punch to the man's right shoulder, sending him spinning and collapsing back onto his bed. Mongo was on him in an instant, wrenching both arms behind his back until the man bucked and bellowed in protest.

Kodiak yelled across his shoulder. "One secure!"

In spite of the noise from the room across the hall, the man in Anya and Gwynn's room slept peacefully, curled up like a child beneath a ragged sheet. Gwynn cast a mischievous glance at her partner, and the Russian nodded.

Gwynn slipped onto the edge of the man's bed and slid closer until her face was only inches from his. In seductive Spanish, she whispered, "Emilio . . . Emilio . . . Wake up. I'm here to make all of your dirty dreams come true."

Emilio opened one sleepy eye and then the next. As the beautiful olive skin of Gwynn's face came into focus, he smiled, but his ecstasy was short-lived. The next thing he saw was the muzzle of Anya's Glock pressing between his eyes. Delight morphed into horror in an instant, and the man tried to retreat, but the concrete block wall behind him and the heel of Gwynn's hand beneath his chin left him pinned with no avenue of escape.

In trembling Spanish, Emilio said, "What do you want? You can have anything you want. Just don't kill me, please."

Anya leaned closer as Gwynn knelt to gain a stronger position over the terrified man.

In Russian, Anya hissed, "I want the person back who you burned last night. Can I have that?"

Emilio's eyes widened even more. "I don't know what you're saying. Is that Russian? I don't speak Russian."

While Anya pressed the muzzle more aggressively into the man's face, Gwynn said, "We know exactly what you're doing at the clinic. It stops today. Do you understand?"

Emilio gasped. "But I can't do anything about it. I'm just an anesthesia tech. I just make sure they're breathing while they're asleep. That's all. I swear!"

"Who's the man in the other room?"

"He's my brother. Please don't hurt him. His wife made him leave. He's just sleeping here. He doesn't have anything to do with the clinic. Please don't hurt him."

Gwynn smiled. "Good. Now we know who to kill first if we see one more dead body being taken to the crematory."

"No, please. I can't do anything to stop them. Please don't hurt my brother."

Just as the words fell from Emilio's lips, a thud sounded from the other room as Mongo dragged Emilio's bound-and-gagged brother from his bed and across the hall. The giant filled the opening where the door had been, and one of his victim's ankles was clamped in his iron grip.

Mongo whipped the much smaller man through the doorway and deposited him on the floor beside Emilio's bed. "This guy? Is this who you don't want us to kill?"

Emilio's brother squirmed and whimpered beneath the flex-cuffs and duct tape.

Mongo planted an enormous boot on the man's face. "One more, Emilio. Just one more white van driving away from that clinic with a body on board, and you get to watch me rip your little brother apart and play in his blood."

Emilio broke down into gasping tears. "I can't stop them. I can't. And they'll kill me if I try to leave. It's what they do. Please . . . you've got to understand."

Those were the words Anya longed to hear. "Oh, they'll kill you, will they?"

Emilio trembled. "Yeah, they'll kill me. No one can ever leave that place alive."

Anya holstered her pistol and spoke in her Russian-accented Spanish. "That leaves you in a terrible position. If you try to quit, they will kill you. If you don't quit, I will kill you. It sounds like you get to decide who will kill you."

Tears poured from his dark eyes, and he rolled his head from side to side. "Please don't do this."

Anya said, "There is one other option. Tell me about Gedeon Zhukov. What was he doing at the clinic last night?"

"I don't know who that is. What are you talking about?"

Anya slapped him twice, leaving him recoiling in both fear and pain. "Do not lie to me. What was the Russian in the white shirt and gold chains doing at the clinic early this morning? He left at the same time as you. His name is Gedeon Zhukov. Now, tell me what he was doing there."

"He was picking up the money. That's all I know. He gets the money. I didn't know his name, I swear."

"How much money?" Anya demanded.

"I don't know. I'm just a tech. I don't know anything."

"American dollars?" Anya asked.

Emilio's breathing continued to accelerate, so Anya took a step back. "I need for you to calm down. We're going to keep both of you tied up until we're finished talking, but no one is going to die here today unless you stop talking. Understand?"

He swallowed hard and stared down at his brother.

Kodiak took a knee beside the man on the floor. "Relax. We're not going to hurt you anymore. We're just going to talk. Just relax so your brother can give us what we need."

Mongo hoisted Emilio's brother onto a chair in the corner of the room. "Sit there and be cool."

Anya repeated her question. "Was the money that Gedeon Zhukov picked up in American dollars?"

Emilio shook his head. "No, it was Cayman dollars. I saw it before he closed the bag."

"Good, Emilio. Continue breathing, and this will be over soon. This is promise from me. How big was bag?"

"I don't know. Maybe fifty or seventy-five centimeters long. It was round with handles like a tube."

"Good. Now tell to me man's name who received transplant."

"I don't know. He was French, but I don't speak French. I swear, I don't know."

Anya softened her tone even more. "Okay, I believe you. Now, tell me the surgeon's name."

"It's a Russian name. It's something like Divanoff, maybe."

"Could it have been Dima Ivanov?"

"Yes, that's it. Dr. Ivanov."

"Okay, this is good. What time are you supposed to go to work tonight?"

He turned his head toward the crooked table beside the bed where his watch lay. "Nine o'clock. What time is it now?"

"You have plenty of time," Anya said. "We are going to leave, but if you call the police, I promise I will kill both of you before the sun comes up again. You are going to work tonight and pretend none of this happened. Do you have any transplant operations tonight?"

"I don't know. They don't tell me. I just go to work and do what they say. I never see the schedule. It is usually no more than two every week. Mostly, it's just cosmetic surgery, not transplants."

Anya withdrew two hypodermic needles from her pocket and tossed one to Mongo. Two minutes later, the two brothers were sound asleep, back in their beds, with no evidence the four operators had ever been inside the small house.

26

VOSPRINIMAYEMAYA BEZOPASNOST'
(PERCEIVED SECURITY)

"Well, that was exciting," Gwynn said as they slid back into the SUV.

Kodiak laughed. "Yes, it was. I like it when nobody shoots at us. What's next on the agenda for tonight? I could get used to this kind of cakewalk work."

Gwynn made a noise no human should ever make. "Did you say cake-walk work?"

Kodiak gave her a wink. "Ask your partner how our last mission together went down."

Gwynn turned to Anya, and the Russian pointed toward her scarred, discolored face.

"Oh."

"Exactly," Anya said as she checked her watch. "I think we have time to have walk-in appointment with Dr. Ivanov."

Kodiak grinned. "You don't waste any time, do you?"

She shook her head. "We have very small window of time to do much work. Emilio is . . . maybe what you call wild card. I think he might tell his boss at clinic about us. If that happens tonight, we will need maybe more help than just four of us."

Mongo tapped his watch. "It's just past five now, so that gives us plenty of time to make some strong first impressions on a few people before Emilio gets to work and spills his guts at nine."

Skipper provided navigation to Dr. Ivanov's temporary residence on the edge of the more pleasant side of Punta Cana. Unlike most other property gates in the city, his wrought iron double gate swung outward and rested against steel pins, preventing it from being forced inward by vehicles whose drivers believed themselves capable of crashing through.

Gwynn eyed the gate. "Neat. It looks like somebody knows a thing or two about keeping people out."

Mongo unbuckled his seat belt. "Pull forward twenty feet, and I'll take care of it."

Kodiak released his belt and reached for the door handle. "I'll give you a hand."

Mongo waved him off. "No need. I've got it. You know as well as I do that there's no such thing as security . . ."—the two completed the phrase in unison—". . . there's only perceived security."

The beast of a man pressed his back against the right half of the gate and bent his knees slightly. His bear-claw fists clamped around two of the vertical rods just beneath a horizontal bar designed to provide strength and rigidity for the gate that was in its final seconds of life. Wearing the grimace of an Olympic powerlifter, Mongo rose six inches, bearing the weight of the massive gate, and forced it across the pins at its base. The left gate provided less of a challenge than the right, and soon, the formerly imposing-looking obstacle gave way, granting welcome access for the SUV.

Mongo slid back inside, and Gwynn said, "Okay, that was impressive. Kodiak, could you have done that?"

Before he could answer, Mongo said, "Sure, he could've. He just wanted to let me show off a little. Ain't that right, buddy?"

Kodiak scoffed. "Anything for you, big guy."

Gwynn accelerated up the short, sloping driveway and positioned the SUV in front of the garage door to block any car attempting to flee. Anya vanished around the corner of the house before the rest of the team could dismount.

She was back almost as quickly. "Telephone line is cut. If there is alarm, it is no problem now."

No faces appeared in the windows along the front of the house, so Gwynn said, "Maybe we should go in the back."

"Good plan," Kodiak said. "I'll seal the front."

In seconds, he had the pair of knobs on the double doors tied together with several wraps of 550 cord. It wouldn't stop a marauding horde of elephants, but it would certainly limit a scared doctor's ability to escape.

With the team reunited by the back door, Anya gave the knob a test, but it didn't budge.

Kodiak took a step back and said, "I've been practicing my lock-picking skills. Do you mind if I give it a try?"

Anya stepped aside, granting him full access to the lock at the same instant the heel of his boot landed against the mechanism. The glass in the frame shattered, and the door exploded inward.

As they followed the flying debris through the opening, Mongo said, "Nice job. That picking practice is really paying off."

They pressed into the interior of the house, scanning as they moved. The first floor of the property was wide open, with only half a dozen narrow wall sections supporting the second floor.

A pair of beefy guys, who were obviously on the security payroll, bounded down the stairs, one with a fighting knife in his left hand and the other raising a Makarov pistol.

Anya shouted, "*Vniz! Vniz! Vniz!*," giving the two men ample time to follow her order to get down, but neither complied.

The hiss and crack of four suppressed rounds from a pair of Glocks followed the noncompliance of the charging Russians, and they collapsed into pools of their own blood. Smoke rose from the muzzles of Kodiak's and Anya's pistols as they stepped over and around the bodies.

With the first floor clear, the team laced their way up the stairs, moving quickly but carefully through the fatal funnel every stairwell represented for assaulters. They made the top landing and divided themselves into two teams. The interior doors proved to be little more than temporary annoyances as they pressed through each as if they were nothing more than paper.

Behind the second door Anya kicked in stood a man with a cell phone pressed to his face and terror in his eyes. She yelled, "Contact single," and raised her pistol to bear on the man's face. "Drop the phone," she ordered, first in English and then in her native Russian.

The man followed her command and raised his hands above his head.

Gwynn stepped around her partner and cleared the rest of the room and attached bathroom. "Clear."

Kodiak and Mongo cleared the rest of the second floor and took up positions at the base of the stairs to guard both the demolished rear door and the tied front one.

Gwynn crushed the cell phone beneath the heel of her boot, and Anya shoved the man onto the edge of the bed.

They locked eyes, and she hissed in Russian, "Are you Dima Ivanov?"

The man stared back at her without a word.

Without lowering her pistol, she drew her knife and pressed it against the man's thigh. "Answer me now, or watch yourself bleed to death."

He said, "You have no idea what you are—"

Before he could complete the foolish sentence, Anya pierced the fabric of his slacks and the skin of his leg with one powerful motion. The man threw both hands toward the blade and bellowed in agony.

Anya leaned closer. "Easy. Stay calm. I do not want you to pass out before you swear to me you will never perform another organ transplant on this island."

He growled like a wounded animal as he beckoned to his security team.

Anya laughed and withdrew the blade from his thigh. "They are dead, and you are next."

She pressed the tip of the blade beneath his chin. "I will give you one more opportunity. You will never take another penny from Mikhail Kuznetsov. You will never return to clinic. And you will never perform another black-market transplant. Look into my eyes and swear this to me."

Instead of acceptance, resolution and defiance consumed his eyes. His pain seemed to end, and his fear melted away. "Whoever you are, you will never leave this island alive. You are fools, and you will pay for what you are doing." With that, he threw himself forward onto Anya's threatening blade until the steel drove through the soft flesh beneath his chin, through his throat, and into the base of his brain.

Anya closed her eyes, withdrew the knife, and stood. "This is more than black-market organ transplants. We have discovered something far more sinister. We cannot allow Emilio to return to clinic. He is not part of this, and we must save him."

Gwynn watched the macabre scene play out in front of her in utter disbelief and felt an unstoppable chill crawl through her soul. "What is this thing, Anya?"

"I do not know, but we have to talk with Ray."

They descended the stairs and gathered Mongo and Kodiak.

As they pulled from the driveway, Anya said. "Stop. We must put gates back in original position."

Mongo and Kodiak accomplished the task in record time and climbed back aboard.

"What happened up there?" Mongo asked.

Anya told the story in gruesome detail, and the big man slowly shook his head and said, "What could be bad enough to make one of the world's best transplant surgeons throw himself on your knife?"

She said, "There is only one thing stronger than desire to remain alive, and this is fear of consequences worse than death."

The drive back to the house was silent, but the voices inside the heads of each of the SUV's occupants roared in endless echoing cries trying to understand what the world around them had just become.

"What do you want to do about Emilio?" Kodiak asked when they pulled into the driveway.

204 · CAP DANIELS

Anya considered the question. "Bring him and his brother here. We will make decision after we know they are safe."

Mongo and Kodiak disappeared, and Skipper's phone back at Bonaventure in St. Marys rang only once before she said, "Op center."

Anya didn't give her an opportunity to say anything more. "We have situation."

She briefed the evening's events, and Skipper sighed. "Oh, boy. Nothing about this is good. Do you need the rest of the team?"

"I need airplane and pilots to take innocent people to safety, but I think I do not need more boots on ground."

"How quickly do you need the plane?"

Anya said, "Do not wake Disco and Chase, but have them come after they have slept."

"Are you sure that's soon enough?"

"Yes, we will protect them until then. I have now question about communication security."

"What are you talking about?"

"We need to have conversation with Special Agent Ray White at Department of Justice, but it must be secure and private conversation."

"That's easy," Skipper said. "The DOJ has plenty of secure telephone lines. We can route a patch through the op center here and have you connected in minutes."

"You do not understand. This is conversation for only Ray White and not for Department of Justice."

"Oh. That's different. Where does he live?"

"Georgetown."

"Can he get himself to Silver Spring, Maryland? We have a friend there who can make it happen."

Anya said, "I think so, but is necessary that you make arrangements for this. We cannot have record of us talking with him on satellite or cellular telephone."

"Okay. I've got his number, and I'll set it up. When do you want it to happen?"

"Right now," Anya said. "You must make him understand how important it is. You can do this, yes?"

Skipper asked, "When was the last time I failed you?"

27

VYGLYADIT MILO
(LOOKING CUTE)

Supervisory Special Agent Ray White's cell phone rang at 9:42 pm, and the lifelong federal agent at the terminus of his career considered letting it go to voicemail, but something about the Georgia area code changed his mind. "White."

"Special Agent White, it's Elizabeth Woodley from St. Marys."

White didn't respond.

"Ray, it's Skipper. I need to talk with you about our mutual friends on vacation in the Caribbean."

"I'm listening."

"There's been a complication with their, uh, reservations. I'm sending their travel agent to your house right now to pick you up. She won't ring your bell, but she'll be waiting for you at the curb in fifteen minutes."

White glanced down at the ragged sweatpants and Soggy Dollar Bar T-shirt. "Fine. I'll be on the street in fifteen, but I've got a question. Are they okay?"

"So far."

* * *

As if running on the metro schedule, a black Toyota Land Cruiser double-parked three spaces away from the steps leading up to White's brownstone. No one stepped from the car or gave any signal the driver was, in fact, the travel agent Skipper mentioned, but somehow, White knew the driver was waiting for him.

Subconsciously, he checked the street and sidewalk for prying eyes and found none, so he gripped the door handle and pulled. The woman behind the wheel was not what he expected. Long red hair pulled back into a pony-tail cascaded down her back, and a pair of striking green eyes looked back at him as he tried to think of something appropriate to say. All he could come up with was, "Are you the travel agent?"

She cocked her head and stared back at him. "Do you have your cell phone with you?"

White involuntarily patted his right hip pocket. "Yeah, I've got it."

The beautiful redhead said, "Take it back inside and put it exactly where you put it every night when you go to bed. I'll make the block and pick you up right here in two minutes."

White stood in silence, glaring at the driver. For the first time, he noticed what he'd missed when he locked eyes with one of the most beautiful women he'd ever seen. The pedals of the SUV had been modified to extend far above the floorboard, and the driver's seat was a customized version obviously designed and built specifically for her.

The woman waved the back of her hand toward him. "Close the door, and go put your cell phone away. You can bring your gun if you want, just in case you think I represent the threat of physical violence."

White almost chuckled as he closed the door and headed back up his stairs. Exactly two minutes later, after plugging in his cell phone on the bedside nightstand, he was back on the street and stepping into the Land Cruiser. He buckled his seat belt and said, "I'm Ray White."

"I know who you are. You can call me Ginger, and my car is swept daily by me, so we can talk in here. You're running an op in the Dominican Republic, right?"

"Not exactly." He took the next three minutes bringing Ginger up to speed on the operation from his perspective. He closed with, "So, I'm not technically running the op, and it's not an officially sanctioned mission."

Ginger listened intently as they drove, and when White stopped talking, she said, "I don't know your operators, but I know Skipper, and if she's going to this extreme to put them on the phone with you, they're obviously under the impression that you're in charge."

"Where are we going?"

Ginger pointed through the windshield. "Right there."

She turned into her driveway and thumbed the button to open the garage door. The door rose, exposing the interior that could've been an operating room. The light was brilliant, and every surface shone as if polished only minutes before.

"Forgive the mess," Ginger said as she placed the car in park. "I've been too busy to clean up out here."

When she opened her door, a switch activated the complex electronic mechanism to deploy a set of three steps from her door to the ground. White rounded the front of the Land Cruiser and stepped beside the woman whose head barely rose above his waist.

She typed a long security code into a keypad beside the door, and a series of tones sounded before the door clicked open. "Yeah, I'm short. Get over it. What do you drink?"

White stopped just inside the door. "I don't drink. I had a brain tumor, and I'm supposed to cut out alcohol."

"How about some tea or even water?"

He held up a hand. "I'm fine, but thank you."

Ginger carefully lifted an empty glass from the countertop and stuck it in Ray's hand. Instinctively, he closed his fingers around the glass, and Ginger said, "Thank you. Now, I have your fingerprints. Let's go make a call."

She led him through the kitchen, down a flight of stairs, and into what should've been a routine basement beneath a routine house in any neighborhood in Maryland. But that's not what he saw. After passing through two panic room doors heavier than anything at the DOJ, they entered a war room to rival the one in the basement of that big Casa Blanca on Pennsylvania Avenue.

"This is impressive."

Ginger settled into her custom-fit rolling chair and pointed toward its non-customized cousin. "Thanks. Put on that headset."

White obeyed, and soon, Skipper's voice filled his head. "Hello again, Agent White. This is a secure line, and I'm ready to patch in the rest of the team if you are."

"I guess I'm as ready as I'm going to be. I have no idea what any of this is about, and I'm locked inside Fort Knox somewhere under Virginia."

Skipper said, "Welcome to our world. Stand by for the team. Oh, and I almost forgot. For the purposes of this conversation, your name is DC."

Gwynn was first to speak when the connections were made. She spent five minutes detailing everything they'd encountered in the previous twenty-four hours.

When she finished, he said, "The doctor just threw himself on the knife?"

"Yeah, he did. What do you think it means?"

"Oh, there's no doubt what it means. He was more afraid of what somebody was going to do to him than he was of dying. Nobody kills himself over black-market transplant surgeries in the third world. These guys are into something far worse than killing people for their guts. What we have to do is figure out what it is and then find a way to stop it."

Skipper interrupted. "I haven't figured it out yet, but I do have an interesting little morsel you might want to chew on. I flagged everyone's passport who works in the clinic in LA so I'd get notified if any of them landed in Moscow."

"Did they?" Gwynn asked.

Skipper said, "Nope, but one of them just cleared customs at Punta Cana International, and his name is Dr. Maxim Bortsov."

"Bortsov's here in Punta Cana?" Gwynn asked.

"It's either him or someone using his passport," Skipper said.

Anya asked, "Can you find hotel reservation for him? I would like to have conversation with him now that we are outside jurisdiction of United States."

"Already looked," Skipper said. "And I came up with squat. I also looked for rental car reservations with the same results. Wherever he's staying and whatever he's driving isn't commercial. My guess is he's staying with his half brother, Mikhail Kuznetsov, the clinic owner, and he's probably got a local driver."

"How did he get here?" Anya asked.

Skipper said, "He arrived on a chartered jet owned by a company called World-Wide Aero Services."

Anya asked, "Does he have reservation for return flight?"

"That'll take a little time to work out, but I'm on it. What are you thinking?"

The Russian said, "I have now wonderful plan. When you tell Chase and Disco to bring Gulfstream back, have them also bring flying uniforms. I have feeling Dr. Maxim Bortsov is going to need luxurious ride home to United States."

"Oh, that's brilliant," Skipper said. "And Chase will look adorable in a charter pilot's uniform."

Anya sighed. "Chase looks adorable in everything."

They spent half an hour detailing Anya's plan until White said, "There's only one problem."

"What's that?" someone asked.

White thought carefully before saying, "I've got to sell it to the attorney general. Otherwise, we don't have anything. It's too risky to try it on our own and roll the dice with customs."

Skipper said, "We're leaving out one other important decision-maker in this whole thing. If Chase says no, it's a hard no. We've done some crazy stuff over the years, but this one is out there, and it may be too much."

Silence filled the air for a moment until Anya said, "Wake him up. I will ask him, and he will do this for me."

Skipper said, "I'm not walking into Chase's bedroom, reaching over Penny—remember Penny? She's his wife—and telling Chase you want to talk him into something in the middle of the night. It ain't happening."

Anya giggled. "When you say it that way, I agree. Is terrible plan but might be fun to try."

White cut in. "All right, this whole thing is insane. Way too many people are involved, and we don't have any control over most of them. I think we should rein it in before it gets out of control."

Anya refocused the conversation in her stoic, Russian tone. "Is out of control what these people are doing. They are killing innocent people who only want to have cosmetic surgery and selling their organs to wealthy people who believe they are too important to be on legal waiting list. This is what is out of control. What we are doing is stopping them, and there is no limit we should put on ourselves in case like this."

Once again, silence seemed to stop the ticking clock before Anya continued. "Ray, you will tell to attorney general what we must have and what we must do. If she tells to you no, you must bring Gwynn home and allow me to do what is necessary."

* * *

Ginger returned Ray White to his home in Georgetown, and the career federal cop never said a word until the analyst rolled to a stop in front of the brownstone. "Do you think they can pull this off?"

Ginger said, "I've known Skipper, Anya, and Chase's team for a long time, and I've never seen them fail. I'll be honest with you, though. Their greatest weakness in all of this is your agent, Gwynn."

White pulled his hand from the door handle. "What do you mean?"

Ginger checked her mirrors—a habit the Central Intelligence Agency taught her before she left the public sector to go to work for the real good guys. "I've never met Gwynn, but it's clear that she's a by-the-book kind of cop. This vigilante stuff doesn't come naturally to her. Am I right?"

White sucked air between his front teeth. "She used to be exactly what you describe, but that Russian's corrupting her a little more every time they work together."

"A little corruption in the name of righting a cosmic wrong isn't such a bad thing, is it?"

White seemed to consider her question. "Maybe not." He opened the door and stepped to the sidewalk. "I don't know how you got dragged into this thing, but thanks for helping."

Ginger shrugged and pulled the SUV into gear. "It's what I do. Call me after you talk to your boss. My number is written on one of your business cards in your wallet." She gave a mock salute. "Good night, Agent White. Oh, one more thing. I'm not going to run your fingerprints. It's obvious you're one of the good guys."

28

Chto Neobkhodimo Sdelat'
(What Must Be Done)

Supervisory Special Agent Ray White pulled the door closed behind himself inside the inner sanctum of the Attorney General of the United States only minutes after the nation's top cop finished her second cup of coffee.

"What is it now, Ray?"

He settled into a wingback. "You're not going to like it, but I'm asking you to hear me out. I've poured my heart and soul into this place for most of my life, so you can do that, can't you, ma'am?"

The AG lifted her empty cup and stared inside. "It's about your angels, isn't it?"

Ray shook his head. "No, ma'am. It's about the Russian mafia selling the organs of murder victims to wealthy, privileged buyers."

"Murder victims? Americans?"

Ray nodded. "Among others. We've got a chance to stop them, though, and I believe it's well within both our power and the law."

He laid out the plan, and the AG took notes. When he was finished, she said, "Just shut up and sit there, Ray. I need a minute to think."

Ray obeyed and lowered his eyes to avoid pressuring his boss.

Long before he expected her to answer, she said, "Do it, but nobody from your office is doing the interrogation. Find somebody else—preferably somebody from outside of our agency."

Ray had played the game far too long to look that gift horse in the mouth, so, without a word, he rose and left the attorney general in his wake.

Back in his office, White pulled out his wallet and thumbed through the few business cards he carried where his cash should've been.

Ginger picked up on the second ring, and White said, "How'd you do that number-on-the-business-card trick?"

"Not all pickpockets are thieves. What did the boss say?"

"She told me to make it happen, but the interrogation needs to be done by another agency."

"Another agency?" Ginger asked. "Like whom?"

White said, "I don't know. Maybe Treasury."

"That's crazy, but I'll pass along the good news. Thank you, Ray. Does this mean you're back in the official loop?"

"Not until they're back on American soil. The DOJ has no official jurisdiction in the Dominican Republic."

"We'll be in touch," she said.

The chain of communication had a prescribed route, without which, information would fall through the cracks. Ginger knew the system better than most, so her call didn't go to the DR.

Instead, Skipper answered the call. "Op center."

"It's Ginger. It's a go, but the interrogation has to be done by someone other than the AG's office. I don't understand it. I don't want to understand it. I just wish that hunk of a special agent was into four-foot-ten-inch redheads. He's a hottie."

"I'll have to take your word on that one. The team will be happy to hear the good news. They were going after those guys, regardless of the attorney general's decision, but this keeps most of it aboveboard."

Skipper's next call was answered a thousand miles to the south.

"You have for me good news, yes?"

The analyst said, "Good morning to you, too, Anya."

"Yes, good morning, but tell to me decision."

"Go get 'em," Skipper said. "But before you bring them home, make sure you've got a contact outside the AG's office to handle the interrogation."

"I think I know perfect person for this, but he will not answer phone for me."

"Why wouldn't he answer?"

Anya said, "Is okay. He likes friend Gwynn, so he will take call from her."

"I've got one more thing," Skipper said. "You asked about a reservation for Maxim Bortsov's return flight back to LA. He does have a reservation. It's the same plane and crew that brought him to the Dominican Republic. They're scheduled to leave for LA tomorrow morning at eight a.m."

"This is perfect. Thank you," Anya said. "I will tell everyone, and we will go to work. This means Chase knows plan and is coming with airplane, yes?"

"Go to work, Anya. Chase will let you know when he arrives, and he'll have everything you asked for."

Anya briefed the remainder of the team and said, "Mongo, you and Kodiak will go to airport. You know what to do."

Mongo said, "Indeed we do, and we're some of the best in the world when it comes to breaking things. This one will be a piece of cake and more fun than should be legal."

Kodiak asked, "What are you and Gwynn going to do?"

"We are going to visit son of old friend," Anya said.

Kodiak narrowed his gaze. "Are you sure that's a good idea?"

"Is best idea," Anya said. "And will be just as much fun for me as you will have at airport."

They pulled from their driveways simultaneously. Mongo and Kodiak headed for the airport while Anya and Gwynn turned the opposite direction.

"Where are we going?" Gwynn asked.

Anya drew a slip of paper from her pocket and read the address. "We are going here to have conversation with person I used to know."

When they pulled into the drive, Gwynn studied the car parked against the house. "No, Anya. This is not a good idea."

"You do not have to be involved, but this is something I must do."

Gwynn gripped the wheel until her fingers throbbed from the blood rushing to the tips without an avenue of return to her heart. "Are we going to kill him?"

Anya opened her door. "I hope not, but I cannot make promise. I will call you when I am finished."

"Oh no, you won't," Gwynn said. "You're not going in there without me."

She shut off the SUV and followed Anya to the door. By the time she made it onto the small patio, Anya was already conversing through the intercom with Gedeon Zhukov in their native language.

"My name is Anastasia Belyaeva. I am friend of your father, Miroslav. Please, may I come inside?"

Gedeon Zhukov opened the door a few inches, stopping the door with his foot, and peered through the opening with one eye. "You know my father?"

Anya leaned toward the opening. "Yes, I knew him very well when he was major in KGB."

"What did you say your name was?"

"I am Anastasia Belyaeva. Please allow me to come in for only short time. I have things to tell you about your father."

With some degree of hesitance, Gedeon stepped back, allowing the door to swing inward, and Anya exploded through the opening, striking Gedeon in the neck. He stumbled backward and collapsed onto the tiled floor, grasping at his neck with both hands. Anya sent the heel of her boot solidly between his legs on her way to plant herself on his chest.

Gwynn stepped inside and closed and locked the door behind her. She drew her pistol, uncertain of what might happen next. If Zhukov had security like Dr. Ivanov, she would be ready to dispatch them without hesitation. Zhukov was obviously no threat to her partner, so Gwynn's focus remained on the rest of the house. Whatever Anya was doing couldn't be stopped, so she had no choice other than to make the scene as safe as possible while Anya settled an old score.

Ninety seconds later, Gwynn was back with her pistol holstered, and Zhukov was bound and gagged on a straight-backed kitchen chair. Gwynn watched as Anya performed the strangest ritual she'd ever seen: stroking Gedeon's nose as if comforting a frightened dog.

"Is okay. I will only hurt you as badly as your father chooses."

From behind the gag in his mouth, Zhukov tried to voice his confusion.

"Do not worry," Anya said. "It will all make sense very soon. Where is cell phone?"

Gedeon grunted and fought against his restraints, so Anya slid a knee onto the chair in front of him. "You are being uncooperative. Do not make me hurt you."

He bucked wildly and threw his head toward Anya in an obvious attempt to shatter her nose with his forehead, but she was too fast. As he lunged forward, she met his face with a rising elbow, doubling the blow's force because of his attempted headbutt.

He groaned as blood poured from the bridge of his nose. Anya leapt away and grabbed the saltshaker from the table behind her victim, then she unscrewed the top and held the uncapped shaker above Gedeon's head. She grabbed a fistful of his hair and yanked his head backward until he was staring up, directly into the open top of the saltshaker.

"This will be very painful for you. Do you wish to continue fighting, or will you be calm and quiet?"

He growled and continued pulling against his restraints. The instant the contents of the shaker met his open, bloody wound and his eyes, Gedeon turned into a raging, wounded animal. He yanked and jerked until Gwynn thought the chair might explode beneath him.

As he continued his tantrum, Anya turned on the sink and pulled the sprayer from its rest. She reclaimed the fistful of hair she'd released and controlled his head, if nothing more. She sprayed water into his face and eyes until the salt was washed away and the man was left gagging on the water that found its way up his nose.

Anya pulled the gag from his mouth. "I will ask again. Where is cell phone? If you say anything other than answer, the pain will get much worse."

His eyes shot to the room he'd likely been sitting in when Anya's voice came through his intercom, and Gwynn stepped beside the recliner in the center of the space. She lifted a cell phone from the arm of the chair and held it up. "Look what I found."

She handed the phone to Anya, who scrolled through the contacts and then held the phone in front of Gedeon's burning eyes. "I think we will make call to your father. He has iPhone, yes?"

He growled. "What do you want?"

Anya smiled down at him. "I want to have talk with your father so he can make decision."

"What decision?"

"Decision for you to live or die," Anya hissed.

Gedeon gasped. "What are you talking about?"

She continued scrolling through the phone. "While we are waiting to make call, tell me about money you took from clinic in bag."

He shook his head wildly. "I knew I saw you before. You took my picture!"

"That is right, Gedeon Zhukov. I took picture, and now, I will take life if this is decision Colonel Zhukov makes for you. Now, tell me about money inside bag."

"You want the money? Take it. I don't care. Take it!"

"I do not want money. I want conversation with your father. Since you will not tell me about money, we will make call now."

Gedeon said, "I have never shorted him. He always gets what is his. Always."

"This is not about money, Gedeon. This is about something your father took from me that I can never have again."

"What do you want? I can give you anything you want. Just tell me what you want, and stop this."

Anya softened her tone, somehow making her even more terrifying. "I want from you decision. Only one simple decision. Do you want to have conversation with father on speakerphone or FaceTime phone?"

The man shuddered as fear overtook him. "You don't have to call my father. Just tell me what you want."

"Okay, decision is made. Will be FaceTime call."

"No! Please, just tell me what you want."

Anya pressed her thumb against Alexi Zhukov's name in Cyrillic script on the phone's screen. "Do you believe in God, Gedeon?"

The confusion in his eyes grew even darker.

Anya spoke softly. "If you believe in God, you should pray your father answers telephone. If he does not, you will very soon meet God and become believer too late."

"You're insane!"

Anya smiled. "Yes, I am, and your father helped KGB make me insane."

The phone stopped ringing, and former Colonel Alexi Zhukov spoke in his deep, unnerving voice. "*Privet, syn moy.*"

"We will have conversation in English," Anya said, still pointing the camera directly at Gedeon's bloody face. "My name is Anastasia, and you raped me four times at State School Four in forest beside Volga River. I have now your son, and he is not hurt . . . yet."

"Who are you? You have no idea who you are playing with."

Anya growled. "Stop talking, you weak, pitiful man. I have your son, and you will decide what happens to him. You know what you did to me, and probably hundreds of other girls like me, while you were turning us into whores for Mother Russia. For this, someone will die, and you must make decision who it will be."

"You must be out of your mind."

"You heard me, Colonel. You will kill yourself, and I will watch you do this, or I will kill your son, and you will watch me do this. You must choose now."

The old colonel lost the ability to continue in English. "You will be dead before morning. You can't threaten me, and you can't kidnap my family and threaten to kill them. You are a dead woman, and you don't even know it yet."

"Make decision."

Gedeon cried out, "*Otets, pozhaluysta.*"

Anya slapped him hard enough to send stars circling above his head. "We will have conversation only in English."

Gedeon repeated his plea. "Father, please do something. This woman is insane. She will kill me. Her name is Anastasia Belyaeva."

Anya placed a thumb over the cell phone's camera lens and looked into the eyes of a man she hadn't seen since she was an innocent child an eternity before. "I will now watch you kill yourself for what you did, or you must watch me kill your son. One of these things will happen. You have thirty seconds to make decision."

29

VODITELI SKOROSTNYKH AVTOBUSOV
(HIGH-SPEED BUS DRIVERS)

Mongo zoomed in on and panned the map of the Punta Cana International Airport on his tablet as Kodiak drove southeast out of the crumbling reality of the third-world city. The façade of ultra-luxury and tropical paradise at the eastern extent of the island, where the blue Caribbean lapped at the rocky shoreline, could lure almost any tourist into believing the abject poverty on the interior of the island was only a myth, but the reality of the island remained, in spite of the fictitious world inside the walls of the resorts consuming the shore.

Mongo let out a chortle. "It's like they build the VIP terminal to be attacked. They stuck it all the way at the east end of the airport with a single fence and forestation to the south and east. The fuel farm lies off to the west, and there's nothing but a runway and wide-open flat land for five miles to the north. A Boy Scout could break into that place and burn every plane to the ground without getting his merit badges dirty."

Kodiak said, "That sounds exactly like the kind of mission we could screw up by the numbers."

"It's not all a nicely wrapped package with a bow on top," the big man said. "The VIP terminal sits right on the parking apron, so if there's anybody in the terminal, we're going to have an audience."

"Let me see," Kodiak said, leaning toward his fellow former Green Beret. Mongo tilted the tablet so he could see.

"Hmm. How about that?" Kodiak said. "Is that a golf course?"

"Yeah, but the trees separate the golf course from the airport. You know those country club people don't want to listen to jet engines while they're putting."

"You play golf?" Kodiak asked.

Mongo laughed. "Do I look like a golfer?"

"You look like the kind of guy who could hit a golf ball a mile or two."

Mongo said, "Back at Fort Bragg, in my misspent youth, we used to hide in the tree line beside the driving range and shoot at golf balls with shotguns."

"How did you keep from going to jail?" Kodiak asked.

"The MPs were more scared of us than they were of the officers playing golf, so it worked out for us grunts."

Kodiak chuckled. "It sounds like I missed a good time. Let's do a drive-by and scope it out."

They drove the access road to the VIP terminal and memorized every detail of the layout.

Kodiak pointed toward the business jet parked at the southeastern corner of the ramp. "That must be our target."

"Can you read the registration?" Mongo asked.

Kodiak slowed the SUV and pulled as close to the fence as he could get. With the binoculars pressed to his face, he said, "Yep, that's her, and from the looks of things, she might be partially blocked from view by that hangar."

Mongo spun in his seat and studied the line of sight. "Let's head over to the terminal and get a better look."

Kodiak pulled into the parking lot and drove beside the terminal building.

Mongo put on a big, goofy grin. "Would you look at that? It's like a gift from God. Somebody put that big old hangar right in the way."

Kodiak said, "Normally, I'd say we shouldn't do anything until well after dark, but I'm good with wiring it now if you are."

Mongo shrugged. "I don't see why not. We'll be in and out in three minutes. I just wish we had a distraction, though. That would make me feel a lot better about not getting busted."

Kodiak checked his watch. "What time are Chase and Disco supposed to arrive?"

"I don't know, but I know somebody who does."

Mongo dialed the number, and Skipper said, "Op center."

"Hey, it's Mongo. What's Chase's ETA?"

"According to the flight tracker, they're two hundred miles out, so they'll be there in half an hour or so."

"Do you have comms with them?" Mongo asked.

"Of course I do. Do you need me to patch you through?"

"You're the best," Mongo said.

"Stand by. It'll only take a few seconds."

Mongo thumbed the speaker button and waited for the connection. Almost before he could lay the phone back down, Chase's voice came through the speaker.

"Hey, Skipper. What's up?"

"I've got Mongo and Kodiak for you."

Chase said, "Hey, guys. What's going on?"

"Things are fine down here," Mongo said, "but we need a little favor."

"Name it."

"When you get here, the VIP terminal is on the south side of the runway, all the way at the east end of the field. We need to spend a couple of minutes with our target aircraft on the ramp without being interrupted. Do you think you could get the attention of anybody inside the terminal long enough for us to get in and back out?"

"Misdirection is what I do best," Chase said. "Get in position, and we'll be on the ground in twenty-seven minutes. We'll be the ones in the big grey Gulfstream."

"We know the plane," Mongo said.

"Oh, I know, but I still like saying we're the ones in the big grey Gulfstream."

Mongo rolled his eyes. "We'll see you in twenty-six minutes, but you won't see us."

They parked in a crushed shell lot beside an abandoned construction project that looked as if it could've been an addition to the golf course that never happened. It took less than five minutes to cover the quarter mile of forested area to the fence line.

They took a knee, and Kodiak eyed the fence. "It's a little taller than I expected."

"What's the matter, little guy? Are you afraid of heights?"

Kodiak said, "Yep. That's why I always carry a pair of these." He produced a pair of industrial cutters from his cargo pocket and made short work of cutting a slit in the fence large enough even to get Mongo through without a problem. Just as he made the last cut, the wheels of the *Grey Ghost*, Chase Fulton's Gulfstream IV, touched down with a chirp on the runway only a few hundred feet to the north.

Mongo slapped Kodiak on the back. "Perfect timing, little buddy."

Kodiak groaned. "I'm not Gilligan, and you're not The Skipper, so quit calling me little buddy."

They kept themselves out of sight in the trees until the *Grey Ghost* taxied onto the VIP ramp and Disco and Chase descended the stairs, dressed like good little charter pilots, with gold stripes on their epaulets and black hats perched on their heads.

Kodiak said, "Check it out. They've even got those little rolling suitcases that charter pilots drag all over the world."

Mongo said, "Maybe if this saving-the-world gig doesn't work out, they'll still be able to make a living as high-speed bus drivers."

Chase took a glance around the perimeter of the ramp, and his eyes came to rest on the cut fence. Even though he couldn't see his teammates tucked into the tree line, he gave them a barely perceptible nod of approval.

Sixty seconds after Chase and Disco disappeared into the terminal building, Mongo and Kodiak pressed through the fence and headed for their target. Both of them kept an eye toward the terminal until they reached the jet waiting patiently to return Dr. Maxim Bortsov to LA the following day.

Kodiak said, "Get me up there," as he stared at the massive engine nacelle several feet above his head.

Mongo took a knee and cupped his hands just as they'd been taught on the obstacle course at Special Forces selection, when they were both too young to need a hand. Kodiak made three strides and landed a boot in Mongo's massive hands. The giant instantly became a catapult, launching Kodiak upward and into the opening of the turbine.

Less than a minute later, Kodiak said, "I'm coming down."

He slid from the engine and into Mongo's waiting arms, and they made their escape even more hastily than they'd approached. With a few twists of wire, the hole in the fence was repaired well enough to fool the casual observer, but their handiwork would be discovered sooner or later.

Back in the SUV, Mongo dialed Chase's number. "Hello, sir. This is Courtesy Crew Carriers, the preferred ground transportation service for discerning flight crews from all over the world. Could I interest you and your copilot in a ride to your hotel?"

"That would be marvelous," Chase said. "We'll meet you outside the VIP terminal."

Kodiak pulled into the parking lot just as Chase and Disco emerged from the building with their wheeled bags in tow.

"You two look ridiculous," Mongo said as they slid onto the back seat.

"Please don't remind us," Disco said. "This is humiliating."

"What did you put in that engine?" Chase asked.

Kodiak said, "Oh, it's just a little housewarming gift. I know how much you charter pilots like surprises, so we left one for your colleagues from World-Wide Aero Services."

Chase met Kodiak's eyes in the mirror. "It won't get anybody hurt, will it?"

"It shouldn't, but it'll render the airplane unusable for a while. I'm sure they're well insured, though."

The twenty-minute drive back to the rented houses gave Mongo and Kodiak time to brief Chase and Disco on exactly what was going on.

When the briefing was over, Chase said, "This is a lot more complicated than I like. I'm a big fan of get in, kill the bad guys, and get out."

Mongo said, "Me, too, but the rules are a little different on this one. I'm still not completely sure how we got wrapped up in this whole thing."

"Every time we've asked Anya for help, she's been on our doorstep the next morning, so there was no chance I would tell her no when she asked for our help for the first time."

"I get it," Mongo said. "It just seems strange working with her without you."

Chase said, "Speaking of our favorite Russian, where is she?"

"We don't know for sure," Mongo said. "She told us she had an old score to settle, or something like that, and it was a no-boys-allowed operation. We didn't question her. We just did our job."

30

Pravo Khranit' Molchaniye
(The Right to Remain Silent)

Anya Burinkova slid her thumb from the lens of the camera phone, exposing her face to Colonel Alexi Zhukov. "Make your choice."

The weathered Communist glared at her as if begging what remained of his mind to bring that face back to his memory.

Anya said, "I was young and beautiful when you tore the innocence from my body. Now, you will make decision."

The colonel leaned closer to his phone. "Who are you?"

"I am Avenging Angel. If you are not dead by your own hand in thirty seconds, your son will be dead in thirty-one."

"What do you accomplish by killing my son?"

Anya whispered, "Twenty-four."

"What assurance do I have that you will not kill Gedeon, even if I kill myself?"

"Eighteen."

Gedeon gagged, choking on his own terror. "Father, please!"

"What will you do if I hang up?" asked Alexi.

"Eleven."

Alexi narrowed his gaze. "You are a dead woman if you do this. There is nothing I will not do to find you and kill you with my own hands."

"Six."

Anya drew her pistol and made a show of pressing it to the back of Gedeon Zhukov's head and drew the camera close to his face.

Alexi bellowed, "Stop this! I can make you wealthy beyond your imagination."

"Two."

"You must stop this!"

Anya pulled the trigger.

The cell phone exploded in her fingertips, and Gedeon Zhukov lay on the floor beside the chair, his eyes wide and his lungs breathless.

Gwynn sent a thundering knee shot to his gut, and the air he'd held in his chest for the previous seconds exploded from his mouth and nose. He lay gasping and trembling with every forced breath.

Gwynn said, "Relax, man. You're not dead. I yanked you out of the way at the last second, so now you owe me your life. Tell me about the money."

He opened his mouth to speak, but the words wouldn't come.

Anya hit him in the face with another blast of water from the sprayer. "You will tell her about money, or I will drown you slowly."

He jerked and sputtered through the spray. "I told you. Just take the money."

Anya took a knee beside his face. "We do not want money. We want truth about money, and we want you to tell us about Americans in business with you."

Gedeon stared between the two women. "Are you some kind of police?"

Anya lowered her face to within inches of his. "I am killer trained by KGB and SVR. I have thousand ways to make you talk, and you will enjoy none of them. You will probably not survive most of them, so is best to answer questions now or I will show to you what I learned from your father."

As he lay motionless, the look on Zhukov's face said he was confounded by the decisions that lay ahead of him. Finally, he said, "You want to know about the Americans?"

Anya glanced at Gwynn and turned quickly to Zhukov. "Yes, tell me about Americans. What are they doing?"

He frowned and leaned toward his inquisitor. "And you are an officer of the SVR?"

Anya sidestepped the question. "I am asking questions. You are answering questions. Tell to me what Americans are doing inside clinic."

He shot a thumb toward Gwynn. *"Politsiya?"*

Anya said, "Not Russian police."

"Amerikanskaya politsiya?"

"Tell me about Americans, now!"

"You understand that my father will find you and kill you, yes?"

Anya smiled. "Your father proved he valued his life more than yours. Now, talk, or what he believes will actually come true."

"They're harvesting organs for transplant into wealthy patients."

"Yes, we know this, but we need to know who exactly is doing this."

"The Americans."

"All of them? There are over three hundred million of them."

"No, of course not all of them. Maxim Bortsov is American citizen, but he is Russian at birth. Mikhail Kuznetsov is half brother to Bortsov and is also American citizen, but he does not go to U.S. He goes only to Russia, Italia, and here in Dominican Republic."

"Italia?" Anya asked. "Does he have also clinic there?"

"Of course. Would you please take off the handcuffs?"

Anya held up one finger, and Gwynn unlocked one of Gedeon's hands. She laced the cuff around the leg of the coffee table and relocked it.

Anya said, "So far, you have told us only what we already know. We do not need you for this. Tell to us rest of story. I will not ask again. You will tell everything you know, or you will die locked to your table." She drew her pistol for the second time and press-checked the chamber. "I have no more patience for this."

Gedeon held up his free hand in surrender. "Okay. I will tell everything I know. You know about the heroin, right?"

The bell towers in Anya's and Gwynn's heads turned to ringing explosions, but neither woman changed her expression. The interview had just become the home court for Special Agent Gwynn Davis, so Anya surrendered the inquisitor's stand.

Gwynn scoffed. "Of course we know about the heroin. That's obviously the primary reason you and the other Russians are so deeply involved in this thing. Why don't you give us the details about the Americans' involvement in the heroin operation?"

"They weren't involved at first," Gedeon said. "But Bortsov is the one who came up with the idea to ship it with the ashes."

Gwynn's mind turned itself inside out as she tried to piece together what Gedeon just said. She had a thousand follow-up questions, but an enormous element of the art of interrogation was knowing when to shut up and listen.

Gedeon continued. "When they started the crematory, nobody believed it would work. Nobody knew there was a market for international cremation service. It costs five thousand dollars in America, but we do it for pennies. We could do it for free and still make millions of American dollars every month."

Gwynn grimaced as Gedeon trailed away from the operation of the business. "Tell me how you get the bodies here from the States."

"That is the easy part," Gedeon said. "We don't."

"I'm not following," Gwynn said.

"That's because you're some kind of cop. Your mind doesn't work like ours. The bodies never leave the States. The agents in America pick up the bodies with the promise of shipping them here, but nobody ships any dead bodies to the Dominican Republic. They take the money, dispose of the bodies, and walk away. They keep whatever they collect. It's only pennies compared to the rest of the operation."

"You mean the part where you ship the heroin back to the U.S."

"Of course," he said. "We have all the bodies we need right here on the island. The clinic produces some. The streets produce the rest. When the family in the States receives their ashes, they don't know if the contents of that urn had been a Dominican street rat or a facelift that went wrong a week before. It's simple. That's why it works."

"Where are you shipping the ashes and the drugs?"

"Are you kidding me? LA and Miami. Where else? From there, the heroin is separated from the ashes, cut down, and distributed."

"And Bortsov is running that operation?"

Gedeon said, "No, not anymore. He started it, but he's hands off now. He just collects the cash while a bunch of Russians do the dirty work. Slavs were slaves fifteen hundred years ago, and it looks like nothing has changed for most of us."

"You seem to be doing okay," Gwynn said.

He rattled his handcuffs. "I'm chained to a chair on the floor of a rented house in a piece of crap country that shouldn't exist, and I'm being interrogated by a couple of crazy women who are probably going to kill me when this is over. Would you call that doing okay?"

Anya said, "We will probably not kill you, but is not promise. I have one more question before decision is made. Why are they paying you? What do you do for them?"

"Come on, comrade. You're smarter than that. I provide security for them. I keep the local police off their backs, and for that, I get a percentage. You know how things like this work."

Anya said, "It does not look like you can provide anything, especially not security right now, so I think is time for you to take small nap." She slipped a needle beneath his skin and pressed the plunger.

Seconds later, Gedeon Zhukov's eyelids grew far too heavy to hold open.

Gwynn uncuffed him as he lay there like a rag doll. "What now?"

Anya said, "We must now make phone call to check on boys."

They carried Gedeon's limp form to the SUV and shoved him in the cargo space behind the rear seats. Gwynn cuffed him to the D-ring mounted to the floor, just in case the narcotics wore off earlier than expected.

Inside the car, Anya dialed the phone, and Kodiak answered. "How'd it go?"

"We have audio recording from Gedeon Zhukov about entire operation, and he is now inside trunk."

Kodiak said, "It sounds like you've had a productive day. We took care of the thing at the airport. It should be fun to watch tomorrow morning."

"What about Emilio Parra, the anesthesia technician?"

Kodiak said, "He's nowhere to be found. He and his brother just disappeared. The house is empty, and the car is gone. It looks like they just vanished into thin air."

Anya said, "It does not look like they were taken?"

"No," Kodiak said. "Most of their stuff was gone, so either they packed up and hit the road, or somebody did an excellent job making it look like that's what happened."

"I do not like this," Anya said. "I believe he was innocent. We should have never left him."

Kodiak said, "I agree, but it's too late to worry about that now. Things are happening too fast to start a manhunt for two scared kids in the DR."

"What about crematory?" she asked.

"It's burning to the ground as we speak, but we were able to salvage a nice sampling of product from inside."

She said, "Good work," and changed her tone. "Chase is here, yes?"

"Yeah, he and Disco showed up while we were sabotaging Bortsov's charter plane. We're all back at the house now."

"We will be there in five minutes."

Anya hung up, and Gwynn said, "You're a little too excited about Chase being here. You've got to turn that off."

"I cannot do this. I am always happy to see him."

They backed into the driveway of Kodiak's and Mongo's rented house, and the big man ambled through the door. He made short work of carrying Gedeon Zhukov inside, placed the man on a bed in one of the back rooms, and cuffed him to the frame.

Anya hugged Disco and kissed him on the cheek. "Is good to see you. Thank you for doing this for us."

Disco withdrew. "Uh, sure, but I didn't do anything other than drive the bus. Chase is the one you should be thanking."

Her set-up worked just as she'd hoped, making Chase Fulton the next recipient of her affection.

He returned the hug and lingered an instant too long. "What else can we do to help?"

Anya said, "We have only one thing to do before leaving."

She had everyone's attention. "We must find way to make Mikhail Kuznetsov, Bortsov's brother and owner of clinic, also get on plane with us tomorrow."

Окн. Окн. Этот Звук
(Ооh. Ооh. That Sound)

Disco leaned back in his chair and tapped three fingers against his chin. "I've got an idea."

Anya turned to face him, and every head in the room followed.

He said, "I'm an old A-Ten driver, so I know a thing or two about sending messages. If you've never watched an A-Ten engage a target, let me tell you about the experience. That airplane is built around a gun called the GAU-Eight/A Avenger, seven-barrel, Gatling-style autocannon. It can throw down thirty-nine hundred thirty-millimeter rounds per minute. The sound that thing makes is unlike anything else on Earth, but the rattle is always a little late to the party."

"Late to the party?" Gwynn asked.

"The depleted uranium rounds leave the muzzles at over thirty-three hundred feet per second, so they arrive at their destination well ahead of the brrrr. Needless to say, the combination of metal on target and that sound sends an unmistakable message to the unfortunate troops on the ground. Universally, they have only one desire when they see and hear it. They want to be anywhere but in front of the Warthog rolling in above them for a second gun run. I think that's the message we need to send to Mikhail Kuznetsov. If we can make him want nothing more than to be anywhere else, his brother's chartered jet will start to look like a golden chariot to Heaven."

Kodiak clicked his tongue against his teeth. "I dig it, but how do we make it happen?"

Anya smiled. "Perhaps having Russian angel whisper into his ear would make same impression as impact and brrrr."

Gwynn said, "Then lucky for us, we just happen to have one such angel in our midst."

The call went through to the op center, and Skipper provided three telephone numbers for Mikhail Kuznetsov in seconds. She said, "It sounds like you're speeding up the timetable."

"Perhaps," Anya said. "But this is okay. We have only one more thing to do, and we will be ready to come home to welcome parade."

Anya drank a bottle of water and practiced her speech before dialing the phone.

A woman answered the first number, and the Avenging Angel came to life.

"I must speak with Mikhail Kuznetsov. Is very important."

"Who is this?" came the response in defensive Russian.

Anya said, "This is person with information Mr. Kuznetsov needs to know. It is message about heroin, ashes, and missing persons."

The line went silent for a long moment before a man's angry voice growled from the other end. "Who is this, and what do you want?"

"Who I am is not important," Anya began in their mutual native language. "Information I have *is* important. Gedeon Zhukov told us everything about opium and organ transplant business."

"Whoever you are, you are dead. You don't know who you're playing with."

Anya continued in her confident, measured tone. "No, Mikhail, Gedeon Zhukov is dead. I killed him, and I made his father, Colonel Alexi Zhukov, watch. You will now listen to recording."

Gwynn pressed play on her cell phone's voice memo app, and Gedeon Zhukov's trembling voice poured through the air as he explained the details of the operation.

Gwynn stopped the audio, and Anya said, "This is not all. We have Emilio Parra. We also have Dr. Dima Ivanov's body. If you would like to see picture, I will send to you, or maybe better plan is for you to see his body for yourself."

Kuznetsov roared through the phone in furious Russian. "You will be dead before the sun comes up!"

"Do not make such threats. It is you who will be dead soon, comrade, but first you will watch your brother die same horrible death that is waiting for you."

Anya didn't wait for another outburst from Kuznetsov. She ended the call and said, "Rounds are now hitting ground all around him, and brrrr is coming."

Gwynn said, "How long do you think it'll take for Mikhail and Bortsov to run for the hills?"

Anya checked her watch. "I think we should leave now to beat them to airport."

Anya, Gwynn, and their team made it to the VIP terminal before Bortsov and his brother, but not before their flight crew. The first officer was performing the walk-around inspection while the captain checked the weather and filed their flight plan back to LA. Chase and Disco, clad in their cute little charter pilot uniforms, rested comfortably on a pair of over-stuffed recliners inside the terminal as if killing time like every charter pilot had done for thousands of hours in their career. The waiting game took up far more of their time than the flying, but the pay was good enough to keep them in the cockpits and in the overstuffed chairs.

"Where you guys headed?" Disco asked as the charter captain pushed himself away from the weather station.

"LA a day early. How about you?"

Disco shrugged. "We're deadheading back to Sacramento. Our passengers decided to stay another week. I guess the resort is a little slice of heaven, but we'll never see it."

"You got that right," the captain said. "Fly safe. There's a nasty storm over West Texas with tops up to forty-two thousand."

Disco motioned toward the ramp with his chin. "We're in the G-Four, so we can get above that, but thanks for the tip."

The trap was officially baited, and the waiting game continued.

While Chase and Disco played masquerade inside the terminal, the rest of the team readied the plane for departure and loaded the precious cargo. The partition between the cargo section and the passenger section of the *Grey Ghost* provided exactly what the team needed to hide themselves and their still-unconscious passenger, Gedeon Zhukov.

Chase watched through the window as the auxiliary power unit cart was rolled beside the waiting jet and connected, providing power and air-conditioning inside the plane without using battery power or starting either of the turbines.

Disco glanced toward the waiting plane. "It looks like they're getting ready for their passengers."

Chase nodded. "Yep, but if Kodiak and Mongo did it right, they won't be going anywhere anytime soon."

At that instant, the double glass doors behind them flew open, and two men burst through, wheeling a pair of enormous bags behind them. The charter captain reached for the bags, but both men yanked them away.

One man said, "No! These stay with us."

His Russian accent made it clear that the team was on the right track. The men could've been brothers by their appearance, or at least cousins. Their shared features were unmistakable. As quickly as they'd come through the front doors, they were out the opposite doors and onto the tarmac. The captain jogged ahead of them and up the boarding stairs.

A lineman approached the plane and waited for the coming hand signals from the cockpit. The cabin door was closed, and the captain gave the starting-engine-number-one signal. The lineman echoed the signal and pulled his earmuffs into place.

Engine number one whistled to life and appeared completely normal, so the captain signaled for the start sequence of the number-two engine. The lineman spun a finger in the air, and the starter was engaged. The jet spun up to speed, and the pilot introduced the jet fuel into the spinning turbine. The engine started and continued to increase in RPM while the pilots scanned the engine instruments for any signs of trouble.

With both turbines spinning, the pilots began their before-taxi checklist. Thirty seconds into the checklist, the number-two engine belched an enormous cloud of black smoke and bright orange flames. A bright-red light and audible warning sounded inside the cockpit at the same instant, and both pilots reached for the fire handle out of muscle memory from seemingly endless hours of repetitious training.

The pilots' near-instant reaction shut off the fuel, oil, and bleed air systems of the number-two engine. That didn't do the trick. They still received the fire warning in the cockpit, so the captain triggered the small explosive valve that emptied halon directly into the engine nacelle. The fire warning continued, so the captain was forced to blow the valve on the second bottle of halon to finally defeat the incendiary grenade Kodiak had placed inside the turbine. The grenade's thermite burning over four thousand degrees was more than the system was designed to manage, but the pilots finally won the battle.

The main cabin door flew open, and the two Russians came down the stairs even faster than they'd climbed them, but not even an engine fire could stop them from dragging their baggage behind them.

A pair of firetrucks turned from the taxiway and onto the VIP ramp and took up positions in front and behind the burnt engine. Firemen clad in silver reflective suits poured from the trucks and stood ready with hoses should the fire reignite.

The captain bounded down the stairs only seconds behind his passengers, leaving the first officer aboard to deal with the aftermath of the fire.

The trio ran for the terminal, and after the captain ripped open the glass door, he headed straight for Chase and Disco.

Apparently noticing the difference in stripes on their epaulets, the captain turned immediately to Disco. "You said you're deadheading to Sacramento, right?"

Disco looked up as if bored out of his mind. "That's right."

The captain motioned toward the two men behind him. "My passengers need to be in LA as soon as possible. Since you're deadheading, could you take them on?"

Disco peered across the captain's shoulder. "What happened out there? Did you have a hot start?"

"Yeah, you might call it that. Can you take them or not?"

Disco inspected his fingernails. "We'd have to check with company and get some paperwork started."

The captain glanced over his shoulder as the man with the Russian accent shoved him aside. The man dropped what appeared to be at least fifty thousand dollars in cash onto Disco's lap. "You will take us to California, now."

Disco didn't change his pace or expression, but he glanced to Chase, who'd put on a face expressing great interest in the pile of banded bills.

Disco said, "If we get caught, we'll lose our jobs, and I'm close enough to retirement to care about that sort of thing."

The Russian doubled the stack of bills, and Chase grinned. "Come on, Cap'n. That's enough to live on while we're looking for another job. Let's do it."

Disco seemed to consider the options before saying, "Will Sacramento do?"

The Russian said, "No, we must land in LA," and dropped a third stack of cash, but this time, it landed on Chase's lap.

Chase unzipped his flight bag, deposited the cash, and looked up at the charter captain. "Are you type rated in the G-Four? If he won't do it, you and I will."

Disco laid a patient hand on Chase's arm. "I need your assurance that you don't have anything illegal inside those bags."

The Russian unzipped the top of his rolling bag and pulled the material apart. "It is cash—although less than before—clothes, and shaving kit. Nothing more."

Disco made a show of peering inside the open bag. "Legal cash?"

"Perfectly legal," the Russian said.

Disco licked his lips, glanced at Chase, and deposited his stack of cash into his flight bag. "It looks like we're going to LA."

POMNI NAS?
(REMEMBER US?)

Chase did the hasty walk-around inspection, and Disco filed the flight plan. Before the firetrucks left the VIP ramp, the *Grey Ghost*—with her two passengers, two crew, four covert operatives, one kidnapped Russian citizen, ashes, and heroin on board—taxied to the runway and blasted into the Caribbean sky, heading northwest.

The *Grey Ghost* covered the twenty-eight hundred nautical miles in just over five hours, touched down at the Hollywood Burbank Airport, and taxied to the ramp.

As Disco brought the plane to a stop, Chase climbed from his seat and stepped into the passenger cabin. "I assume you'd like some anonymity. If you'll give me your passports, I can get us through customs and immigration without any uniforms asking questions or searching bags. It's part of the VIP service we provide . . . especially for cash customers."

The two men produced American passports, which surprised Chase, but he showed no reaction. "Thank you. If you'll keep your seats, I'll be back in just a few minutes. The captain has the APU running, so you'll be perfectly comfortable. It shouldn't take more than ten minutes, fifteen tops."

He hopped down the stairs, leaving the two men waiting without passports in the luxurious leather seats of the Gulfstream.

Hydraulic sounds, and even a light jostling, made their way through the airplane, and one of the passengers called into the cockpit. "What was that sound?"

Disco leaned into the aisle. "It was just the lineman connecting the fuel hose. We burned a lot of gas in the last five hours."

Disco completed his responsibilities in the cockpit and climbed from his seat. "Let me go see what's taking so long. I can usually get things done a little quicker than the copilot. You know how it is. Seniority has some clout the young guys haven't earned yet. Sit tight. I'll be right back."

He descended the stairs and trotted into the terminal, where Mongo, Kodiak, and Anya waited by the counter.

Gwynn pulled a man in an open-collared shirt and jacket toward them. "Guys, this is U.S. Deputy Marshal Will Parish. He and I have a dinner date later, but right now, he'd like to take a look inside your fancy airplane, if you wouldn't mind."

Disco tipped his cap. "Nice to meet you, Marshal Parish. Consider the plane to be yours, and make yourself at home."

The marshal led four younger men, dressed in similar attire, from the terminal and across the ramp. The next set of feet to hit the ramp were those of one of the finest drug-sniffing dogs in federal service. She was the only one in uniform. Her harness held a badge and nameplate declaring the sniffer to be Lieutenant Labrador Lancelot of the United States Drug Enforcement Administration. Although none of the officials had any jurisdiction in the Dominican Republic, the instant the brothers crossed the U.S. border with almost four million dollars in cash in their rolling bags and ten kilos of heroin tucked away in the cargo compartment of their chartered jet, the jurisdiction light turned green.

When Dr. Maxim Bortsov and his half brother, Mikhail Kuznetsov, descended the stairs, they did so with their hands cuffed tightly behind their backs and shackles on their ankles. A pair of blacked-out SUVs drove through the gate and onto the ramp. Anya and Gwynn followed the SUVs onto the tarmac and stepped in front of the cuffed men.

Anya stared into Bortsov's face. "Remember us? I am no longer envious of people who need you to make them feel beautiful. I learned I am still beautiful to people who love me."

Gwynn stepped beside her partner. "And I think my eyes are just fine without the rest of me ending up in your furnace and mixed with a kilo of heroin."

Mikhail Kuznetsov turned a dark eye toward his brother and hissed in Russian. "You fool! You brought these people into my house. I should have known you would destroy everything I worked so hard to create."

* * *

Under excruciating interrogation by the U.S. Marshals Service and the DEA, Bortsov and Kuznetsov were presented with the audiotaped statement by Gedeon Zhukov, who found himself under the protection of the Witness Security Program, alongside Emilio Parra, who'd fled the Dominican Republic for San Juan to escape the wrath of his Russian overlords. Skipper's handiwork in flagging everyone's passport made finding Parra and his brother a piece of cake.

With mountains of evidence against both of them, each brother turned on the other with rage beyond comprehension. The federal judge denied their negotiated plea agreements and deposited both of them in the same federal prison, in general population, for the rest of their natural lives, which turned out to be far shorter than either could've expected. The two men learned just how deeply the hand of the Russian mafia—the Bratva—reached into the prison system as each felt his own blood flow from his body and into the barren earth of the exercise yard.

* * *

In the hallowed halls of the Robert F. Kennedy Building at 950 Pennsylvania Avenue NW, Special Agent Gwynn Davis and Ana Fulton sat across the desk from a man they both respected more than they'd ever admit, and felt the weight of the end of something grander than all of them—something neither would've chosen but both would treasure for the rest of their lives.

Supervisory Special Agent Ray White straightened his tie instead of shucking it loose, as was his typical custom, and fought back the tear he felt welling behind his eye. "This will be my last formal act as commander of Task Force Avenging Angel and as a lifelong federal law enforcement officer."

The three of them felt the same weighty emotion pour over them as White fought his way through his declaration. "The two of you have been royal pains in my ass, and there were times I wanted to strangle both of you, but I've never worked with any team who accomplished more than you."

Laughter took them instead of the streaming tears that were yet to come.

White continued. "Anya, you're the worst cop I've ever met, but I've never seen anyone who could solve a case more completely than you. When you turn in your badge, please make sure they grind it into powder and then scatter it to the wind. God forbid you should ever have it back."

The laughter waned, but the smiles endured as White said, "And Davis, you were one of the best cops I've ever seen until she showed up and corrupted you. Now, you're almost as bad as she is, and I hope you take that as the enormous compliment it is. If you stay with the department, you'll be in this seat before you know it, but whatever you do, don't even think about hiring her again. Do either of you have anything to say?"

Gwynn squeezed her eyelids closed and let the tears come. "The past three years will forever be the most terrifying, most educational, and most wonderful of my life, and I wouldn't trade a single second of that time for all the money on Earth."

Ray said, "You two have done the world, and especially the country, an enormous service. You've saved thousands of lives and ripped evil from dark crevices all over this nation. The country owes you a debt it'll never pay, but both of you should be proud of what you've accomplished." He cleared his throat. "Anya, do you have anything to say?"

She bit her lip and sat in silence as the power of the emotion poured through her, but words wouldn't come.

Ray sighed, swallowed hard, and pulled a stack of papers from his desk drawer. "Anya, this is everything the Department of Justice knows about you." He turned and slowly fed the stack to the shredder behind his desk. "You've been free to go for over a year, but you wouldn't walk away, and that speaks volumes about your character, your loyalty, and your devotion to what is ultimately right. Your adopted country thanks you, I thank you, and now, you're no longer simply free to go. You must go. You've more than fulfilled your commitment, and you've far exceeded any expectations of the attorney general."

He paused, gathered himself, and said, "With that, Operation Avenging Angel is officially closed. The mission is complete. And the team is disbanded. This time next Friday, I will be officially retired, and the two of you will have to be pains in somebody else's ass."

They stood, hugged, and cried together.

When they parted, Anya's badge and credential pack lay on the center of Ray's desk, and the Russian stood in stoic silence beside her chair. "You are wrong, Ray. We are not finished. There is one more mission that must be done, even if I must do it alone. Although we have crippled the beast that is Bratva, its heart still beats, and its head still rests atop what remains of a dying body. We must fight one final battle to finish war against the Russian's wrath."

Keep reading for a preview of The Russian's Wrath, the next book in the Avenging Angel — Seven Deadly Sins series...

1

ONA DOLZHNA ZAPLATIT'
(SHE MUST PAY)

Chicago, IL, Late Summer 2015

Cigar smoke rose like a spirited demon escaping the pits of Hell and slithered through the dead-still air of the mahogany-paneled sanctum where four men sat, speaking in Russian and sculpting the demise of Anastasia Anya Burinkova.

"This little traitor has cost us a quarter of a billion American dollars, and it must end now."

The man's glistening dark hair was combed straight back, exposing seven decades of a furrowed brow.

The man to his left, and a quarter century his junior, leaned forward and pointed his Cuban at the older man. "Ilya, you are correct about this vermin who turned her back against her own people, but I believe your estimate of our losses is quite low. If she is allowed to continue, she will more than double your number in another year."

The older man groaned. "Perhaps you are right, Yakov, but if you are telling the truth about this mysterious source of yours, we will rake the flesh from her body and send her bones to the bottom of Lake Baikal."

Yakov said, "Question my source again, old man, and it will be the greatest and final error of your life."

A ruddy-faced bald man, sitting mostly in the shadows of the darkened lair, examined the golden-brown wrapper of his two-hundred-dollar cigar. "Gentlemen, I understand that tensions are high, but I must be the voice of reason here. We cannot turn against each other. This is precisely the sin of comrade Dmitri Barkov's seed. We must remain unified against our common enemy."

Yakov glared back at him. "This is but one more of the lies you've been led to believe, Oleg. Anastasia Burinkova is not the daughter of comrade Barkov. Half of her blood is American, and I'm quite certain you know her father well."

Nikita, a dark-eyed elf of a man, and the fourth and final Russian in the room, snapped his fingers—a habit for which he had become known but could not break, regardless of endless attempts. "Who this wretched woman's father is has no bearing on the necessity of killing her. She must die, and it must be done in the unholiest of ways, by the least human creature we can unleash upon her."

"Agreed," Ilya said. "But before that can be done, we must know every detail of her alliance with the Americans. If Yakov is correct—"

The younger man said, "Do not question whether I am correct. You will soon fully understand just how valuable my informant is."

Oleg said, "Tell us, Yakov. How did you come to recruit this American spy?"

"You forget that I was trained first by the KGB, and then SVR, and after that, FSB. I am a graduate of one of the most prestigious universities in the United States, and I have run more American spies than all of you combined."

Oleg shrugged. "Perhaps, but none of this makes you immune to falling victim to a trap by the Americans. Did this man come to you, or did you seek him out?"

"How I nurtured and developed my spy is none of your business. All that is important to you is that he is trustworthy and extremely well placed inside the American government."

Oleg waved a hand. "You are beginning to sound like an arrogant politician, Yakov. You spoke only of your grand accomplishments, but you failed to answer my question. Did the source approach you, or did you pluck him from the bushes?"

"He came to me," Yakov said, "but only after weeks of small, delicate grooming by me and my operatives. The man is scorned and shunned by his own government."

Oleg took a long draw and let the white aromatic smoke escape his lips. "I thought you said he was well placed inside the American government. Now you are trying to make us believe he is an outcast in his own country. Which is true, young Yakov?"

As his ire rose, Yakov said, "Listen to me, you bunch of dinosaurs. I am risking my life being here in this godforsaken country, and I'm doing it in the name of restoring the motherland to her former glory and might on the world stage."

"Bullshit," Nikita barked. "You are doing this for the enormous fee you are being paid and nothing more. Do not wave the flag of a patriot in our faces. You were for sale, and we bought you. That makes you our property, and by extension, it makes any source beneath your wing ours as well. Do not forget this."

Yakov leapt to his feet. "Let me make one thing clear, comrades. I could walk into Anastasia Burinkova's bedroom tonight, press a pistol to her head, and dispatch her from this world."

Oleg and Nikita laughed, and the dwarf said, "You could walk into her bedroom, but someone could walk out of that same bedroom with every piece of you in envelopes. This woman isn't the kind of person who is easily dispatched. She is a Kremlin-trained red sparrow and assassin."

It was Yakov's turn to laugh. "Yes, she may have been trained in State School Four, as well as the Red Banner Academy, but she is merely mortal, just like all of you. And she has become softened by her station in the West. Her razor grows rusty, and her vigilance now slumbers, when in the past, it would never rest its head."

Ilya crushed his cigar into a heavy crystal tray. "This woman you call 'soft' and 'lacking vigilance' faced off against six of our most established brothers, and now, each of those men is either in an American prison or the grave because they underestimated a beautiful woman who spoke their native tongue while driving daggers through their hearts."

"I know what I'm doing, Ilya. I am what the Americans call a spymaster." He paused and tore open his shirt, exposing the flesh of his chest and neck. "I have played this game—the world's deadliest game—for thirty years, and look at me. I bear no scars, no marks of bullet or blade. I do not fail. I do not get caught. And most of all, I never underestimate my foe nor overestimate my source."

Ilya said, "Okay, Yakov. You have convinced us. Now, tell us what you know about the daughter of Katerina Burinkova and the American, Robert Richter."

Yakov poured himself four fingers of vodka without offering to refill the glasses of his countrymen. "This is what I know about Anastasia Burinkova. She defected to the United States after failing the mission assigned by Colonel Victor Tornovich of the SVR. She was to seduce and recruit an American by the name of Chase Daniel Fulton, a bumbling idiot trained by the CIA. Instead of successfully recruiting him or killing him, she believes she fell in love with him."

Oleg cocked his head. "Victor Tornovich was killed, and his body was burned in Virginia. Was this the work of Burinkova?"

Yakov looked away. "I do not know, but that is irrelevant. What is important to understand is that the American Department of Justice apprehended our target in the city of St. Augustine, Florida."

Oleg continued staring at Yakov. "Pardon the interruption, but am I mistaken that Ms. Burinkova killed four federal agents that night?"

"You are not mistaken."

Oleg nodded. "That is what I thought. Killing four American agents doesn't sound like the work of a woman who is complicit in her cooperation with the so-called Department of Justice."

Yakov said, "At first, she was not cooperative, but the supervisory special agent who was running the operation, known as Avenging Angel, was highly skilled in manipulation. His name is Raymond White, and he is now retired from federal civil service, as they call it."

Ilya said, "So, we are expected to believe that this Raymond White person manipulated a Russian assassin and sparrow into working alongside the American Department of Justice. Is this what you are asking of us?"

Yakov smiled and relaxed in his seat. "No, comrades, it is not me who is asking you to believe this. I am merely asking you to listen to the information provided by my source."

Oleg raised a finger. "No, no, no, Yakov. Remember, you are bought and paid for. Your former source is now *our* source."

Yakov raised his finger in response. "You forget, Oleg, that I am perhaps bought, but not yet paid for."

Nikita said, "Bring in this so-called source, and if we believe you have delivered something of value, you will be paid."

Yakov slowly shook his head. "Do I look to you as if I am a fool? Once you have my source in your hands, you and I both know I will never be paid, and I will likely never be seen again. This is not how I do business. When I see proof of the wire transfer, you will have your source, but not a moment sooner."

The cigar clenched in the dwarf's teeth looked enormous in contrast to his impish head, but the look in his eyes was nothing short of ice. He pressed his cell phone to his ear and said, "Send the money."

Yakov typed a password into his iPad and watched the number appear on the screen. "You transferred only four million dollars. I can only assume you wish to have only half of my source. Do you prefer the upper half or the lower?"

Nikita said, "You'll get the rest when we are satisfied that you have delivered what you promised."

Yakov said, "If I fail to deliver what I promised, I know full well that I will be dead before the moon rises over the Kremlin, and eight million dollars isn't enough to protect me from your reach. Send the rest or I walk away."

Nikita made the call, and Yakov watched the balance of his Swiss account double in size. "Thank you. It has been a pleasure doing business with you, comrades."

He placed his iPad on the desk facing the three oligarchs, and a man's face appeared on the screen. He was in his thirties, clean-cut, and perhaps slightly afraid of what was to come next.

Yakov said, "Comrades, meet former DOJ Special Agent Johnathon McIntyre. You may call him Johnny Mac."

ABOUT THE AUTHOR

CAP DANIELS

Cap Daniels is a former sailing charter captain, scuba and sailing instructor, pilot, Air Force combat veteran, and civil servant of the U.S. Department of Defense. Raised far from the ocean in rural East Tennessee, his early infatuation with salt water was sparked by the fascinating, and sometimes true, sea stories told by his father, a retired Navy Chief Petty Officer. Those stories of adventure on the high seas sent Cap in search of adventure of his own, which eventually landed him on Florida's Gulf Coast where he spends as much time as possible on, in, and under the waters of the Emerald Coast.

With a headful of larger-than-life characters and their thrilling exploits, Cap pours his love of adventure and passion for the ocean onto the pages of his work.

Visit www.CapDaniels.com to join the mailing list to receive newsletter and release updates.

Connect with Cap Daniels

Facebook: www.Facebook.com/WriterCapDaniels
Instagram: https://www.instagram.com/authorcapdaniels/
BookBub: https://www.bookbub.com/profile/cap-daniels

ALSO BY CAP DANIELS

Books in This Series
Book One: *The Russian's Pride*
Book Two: *The Russian's Greed*
Book Three: *The Russian's Gluttony*
Book Four: *The Russian's Lust*
Book Five: *The Russian's Sloth*
Book Six: *The Russian's Envy*
Book Seven: *The Russian's Wrath*

The Chase Fulton Novels Series
Book One: *The Opening Chase*
Book Two: *The Broken Chase*
Book Three: *The Stronger Chase*
Book Four: *The Unending Chase*
Book Five: *The Distant Chase*
Book Six: *The Entangled Chase*
Book Seven: *The Devil's Chase*
Book Eight: *The Angel's Chase*
Book Nine: *The Forgotten Chase*
Book Ten: *The Emerald Chase*
Book Eleven: *The Polar Chase*
Book Twelve: *The Burning Chase*
Book Thirteen: *The Poison Chase*
Book Fourteen: *The Bitter Chase*
Book Fifteen: *The Blind Chase*
Book Sixteen: *The Smuggler's Chase*
Book Seventeen: *The Hollow Chase*
Book Eighteen: *The Sunken Chase*
Book Nineteen: *The Darker Chase*

Book Twenty: *The Abandoned Chase*
Book Twenty-One: *The Gambler's Chase*
Book Twenty-Two: *The Arctic Chase*
Book Twenty-Three: *The Diamond Chase*
Book Twenty-Four: *The Phantom Chase*
Book Twenty-Five: *The Crimson Chase*
Book Twenty-Six: *The Silent Chase*
Book Twenty-Seven: *The Shepherd's Chase*
Book Twenty-Eight: *The Scorpion's Chase*
Book Twenty-Nine: *The Creole Chase*
Book Thirty: *The Calling Chase*
Book Thirty-One: *The Capitol Chase*
Book Thirty-Two: *The Stolen Chase*

Stand-Alone Novels
We Were Brave
Singer – Memoir of a Christian Sniper

Novellas
The Chase is On
I Am Gypsy

Made in United States
Orlando, FL
13 September 2025

64946961R00152